# Final Cut

# Final Cut

Billie Sue Mosiman

**Five Star • Waterville, Maine**

Published in 2003 in conjunction with
Tekno Books and Ed Gorman.

Set in 11 pt. Plantin by Rick Gundberg.

Printed in the United States on permanent paper.

**Library of Congress Cataloging-in-Publication Data**

Mosiman, Billie Sue.
  [Pure and uncut]
  Final cut / Billie Sue Mosiman.
    p. cm.—(Five Star first edition mystery series)
  "Originally published in the United Kingdom under the
title: Pure and uncut"—T.p. verso.
  ISBN 0-7862-4175-6 (hc : alk. paper)
  ISBN 1-4104-0112-X (sc : alk. paper)
  1. Hollywood (Los Angeles, Calif.)—Fiction. 2. Motion
picture industry—Fiction. I. Title. II. Series.
PS3563.O88444 P87 2003
813'.54—dc21                    2002023269

Question by interviewer on *America Online* bulletin board service: "Do you believe that cinema, the way it is defined now, has reached its full potential?"

Oliver Stone: "Not at all. Much more is coming. We have mixed media for now. I feel that 3-D media is on the way."

# 1

"ME: This part's a career maker and the movie's gonna go through the roof!
MOVIE STAR: Tell me about the part."

Julia Phillips,
*You'll Never Eat Lunch In This Town Again*

They were asked to meet on the soundstage at ten o'clock Monday night. The gathering of actors and actresses, film crew, grips, make-up artists, wardrobe and lighting technicians stood milling around uneasily in small groups, talking in hushed voices.

Along with the rest of them, Georgie waited for Cambridge Hill, Hollywood's double Academy Award–winning director, to appear from his office at the back of the set. Cam was to tell the others what the movie was about. No one knew except the powerhouse agents who handled all the hottest properties. Oh, Georgie knew sort of what it was about, though he hadn't seen the script. He had to do the camera work. He couldn't be left out in the cold completely.

However, the agents had read the script. Film deals didn't fly unless the agents knew for sure the property wouldn't embarrass their clients. But unlike other deals before this movie, Georgie found out the agents were sworn to secrecy. Cambridge was offering more than they could comfortably turn down.

They knew how to zip their lips. This time money didn't talk. It shut the hell up.

Olivia Nyad, fresh from the wrap party for the closing of her last film, seemed the most agitated. Georgie watched her chain smoke, fascinated how one person could stand to suck in that much pollution without a break. She had filled two small clear glass ashtrays with scarlet lipstick-smeared butts. She hadn't spoken to a soul the entire half hour they had all been waiting. If anyone had asked the others present why they did not chat with Ms. Nyad, they would have said that she kept herself apart, inviolate. They might have said that she was a true star of the old school, unapproachable even to her colleagues. They would have been right.

Georgie glanced over at Marilyn Lori-Street, a comer and an exceptionally talented actress who had not really been given a chance in any film of worth. The kid smiled blissfully. She sat on a high stool, slim legs crossed to show off enough thigh to turn half the men on the set into jellyrolls. Georgie thought he shouldn't stare, but just couldn't help himself. He'd never get a chance with her, but it didn't hurt to fantasize.

Robyn LaRosa, the movie's producer and principal bankroller, stood talking quietly with one of the other cameramen, Sean Parker. Robyn stood five foot three only because she wore spiked-heel black leather boots. She could have been a fashion model for *Elle* or *Vogue*, except for her height, Georgie thought. The white bodysuit clung to all the right curves and revealed a good cleavage unsupported by any wonder bra. Her hair was a sleek red helmet cut above the ear on one side and below it on the other.

No one dared ask her about the script. She might look like a trendy gal with cream puff pastry between her ears, but it was well known she possessed the temperament of a rogue elephant.

Catherine Rivers, Cambridge's assistant director, sat cross-legged on the floor with an actor no one but Georgie recognized, Jerry Line, and another actor *everyone* knew, the great Jackie Landry. It was Jackie who had been cast for lead opposite Olivia. Catherine and the two men were throwing craps using a square of cardboard as a wall.

Every time Catherine crapped out she cried in a girlish voice and touched one or the other of the men on their crossed legs.

Georgie wished he could join in games like that, but crew didn't often get so chummy with the stars. At least Georgie didn't. He was too quiet, too retiring. He was, God help him, too much of a techie nerd to be given much notice by creative types.

Now it was edging into a forty-five minute wait and Olivia deliberately knocked her latest ashtray to the floor from where it had been perched on a dolly cart used for hauling around scenery.

When heads turned at the crash of glass, Georgie started. He watched her smile sweetly before she said in her famous, low-from-the-diaphragm voice, "I'm trashing this joint if Cam isn't out here in thirty seconds. Who the hell does he think he is?"

Cambridge Hill took that moment to open his office door although he couldn't have heard Olivia's threat. Yellow light spilled across the ominous darkness and he strode through it toward where they stood assembled on the raised platform stage. Georgie took a deep breath. It was about time. Nerves were stretched to the breaking point.

"Here comes the prick now," Olivia said to no one in particular, but not so loudly her words would carry to the man heading her way.

Catherine and the two actors came to their feet, dusting

off their hands on their clothes. Jerry pocketed the pair of red Vegas dice; Jackie dropped the cardboard.

"Thank you for coming," Cambridge said, stepping onto the stage. He did not apologize for the late hour or the wait. Under his right arm he carried a half-dozen bound scripts. In his left hand he held a sheaf of documents. It was this hand that caught everyone's attention. Georgie thought Cam might as well have been carrying a boa constrictor. They had all heard a rumor that this film was going to be under wraps for the duration. Could the papers he carried be rules and regulations they must follow during filming? Why else make them meet in this cavernous warehouse of a soundstage at this time of night when no one was on the lot except the security guards? He had done it before, on his last film.

Nothing surprised Georgie about Cam. He was a legend and entirely unpredictable. Some called him a genius.

Cam plopped the scripts down on a metal folding chair. He pointed to them. "These hold the first scene we're going to shoot. Those of you who will work with me on this project get one before you leave tonight."

"It's not the whole script? You're not going to give us the whole script?" Olivia blinked rapidly behind the pall of cigarette smoke. She looked as if she had just been told her agent had died, her mansion in Beverly Hills had caught fire, and her two Maltese dogs had been fed sushi crawling with salmonella bacteria.

Cambridge turned to her with a flourish. He was as dramatic a figure as anyone who stepped before a camera and enjoyed a reputation that put many of the old Hollywood moguls to shame. His black hair, receding now, but still full on the sides and back, looked as if he'd been combing his hands through it for hours. There was a shadowy day's growth of dark beard stubble on his cheeks and chin. His gray eyes settled on Olivia, piercing her the way arrows pierce a painted target.

"Baby," he said, voice like dry gravel, "it's not even a sure thing yet you'll get the first scene."

Wow, thought Georgie. Cam loves the dangerous edge.

"What is this, Cam? I don't work on pictures without seeing the script." Olivia, not easily surprised and very rarely spoken to that way, looked pissed he'd gotten to her. She dropped the cigarette butt to the stage floor and ground it beneath her shoe.

"Your agent's seen it. You'll have to trust him." Cambridge turned to the others gathered into a close knot in the center floor area. He held up the hand with the papers in it and shook them so that the pages flapped noisily. "No one's getting those scripts on that chair until you sign this nondisclosure form."

A few in the film crew muttered, but the actors looked nonplussed. They'd seen in the trades how Cam had demanded the actors and crew sign affidavits pledging secrecy on his last picture.

Cam continued, "I want anyone working with me on this to sign the dotted line. Crew, gaffers, light directors, everyone. You're not going to get an opportunity to run off and show it to your attorneys because I've already struck deals with the agents concerned. They know what's good for you, so listen to them. Try to pry out of them the whole story plot and it's cause for dismissal. You sign tonight or you're off the film."

"Cut out the dramatics, Cam, and tell us what the nondisclosure says and why we should want to sign it." Olivia had the clout, her star shining the brightest in the Hollywood sky. She said what everyone wanted to say, but didn't have the guts to whisper aloud.

"It says you'll get the script scene by scene before it's shot. No one except Robyn, who's already seen the entire thing, of course, gets the whole script. As I mentioned, the agents involved have read over a copy and returned it. They approve. The nondisclosure also says that Robyn's production company and I will personally bring suit against anyone in this room who lets any part of the script leak to the media. Or if any of you tell your lovers, your spouses, mommas, daddies, or your hairdressers what's going on here on the closed set.

"In other words this script better not get past this room. If it does I will not only fire you and fine you, I'll prosecute your squirrelly ass." He paused and glared, eyebrows knitting together. "And you know I'll do it. This form says you agree to these terms."

"I'm not doing it." Olivia grabbed her small green alligator clutch and turned to leave the stage. Georgie knew she had read about Cam's last movie and contract deal. That one said nothing about prosecution; she knew that too. She was pulling a power play. She liked living on the edge, just like Cam.

"You know how much money you're turning down, right? Your agent told you?" Cambridge called to her back.

She turned and narrowed her eyes. Those dark, exotic, chilling eyes. "You know I don't need the money."

"What about a second Oscar? It's been almost a decade since your first. You're fading fast, Olivia."

Oh, good one, Georgie thought. Now why don't you kick her while she's down.

"Screw you, too, Cam." She paused a beat, not really giving in to the anger yet. "You're guaranteeing me an Oscar?"

Cambridge nodded. Then he said, "I'm playing you against type, Olivia. This film will go down in history. You'll be remembered forever for this part. In this film. In my film."

"I guess you want to cast me as a prostitute or something. Or maybe a space queen on Planet Zytoid. Is that it?"

"You've always played a heroine, Olivia. This time you'll excel in the role of a villain."

"Absolutely not. I positively refuse!"

Cambridge broke from where he stood holding the forms in both hands. This abrupt action startled not only Georgie, but everyone watching. Cam was across the space separating him from Olivia so fast several of the silent bystanders watching this interaction between two strong personalities gasped aloud.

When he reached Olivia where she stood her ground, challenging him, he tucked the papers under his arm and began to gesture to her in typical Italian street fashion. His voice changed and he was Al Pacino shouting at the top of his voice, "You wanna fuck with me? Huh, is that what you want? You wanna fuck with me?"

Olivia's face transformed with sudden spirited laughter. Everyone, including Georgie, joined her, startled by the inexplicable change in face, voice, and body Cambridge was able to bring about. It was as if Pacino had manifested himself in this harried-looking, potbellied, decadent director. Georgie had never seen him do that before. It was something new, something he must have practiced for a while.

"Jesus, Cam, that's good. You do that better than Pacino does that," Olivia said.

Cambridge grinned, showing the spaces between his big square teeth. "I haven't told you the best news of all yet. Stick around!"

He returned to his spot before the group and stared at each of them in turn as he spoke. "What I am about to say now is privileged information. If one of you breathes a word of this and it gets out, your ass is mine and you know I'm not kidding. You'll never work again, not only on my pictures, but *anybody's*. You think I don't have the clout?" He paused, shot a glance at Olivia, daring her to interrupt. "You think the agents in this town have the power and I don't? Well, let me clue you in on a little secret. I have all the top agencies behind me on this. If I can't ruin you, they will. So believe me when I say I am not kidding!"

A shudder ran through the group. Georgie reacted to a chill running up his own back. Agents *did* have the power to put any one of them out of business permanently. If Cam had the agents on his side, he had the power, no question.

"Come over here, Georgie." Cam gestured for him to come forward.

Georgie sauntered forward, knowing all eyes followed his passage. His leggy frame was encased in jeans so worn they had holes in the knees and seat. The latter wouldn't have been so noticeable if he hadn't been wearing flaming red shorts, but that wasn't something he cared about, what people thought of him personally. He cared about Cam. About this picture. That's *all* he cared about.

"Tell them," Cambridge said.

Georgie cleared his throat. He liked handling the camera; he wasn't all that fond of being the centerpiece in a group this way. He tugged on his jeans in an "aw shucks" way, felt stupid as a shit-eating puppy, and finally grinned. "We've bought the patent to a new film process. This will be the first major film of its kind, at least for distribution to theater. Have any of you been to Vegas, seen the 3-D wraparound shots at the Mirage? Or checked out the virtual reality rides at Disney World?"

A few heads bobbed, a few "Yeahs" were muttered.

14

"Have any of you been to a theater where there's a dome with semi-reclining seats?"

Olivia interrupted, "It's going to be 3-D? Without the glasses? Good God. A gimmick film."

"No gimmick. The story carries this one," Cambridge said, dismissing Georgie with a slight jerk of his head. Georgie moved out of the limelight, relieved to drift to the edge of the group.

Cam continued, "3-D, yeah, in a manner of speaking. But without the aid of those dumb-ass red and green cardboard glasses. And it won't be shown at just the one theater. At least one theater in every metropolitan city in this country is already being outfitted with hydraulic platforms and seat-belted seats for the audiences. Two years ago they tried out interactive films on laser discs in seventy theaters nationwide. We all know how those tickets sold like gangbusters. Those same theaters, plus the new ones built since then, will show this film. I've got studio backing on this. It's . . . needless to say, a big outlay of investment monies." He glanced over at Robyn and back again. "Screens are being expanded to wrap around the peripheral vision and heightened for overhead projected images. This film will be the first of its kind to reach mass audiences. The studio thinks it'll pay off. Robyn's partners think it will, too."

Georgie saw Olivia move past Cam to the metal folding chair. She looked tightly controlled, all erect shoulders, stone-faced with determination. She picked up one of the scripts bound in a green metallic folder and flipped over the cover.

Uh oh, Georgie thought. Here it comes, turn on the fan. Turn on a big *industrial-size* monster fan.

Olivia looked up at Cambridge. She spoke with a furious edge to her voice. "*Pure and Uncut*? Are you kidding me? This

15

is a joke, I take it. Sounds like a film about cocaine."

Cam just grinned.

Jackie Landry followed suit, taking up one of the scripts and looking at the title. He frowned, which only made him look even more handsome. He had been called the younger version of Redford and Georgie saw the resemblance. He had the same blond, wholesome, sexy good looks women swooned over. "*Pure and Uncut.* I like it," he said. Behind him Marilyn and Jerry snatched up copies.

"You want *me* to play a killer, am I getting this straight, Cam?"

Cambridge ignored Olivia and began handing out the nondisclosure forms to the film crew. "Pens are in my office if you don't have one on you."

"Cam! Talk to me, goddamn it. This is about a woman named Krystal and she's a killer? Have I got this story line scoped?"

"You got it, baby." He continued handing around the papers.

"You're gonna waste a new 3-D process on a *slasher* movie?" Olivia couldn't raise her voice any higher without hitting a screech.

"It's not a slasher movie. It's a suspense film. Ten leagues and a hundred million dollars beyond slasher junk, Olivia. The lead's a stalker. Think *Basic Instinct*, but hotter and better."

"Now I know you've sincerely lost your mind. I never thought I'd see the day. You've made films that rocked this town on its ear. But now you come up with this tripe? I'm not believing it."

It was as if a fire had been lit under Cam. Georgie saw it happening. He'd seen it before and every time it never failed to make his blood sizzle and zing. Cam whirled and suddenly he was no longer the reasonable, intelligent director or the clowning Pacino imitator. He was a ten-story flame and smoke disaster.

"Look, you stupid bitch, I can hire you or I can send you packing, but I will *not* keep taking shit from you all fucking night, you got that?" From the rage in his tone the people nearest him cringed back in fear.

"I'm not going to direct a *Jurassic Park*, hell no! I'm not going to do a sci-fi flick for special effects; that's what everyone would expect. I'm going to do this thing my way and this script is going to put me right over the top and anyone who acts in it is going over with me. I had the best screenwriters. I worked on the script myself. This has more chills than the last ten suspense films put together. You think Hitchcock made a mark? Wait until this gets finished.

"People are going to be locked into their seats, you understand that? They're going to be bolted down and swung up and down and sideways, they're going to lurch and spin forward and get jerked the hell back. They are going to *live* this movie. They're not going to watch it. They're going to stalk someone with Krystal. If there's a car wreck, the audience will be inside the car. If there's a sudden object flying through the air at you, the audience will see it coming straight for their faces.

"What sells in this country? I'll tell you what! Violence. It's lapped up like mother's milk. We fucking *thrive* on it. We've become the entertainment capital of the world, don't you know that? Not *Hollywood,* but our violent society. It's all the hell this country has to offer anymore. Our crime, our guns, our drugs, our sex, our music. We're into death here, that's what we're all about and if you think any differently, you're sadly mistaken.

"This film is going to give the moviegoer the chance to

17

participate and he won't have to go to jail for it. No prison time. You think your typical movie fan wants to see another dinosaur? Another Freddy Kruger with the knife glove? Another *Star Wars* fight? They're sick of the buddy movies and the la-goddamn-de-da romantic comedies.

"No! I know what they want because I want it too, and you want it." He turned, jabbing a finger at Marilyn, at Robyn, at Georgie, at Jackie, and then at Olivia. "We all want it and we don't want to admit it, but it's there, that craving. We're connected to it on CNN, we export it with our troops overseas, we send it out over the airwaves. And we want it to be real. We want to feel it and wallow in it and *be* it."

He stopped talking abruptly and to Georgie it seemed as if at that moment the frightening truth of what Cam had just said had hit him somewhere deep where he hadn't truly understood it before.

Cam coughed, blinked, glanced around at the staring faces and he saw the same truth reflected back to him.

"Sign the contracts," he said softly, beginning to hand the papers out again. "You won't be sorry. I promise you that. If you'll trust me, you'll be a part of something so big no one will ever forget it. Just sign the goddamn contracts."

Georgie held his breath again while Olivia took the offered pages and walked slowly toward Cam's lighted office for a pen. On the way she lit a cigarette. From the back, with her squared shoulders, she might have been Joan Crawford, one of her idols. She had the screen presence of one of the old stars, the real stars. Georgie admired the hell out of her for that. It was something you couldn't buy, learn from acting classes, or imitate. You had to be born with it.

All the others, upon seeing her give in, brought pens out of pockets and purses and began to sign. Georgie borrowed Jerry Line's pen when he'd finished, then he signed too. He'd been on all Cam's films. He would have signed in blood and sold his soul to the devil to work with him again, no debate.

Cambridge laughed and lumbered over to Robyn. Georgie saw him hug her so hard she lost her footing and he had to steady her as he let go. "This is gonna be beautiful," he said, laughing.

Georgie moved closer, the nondisclosure drooping in his hands. People just mostly ignored Georgie and that helped him drift about anonymously. He might as well be a stage prop for all the attention his movements caused. Whenever Cam needed to know something, he always came to Georgie to find out the scuttlebutt. Georgie the Sponge, he called him kiddingly. Georgie, my man, my friend, the finest cameraman in the business.

And Georgie was that. He was the finest. He just happened to have the personality of a metal folding chair. Good thing he'd never had aspirations to act.

"This better be beautiful," Robyn was saying, her eyebrow quirked up in mock fierceness. "It's costing me enough. It flops, I go bankrupt."

"We have investors, don't be a prima donna."

"No one bigger than me," she said.

"No, baby, no one bigger than you, you fucking shrimp."

Robyn smiled coolly and gave him a peck on the cheek. "I love you, too, you gonorrhea goofball. Want to take me for drinks after? To celebrate?"

"I got an appointment."

"In those dives you hang out in?"

"Yeah."

"You're going to get more than gonorrhea you keep that kind of company."

"I'll watch my dick and you watch yours," he said, slapping her on the rump.

"If I had a dick," she said.

"You *don't?*"

Robyn smiled again, but this time with more warmth. She began to collect the signed nondisclosure forms, taking Georgie's first, giving him a little noncommittal smile. Now Cam and the production company possessed all the power over the entire crew for the duration of the filming.

Georgie had a job to do.

The movie was a go.

# 2

"Hollywood is a place that attracts people with massive holes in their souls."

Julia Phillips, *The Times*, London

In the silent dark of the room, in the center of the womb place, in this darkness thicker than any moonless, starless night, deeper than any cave or dungeon, The Body reclined.

The chair, specially built, cost a princely sum. It was made of supple leather shaped to The Body's dimensions and natural curves. When in the reclining position it held The Body's feet raised, but not so far as to make the blood rush to the brain. The arms of the chair were exactly the length of The Body's arms so that the hands reached just to the end where the fingers, from the second knuckles down, lay over the edge.

In this dark and comfortable place which The Body required, came the dreams of glory and the fantasies of retribution. In this room, it thought of itself as The Body for it was the body that dictated all responses from others, all future events and outcomes. Not a name. Not a gender. Just the shell, The Body.

It seemed now The Body had been gifted with a perfect plan for redeeming itself in the blood of one who had done it such great, irreparable harm. That was why it lay now, giving

21

in to the darkness and taking something back from it.

Cambridge Hill had given them the script. The one script that turned itself into a plan. Had it been years, already? And it had, it had been years, without redemption, without surcease of pain. Before this there was no sure method of extracting revenge without fear, without reaping the proper benefits.

So The Body waited. Closed in the dark, soundproof, lightless room. Lying in the specially made chair. Often, when the control slipped, weeping inconsolably over loss, gripped with sorrow, wracked with frustration.

Now there was a way. A Way. To take the offender away. Away.

Into the ultimate darkness without exit.

But an exit after tremendous suffering, thought The Body. No exit before the plays are made, the scenes wrapped, the work put into the can.

A beeper sounded, reminding The Body to return to the world at hand. Without that auditory intrusion, the sensory deprivation might carry The Body off into some other dimension of madness from which it could not withdraw.

That would be unjust, to embrace true lunacy right at the moment justice appeared within reach. The Body had been tempted. Before acquiring the timer that beeped after three hours, there'd been times in the room that lasted longer than hours and longer than days, perhaps for lifetimes. And The Body lost itself, forgetting the chair, the house where the room was located, the city where the house stood, the state that held the city, the planet that twirled in the solar system.

Right on the mouth of madness The Body teetered willingly, staring down into the throat leading to eternal damnation. Many times. Tempted like an angel promised the right-hand throne next to God. Tempted as heartily as was the great Lucifer, the most beauteous of all.

I have been there and come back, The Body thought, pulling itself upright and to its feet, moving now away through the darkness, hands outstretched to grope for the door latch, the only one set into the four walls, knowing approximately where the latch might be and searching for it with fingertips that trailed along the tufted, buttoned, padded surface.

I have come back from the precipice and if I am good, if I am strong, I will not visit again until this is done.

Until my worst enemy is dead, finally, released from life, dead and done.

# 3

"Where is Hollywood located? Chiefly between the ears. In that part of the American brain lately vacated by God."
                                Erica Jong, *How To Save Your Own Life*

Cambridge Hill sat on a barstool between a rummy who worked as a dock loader for a concrete company and a young slut who was doing a pretty good job of putting the moves on him. Cam had drunk five beers and was feeling more maudlin than raunchy. He turned away from the slut girl, knowing that would offend her and ensure he'd go home alone, alas. But never mind, never mind.

He faced the dock loader. "Jim? That your name, right? Jim?"

"That's it. And you're Cam!"

"Stands for camera."

Jim eyed him suspiciously. "You're kidding."

Cam grinned, showing the full smile with the spaces between his teeth. "Yeah, I'm kidding. It stands for Cambridge. My parents had high hopes."

"So you disappointed them, huh?"

"You could say that. I make movies."

"Sure you do." Jim polished off his whiskey neat and gestured to the bartender for another. "Everybody in fucking LA's making movies. Even my barber's writing a screenplay."

24

"Gonna make a stalker movie. Just signed up the actors and crew tonight."

"You're not making this up, like with the camera?"

Cam shook his head. "It's the truth. I make movies. I direct. You ever see *Soldier*?"

"Hell, yes! I was in Nam and that movie was right on, man. You the guy who made that? Shee-it."

"That's my movie. I was in Quang Ngai. Foot soldier, mine fodder, and I just got lucky to get out alive."

"Marines." Jim held out his hand and shook Cam's hand. "Da Nang. We're getting to be old soldiers, you know that? You ever think you'd be old? I never would have thought it. Old, man, I hate that shit."

Cam slurped up the last drops of his beer and ordered another. "So I'm doing this stalker movie," he said, bringing the subject back around to what he wanted to talk about. He often took his work into the working man's joints, checked out their responses, their ideas. Sometimes he even incorporated them into whatever film he was working on. You could do worse than listen to your audience. They knew what they liked, what moved them, what bored the fuck out of them. Cam's colleagues didn't listen to these people. They looked *down* on the public, feeding them what they thought they should want. Which translated to either mindless drivel or left-wing political diatribes on the latest bleeding heart subject the media helped burble to the top of the cesspool.

"Stalker movie, yeah," Jim said, focused. "Scary movie, huh?"

"Plenty scary. But see, it's a woman stalking a guy."

"Hey, that ain't so farfetched. I know a guy that happened to. He couldn't get rid of the psycho bitch. She like *haunted* him. Everywhere he turned, the crazy bitch was there."

"Well, that's not quite what this will be about, but close."

"So tell me about it."

For the next hour, while the two men drank at the bar like long-lost friends, Cam laid out the plot of his movie to Jim, the dock loader. At the end of the hour both of them were well on the way to inebriation. Cam thought ole Jarhead Jim liked the movie story, but certainly it could be the whiskey talking. Still, it reassured him to have a real person say yeah, he thought it was a damn cool idea.

You couldn't depend on agents and producers and front-money men and actors to tell you if a movie would fly or not. What the fuck did they know? They made movies, they didn't know what movies they ought to be making. They had their heads so far up their asses they breathed methane. And the scriptwriters, Jesus God. One piece of lackluster crap after another came across his desk, like the writers' brains were full of sawdust.

Now that Cam had gotten one opinion—one of many to come since he'd do this again real soon—he remembered the babe and checked to see if she was still hanging around.

Shit no. She wasn't anywhere in the place. Gone home with someone else already. He'd missed his chance, not that he was going to cry about it. She had looked all right, but he wouldn't have fought the local PTA to lay her.

He scanned the crowd that had grown since he and Jim had started talking and saw a couple of possibles at a booth in the back. Lone gals, one dark and one light, sipping pink cocktails, for Christ's fucking sake, and watching for a man to give them a tumble. He thanked Jim for his time and said, "I'm going to find myself a warm body to get me laid."

"Hey, go for it, hoss. I gotta get home to my ole lady anyway before she calls up the cops."

Cam ambled across the room to the girls. So fucking what

if he couldn't handle both of them in his condition. There was always tomorrow morning if they'd stay the night.

Many times he'd been fine in bed, a goddamn stallion, once the sun was up for a while. Blessed with an iron constitution, he never suffered hangovers. Come morning, he could screw the lights out of five women if he could get his hands on them.

God bless hops and malt and cool mountain water, heaven's midnight nectar. God bless the women who spread their legs when they saw him coming.

He grinned lopsidedly at the women and they smiled back. Ah, sweet conquests.

# 4

**Hollywood:** "To survive there, you need the ambition of a Latin American revolutionary, the ego of a grand opera tenor, and the physical stamina of a cow pony."

Billie Burke, *Filmgoer's Companion*

Karl LaRosa knew the car behind him was a tail only after he made his fourth turn, taking him from Hollywood to the freeway that led to North Malibu. Coincidence. No, he didn't believe in coincidence. You got what you worked for; you brought into your sphere what you needed; you hit on the right idea because you focused your mind in the right direction. No, this was not just some driver going his way. This was someone stuck right on his ass.

It could be anyone. An LA gang who wanted his car. It wasn't a new Jaguar. It was, however, a primo sports coupe, 1985. Carjackers might not know the difference.

Or the tail might be a pissed-off client. A damn nutcase. Anyone.

He put the pedal to the floor and took his chances on getting a speeding ticket. None of the thoughts he'd just had concerning the tail made him care much about having to face a cop. In fact, if whoever was behind him had mischief in mind, a cop would be a godsend.

His Jaguar pulled away from the headlights in his rearview. He slipped over two lanes to the fast lane and saw it was clear ahead. The speedometer was already rocking at ninety and slamming on. The motor hummed along like the well-kept, handmade beauty it was. He kept the car in A-1 condition mostly because he loved it, but also because of the long commute he made to and from work. He couldn't outrun a 'vette or a Ferrari, but for some reason he didn't think the tail was one of those sleek expensive jobs. The headlights were too far apart for that.

Still he could see the car behind him gaining.

His foot pressed the floorboard as if more pressure might cause the Jaguar to go faster. Now the speedometer jiggled at one hundred and the motor purred like a contented beast. The speedometer inched over, going into the red line.

He catches me, Karl thought, and plays bumper cars, we are both in serious shit here.

His speed rose another twenty miles an hour. There was a hundred and eighty on the gauge, but he'd never tried burying it and he didn't think he had the guts to try it now. The lane ahead was still clear. It was Sunday night, almost two in the morning. Good thing. If there had been heavy traffic he could never have gone so fast.

He checked the rearview and driver's side mirror. Oh man. It was really coming. The tail was just a car length back. It was coming like a train, straight for his back bumper. That would never do. The Jaguar couldn't hold the road if it got a jolt. Or rather, the Jaguar might hold, but he wasn't sure his driving skills were up to it.

He lifted his foot from the gas pedal. As the tail neared, it fell back to keep from ramming him. When the speedometer read eighty, that's when it happened.

Karl screamed just as if he thought the driver of the other car might hear him. "Hey, don't hit my car!"

Metal rapped metal as the bumpers touched, then there was a surge and Karl fought the wheel, his foot hovering, but not touching the brake. If he hit the brake it was all over. They'd both go catapulting over a side lane and into other traffic.

The lights behind him backed off. They fell back a car length, two, three. Karl slowed more, his heart bongo-ing in his chest in a crazy boom-boom rhythm. Despite the wind coming through his cracked open side window, he felt sweat slip down his forehead and sting his eyes.

As he watched the rearview and side mirrors, he saw the headlights swing over two lanes to an exit and leave the freeway.

"What was that all about?" he asked aloud. "What in hell was that about?"

He moved over carefully two lanes, his speed down to a normal sixty miles an hour. He realized he was breathing fast and he bet if he could see his face in the rearview mirror it would be white as driven snow.

Lucky, he thought. You're a real lucky son of a bitch, Karl LaRosa. Whoever played tag with you decided at the last moment to give it up.

Maybe it had been a drunk, a stupid drunk, his mind warped by alcohol vapors. Or someone on drugs who came to his senses just in time to avoid a horrible wreck.

Once off the freeway and driving down the quiet night streets of Malibu, Karl sighed. His workweek recently was eating up his weekends, running all the days together. Tonight he'd been locked in his office finishing up paperwork on a new client. She'd want instant results, as if the world should bow down to her whims and wishes. Most of them were like that. Now, I want it now. I can't wait, it's got to be now.

Not that he was bitter or cynical, not yet. He'd been in

Hollywood since his college days and he was used to it, used to the get-it-done-by-yesterday mentality. He actually had a lot of sympathy for his clients. This was Barracuda City. It infected newcomers with such apprehension and longing that they couldn't help pushing, shoving, hurrying as if tomorrow was too late and next year, well, next year didn't even exist.

He knew how much they cared and how much they needed success. That's what made him so good. He understood the fire that burned them and so he made allowances. He had patience when others didn't. He was very good as a personal publicity manager and it was his empathy that made all the difference.

He turned into his driveway and hit the remote for the garage door. He drove inside, shut off the motor and sat a moment. He should see if the bumper was dented. Maybe it was all right . . .

Just as he grabbed up his leather zippered case of papers from the passenger seat and opened the car door, he saw something askew.

The door leading into the house was open.

It was never open. Never. It was locked until he unlocked it.

There might be someone inside still. Would he not only be nearly run down tonight, but maybe murdered by a burglar?

He glanced at his car phone. He'd look stupid if he called out someone and there was nothing wrong. Maybe he should check out the situation first. He slid out of the car quietly. He pushed the door shut just until the interior light went off, then pressed harder until the latch took. He moved softly to the door leading from the garage into the kitchen. He touched the doorknob, stood listening.

No sounds. They were gone already or they were in some part of the house where he couldn't hear them.

He peeked around the door, opened it wider, slipped inside. He had no weapon, didn't believe in guns, didn't like them. Frankly, guns scared the hell out of him. Olivia had offered him a 9 mm Glock automatic from her collection, but he said thanks, no thanks, that looks like a killer to me. Now he wished he'd taken it and stashed it in the Jaguar.

Maybe he should just get back in the car and call the cops. That's what a smart homeowner would do.

No, he was already inside now and there were no voices, no secretive sounds of movement. He couldn't detect the presence of another human.

He halted and took stock. The light over the stove was on as he had left it. No one here. No problem here. Nothing seemed out of place. He hadn't known he'd been holding his breath, expecting to see disaster, until now that the air rushed out of him all in a whoosh.

He turned to the door leading to the living room. Lamp on in there. He didn't leave lights on in the rest of the house, only the light over the stove. So someone had left it on. He was almost certain the intruder was gone. The house felt forlorn and empty the way it always did when he first entered.

His footsteps on the tiled kitchen floor rung through the room and no one came running, brandishing a handgun in his face.

He worked up spit enough to call out in a cranky, scared voice, "Anybody in there?"

He paused, listening hard. Nothing. They were gone. He or she was gone. "They're gone, Karl, catch your heart and slow it down." Admonishing himself this way did the trick. Almost. He calmed, was suddenly afraid again when his footsteps creaked over a low board in the wood floor. He couldn't help his irrational fear, but it made him angry, too. Would

Lee Marvin or Robert Mitchum be this scared? Would John Wayne? Hell no.

He straightened up. Glanced around the living room and saw nothing at all disturbed. Everything lay and sat just as he'd left it. His coffee mug on the glass dining table near the far wall of windows. His reading glasses he kept at home, just as he'd placed them that morning on the latest copy of *Variety* on the coffee table. Nothing missing that he could tell. There sat the big CD player unit, the television and VCR, even the Oscar his father had won in the forties for Best Supporting. Hell, if this was a burglary, they'd have surely taken Oscar. No one in the universe would break in and leave behind the gold-plated statue.

Perplexing. Why break in if they didn't want to steal something?

The hair tingled at the back of his neck. He swallowed and it hurt, like the muscles in his neck were tight as newly strung fence wire.

It was something else. Whoever had been here wasn't interested in stealing his things. Whoever it was hadn't been looking for anything special. Then what . . . ?

He hurried now, dropping his leather case to the sofa, running through the room to his bedroom. He didn't know what he expected. A couple of teenagers lying startled and naked on his bed, caught in their illicit guilt. Or a dead body lying across the mattress, throat cut. Or . . . just anything but the soft light twinkling from the bedside lamp and the small, folded note lying on his pillow. He didn't expect that at all.

He straightened again, found that he'd been moving in a crouch, like some kind of animal going to ground and ready to spring. His fists were balled. He opened his hands now, flexing the fingers, and, after looking around the room quickly for signs of anything out of place but finding nothing, he moved to the unmade bed. He stared at the paper on his pillow without touching it. It was a sheet of cream stationery folded in half. His name, KARL, was printed in block letters with black ink.

He picked it up finally and flipped up the paper to read.

*Dear Karl, dearie, dear heart, my love.*

Karl could hardly force himself to read further. So far the words made no sense to him. He could not imagine who might have written them or why.

He read on.

*I hope you can find a way to forgive me for intruding into your privacy. I can't tell you how I got in. I might want to come again, you see. Don't bother to change the locks, by the way. It won't stop me.*

*I've missed you every single day, hour and minute we've been apart. If you'd only give me one more chance I would do anything. You know I'd lay down my life for you.*

*The one thing I can't do is give you up.*

*I love you too much to ever give you up.*

Karl's gaze rose from the end of the page where there were Xs and Os in the place of a signature. Xs and Os, like a lovesick kid would put at the end of a love letter.

He sank onto the side of the mattress and read over the note again. And a third time, his brow furrowing, his mind turning and tumbling, trying to decipher from the printed letters or the words who might have written them.

He refolded the note and closed his eyes.

He had a real problem.

Any one of several women might have written it, he admitted. He did not think himself promiscuous, but he certainly had had his share of relationships. Too many of his affairs ended in recrimination and long sorrow; that's the way it was out here with all the competition and the passion that sometimes got displaced onto people like him who helped a novice become a pro. He told them—didn't he tell them?—not to get serious, no commitment, please, let's not become too fond of our arrangements; it's not you, it's me. I'm not sure I'll ever be ready for another lengthy relationship. My marriage going on the rocks took away my hankering for all that.

Olivia might have written this note.

Or Marilyn.

Maybe his ex-wife, Robyn.

Or Catherine.

Fury at how the note-writer had included the thinly veiled threat "don't bother to change the locks"—overrode his wonder at who it might be.

He stood, flinging the note to the floor. He went through the house checking all the window locks and made sure the kitchen door from the garage was locked. Then he put a chair beneath the doorknobs on the front, garage, and back doors.

No one was coming in while he was here. He'd make damn sure of that! So what if it made him look like a scared little sissy pants. He wasn't going to bed without the doors secure.

When he'd finished, he returned to the bedroom and undressed. He hastily brushed his teeth, yawned widely at his reflection in the medicine cabinet mirror, and didn't remember the note until he crossed the carpet barefoot for bed. He stepped on it, creasing one corner of the folded stationery. He stooped, picked it up and dropped it into the trashcan next to the bedside table.

"To hell with it," he muttered.

He wondered if the Jaguar bumper was damaged as he crawled between the sheets, and was about to worry about who had gotten into his home to write the note, but the deep tiredness in his bones slithered throughout his body as he settled into bed. He fell into sleep as if he were diving through a wave and being lost in an undertow.

Dead to the world and any danger it might hold.

# 5

"Insecurity, commonly regarded as a weakness in normal people, is the basic tool of the actor's trade."
Miranda Richardson, *The Guardian*, London

Cam forced Jackie Landry to redo the shot where he entered the house and found the note on his pillow.

"Cut!"

This was the ninth take. He'd gone through this nine times and had been screamed at nine times. He now rubbed down his face with both hands, refreshing himself. Immediately the girl from make-up rushed over and patted him down with powder so his skin wouldn't shine from the lights. He always forgot and she always had to run over.

"Listen." Cam came right up to Landry on the set, but he was still shouting loud enough for his rant to carry clear across the room. "You don't look scared to me. If you don't look freaked out, this scene doesn't work, I keep telling you that. What's the matter, you didn't get enough sleep, you didn't get laid, what the hell's the matter with you?"

Jackie knew not to talk back. "Let me try it again."

"You're fucking right we're trying it again. Remember? You just got off the freeway and could have been killed. Your heart's already beating like crazy when you drive into the garage. You see the door open. Somebody might be inside.

37

They might have a goddamned Uzi in there, or at least a .45. If you want to ever break to eat lunch, you have to get this right. Now show me scared."

He walked off, turned, walked back again. "You've never been in the service, I know that, but have you ever in your life been in jeopardy? Ever been in danger?"

Jackie, at a loss and feeling horribly harangued, hung his head and mumbled, "I fell off my brother's roof once."

"You what?"

"I fell off a roof. That was pretty scary. I slipped going up after a kite, broke my arm in two places."

Cam threw up his hands and stalked off. "He fell off a fucking roof and broke his arm."

Jackie, chastised, was now in the proper mood. Cam scared the shit out of him. He never knew if he was going to yell at him or sock him in the nose. If he had to retake it again, Cam was going to slug him, he just knew it. And if that happened, he'd hit him back. He wouldn't want to; he knew if he did he'd be off the picture, but no one laid a hand on him without getting twice as much in return.

"Quiet on the set!"

Jackie focused on the garage door. When the cameras were rolling, he walked to it in trepidation. This time the shoot went smoothly. Cam yelled, "Cut!" after Jackie flopped on the bed, pulling the covers over his naked legs, his eyes falling closed on the close-up. Jackie struggled up from the mattress.

"That was great. That wasn't spectacular, but it was great. See, all it takes is acting."

Jackie glanced over at Olivia Nyad as the wardrobe person, Betty Ann, handed him a robe to slip over his jockey shorts. He never wore jockeys. He preferred boxers. His privates had shriveled up like a bunch of raisins with everyone watching him fail over and over to get the scene right. Olivia grinned.

"I don't think it's so funny," he said.

"Honey, trying to get you to look frightened is like trying to put a frown on Fabio. You're too handsome for your own good."

He tried to smile. It was a half-assed compliment, but it was a compliment nevertheless and he needed one just then. "I've never worked with Cam before," he said by way of explanation. Or maybe it was an apology.

"After you work with him this time, you won't work with him again either."

"Why not?"

"Because he eats actors alive. By the end of this film, you'll be shark bait."

Again Jackie sighed. Olivia was probably right. He had heard every actor ought to do one film with Cam, but only one. Many claimed that's all it took to learn the most important lessons about why they became actors in the first place. You found out if you loved the work enough to take that much abuse.

"You haven't worked with him before either, have you?"

"Never had the pleasure."

"He always yell like that?"

"Mostly. It's his method."

He gave her a puzzled look.

"You know. Some of them cajole, some fall in love with us, some are reasonable and depend on appealing to the intellect. But Cam, he's temperamental and that's how he gets his way."

"He's manipulative."

She laughed. "Don't say that so he can hear you. Even though you're right."

Robyn strolled by and tossed off, "Good work, Jackie." He watched her sashay past, his gaze riveted on her ass in the tight white slacks. Robyn was one of the few people in show business who came on a set in tight clothes. Most people wore whatever was comfortable. Sometimes they had to stay eighteen hours and tight clothes could hurt you. But not Robyn. She lived up to her model-like beauty, always showing it off.

"Want some of that?" Olivia asked.

She talked like a guy, which embarrassed Jackie for her sake. "She's so tiny."

"So was Napoleon."

He laughed and the bundle of tension putting a cramp in the back of his neck fled. Olivia might talk like a man in a locker room, but she was so clever it didn't seem to matter to him now. The damn scene was over. He'd gotten through it. But there were a lot more like it to come. He didn't want to think about that just yet. He was a little afraid audiences would think him a pussy all the way through this movie, if he had to be so scared all the time. It wasn't exactly the role of hero he was getting to play here. Maybe something good was coming up in the scenes they hadn't seen yet. Surely he didn't have to go around like a frightened geek through the whole movie. He fervently hoped.

He saw Olivia still watching him. His thoughts slipped out. "We're all nuts to be doing this without knowing the plot."

"We know it. I'm the stalker, you're the stalkee. What's to know?"

"I think it's going to be more than that."

She shrugged and lit a new cigarette. "I can handle it, whatever it is."

She would, too. She'd steal this movie away if he didn't watch out. They were going to share top billing, but given the chance, Olivia Nyad would whittle him down to a nub. He'd be her shadow. Hell, he already was. There had been no Oscar nominations for him.

The fleeting thought that being in a Hill movie might garner him one made gooseflesh break out on his naked legs and arms.

"You can't get your agent to tell you anything about the script?" he asked.

She shook her head. "To tell you the truth, I'm still trying. No luck yet." She rose to join him where he stood on the set. "Want to go get something to eat?"

"Sure, let me change." He knew she watched him walk away. Many men by nature were lecherous creatures. Olivia was the first female he'd met. He wondered what she'd be like in bed. A filthy talker probably, like some bad starlet in a low-budget porno flick. Fuck me, she'd say. Do me hard. Eat me, baby.

He grinned to himself.

He knew, if he played his cards right, he'd get to find out if he was right. Then maybe if she could weasel any information from her agent about the script, she'd tell him. It was worth a try. He hated working in the dark this way.

# 6

"Hollywood has always been a cage . . . a cage to catch our dreams."

John Huston, *Sunday Times*, London

When not immersed in the details of the next day's shooting script, The Body took care of all the necessary tasks to stay healthy. There was food to prepare and consume. Exercises to perform until the sweat rolled down the forehead in rivulets. A shower, preferably cold as ice, for the shock value to the system.

With all of that out of the way, The Body either sat in the dark isolation of the sensory deprivation room or went to the computer and typed out the sadness of a lonely life into a file of the word processor. It was a stream-of-consciousness activity that helped soothe the mind after a day on the set. The Body now typed, fast and sure, but without capital letters and sometimes without punctuation, thoughts running together the way they did inside a confused brain.

—inside Karl's house it was like trespassing but not enough to scare me. he might put in a security system. all the other Malibu bigshots have security systems. but i can get past anything he puts in. i've been studying electronics. i've been studying a lot of things. what else do i have to do with my time, but study. i could go crazy if i didn't keep my mind trained on the future. there was no future inside karl's house. it was spotlessly clean and too neat except for the bed, he didn't make the bed.

   last night i was in her house and it was clean too and i was worried for a minute the live-in maid had heard me enter, but no one came to check. C. was sleeping beside her husband. i'll only go in when she's sleeping. to watch her. to watch her and hate her. she'll never know i was there. i am a phantom. there is invisibility for people me—

The Body stretched, sitting straighter in the desk chair. Thirsty. Should have brought my glass of wine from dinner, The Body thought, rising from the computer.

The room was dark, save for a blue glow from the computer monitor. The Body passed near the mobile hanging over the crib and paused to give it a little swing. Mickey and Minnie Mouse and Goofy went swimming around in a circle in the air above the empty crib.

The Body found the wine bottle and poured a slug of it, filling the wine glass that sat next to the sink. At the door of the room where the computer sat, The Body flicked on the overhead light.

No more shadows. No more darkness. Away with it! Be gone, darkness and lies!

The stuffed toys arranged along the wall shelves. The white crib and the Disney-character mobile hanging now still above it. The child's bright rug on the wood floor, a series of alphabet blocks decorating the expensive fabric.

The computer stood on the white matching desk against the wall opposite the crib, the ramblings there not altogether coherent to anyone but the author.

The Body's eyes closed and the hand holding the wine glass trembled.

This room would never be put to good use. The bed, the toys, all of it a ghostly setting for The Body to save thoughts on a computer's disk. Most of the time the room was a haven and kept The Body from feeling so alone. But tonight . . . tonight it just made The Body lonelier than ever.

The light went out.

The Body left the computer monitor on and went to bed.

The full glass of untouched wine sat sweating and warming on draining board.

Tomorrow Cam would give them another set of pages from the script. The Body would then have something to do besides languish in this cage they called Hollywood.

# 7

"I fucking hated school. I was left back, so I was, like, sixteen in ninth grade. I wouldn't even make the effort to just keep up with it, to do the little bit of work that I needed to do to get by. I wanted to be an actor."

Quentin Tarantino, *Premiere*

Olivia Nyad sat in a white velvet chair across from her secretary Janet Grenda in the sitting area of her bedroom. Jan had been with her for ten years and saved her ass more times than Olivia liked to count. Once in a while she thought she saw a hint of disgust, as she did right now in Jan's eyes. If she really believed what she saw, she would have fired her on the spot. But she might be imagining it. It was too hard to find someone you could trust. She didn't really want to go in search of another personal secretary. How often could you find a confidante in Hollywood who would keep her mouth closed?

"Brad's not going to tell you," Jan said. "You can't push him too far."

"That bastard! I've made more money for him than fifteen of his other clients put together. He owes me." Olivia pulled her peach silk negligée closed over her bosom as if shielding herself from invisible attack.

She could see outside double leaded-glass windows. In the blue wash from the neighborhood streetlights and the rising moon, palm fronds swayed gently in a breeze. Shadows from the palms danced over the softly lighted swimming pool and the terrazzo deck surrounding it. She hated swimming. The pool came with the house.

"Cam made them promise not to tell." Jan had that pleading look, the one she used on Olivia whenever it appeared things were about to get out of hand.

"That fucking Cam." Then Olivia smiled. "I love the hell out of him. Who would have put me in this part, but him?"

"You see? There's a lot to be grateful for. If you can't get Brad to tell you about the script, at least you've got the best part in the film."

"Film!" Olivia spat the word, making it sound like something nasty. "That's what Cam does—films. Know what he said in an interview about Quentin?"

"I can't imagine." Jan shifted the valise of papers on her lap. Fan letters, attorneys' inquiries, stock option reports.

"He said Quentin does movies, which is a far different thing from making films. He insulted him right there in print. One director bitching out another before God and everybody. That's what I love about this town; it eats its young."

Jan smiled at this, agreeing silently. She sat waiting patiently. Olivia knew she was eager to get on with the day's work that sat on her lap, but she'd listen for as long as required. It was part of the job. There were other considerations, too. They had recently slept together, just to get it out of the way. It took years to be honest about the sexual attraction between them and they both thought they should do it and see what happened. Now Olivia only turned to Jan for physical affection if she couldn't find a willing male, but Jan hadn't an ounce of jealousy in her. Sometimes, though she couldn't prove it and didn't possess any real evidence other than the finger-walking creepy feeling up her back, Olivia suspected the other woman of watching when there was a man in her bed.

Which, if it were true, was a turn on.

"So you don't think Brad can be pried open?" she asked Jan again, thinking of the script and wishing, wishing, wishing, she could see the whole thing, all the scenes.

"Not even if you blow him."

Olivia laughed. "That's what I like about you, Jan, how you come right out with my deepest thoughts and most desperate plans." Jan knew she did not find her agent attractive. He wore his gut like a fat belly belt made of diamonds.

Olivia gestured to the valise. "What do I have to sign tonight?" She was tired from the shooting and tomorrow, at dawn, they were going on location again, "somewhere out in LA" Cam had told them, enjoying the mystery, getting a kick out of keeping them ignorant of the shooting schedule.

Jan had graduated from the University of Iowa in business administration. She'd married an actor wannabe who hauled her off to Hollywood, then promptly dumped her. Olivia had met her at one of the ex-husband's amateur plays where Olivia had gone to pick up another friend, a new, hot producer of teen ghoul movies. They had invited Jan to dinner afterward and hearing of her woes, Olivia had asked if she'd like to handle some personal business. She'd hired her within the month when it was clear the woman was a true find. Honest, hardworking, and most of all, loyal.

Jan shuffled through the papers, telling Olivia what was there and what she was supposed to do with it. Without Jan, Olivia would have had to hire four or five knowledgeable business people to advise her. Like the hot director, Quentin Tarantino, whose "movies" were muscling in on Cam's "film" reputation, Olivia had not gone beyond the ninth grade in school. She couldn't spell, she didn't know how to protect herself from the hounding of fans, and she had to depend on Jan to make sure she kept part of her earnings put away in the stock market for a rainy day.

Sure, she had an accountant, two attorneys, a business manager, an investment counselor—a retinue of handsomely paid guard dogs handling her career and income, but it was Jan who was the pipeline. They all moved the paper through her to save Olivia the trouble of meeting with ten different people.

For the next half hour Olivia half listened to Jan summarizing the paperwork while quickly signing sheet after sheet and studio publicity photos to send off to her fan club president to distribute to the fans who wrote asking for a picture of the star.

When finished, she shook her wrist to get out the cramp. "While I'm working on *Pure*," she said, referring to Cam's film, "maybe we can do this once a week instead of every night. It tires me out too much."

Jan looked doubtful. "It'll pile up. It'll take you longer to catch up."

"I don't give a damn. I can't be bothered with this stuff all the time. Don't nag me."

"Whatever you say. We'll make it once a week, then."

The telephone rang. Jan rose, folding closed the valise and setting it aside in the chair she vacated. She answered, looking over at Olivia. She said, "Hold on, let me check."

"Who?" Olivia asked. "It's late." It was eight p.m. She would be asleep by nine. It had been some years since she could stay up partying all night and still do any kind of decent job on a set the next day.

Jan covered the receiver with one hand. "Karl. He says it's important."

"Gimme." Olivia held out her hand for the receiver. She

always had time for Karl LaRosa. Jan scooped up the valise in her arms and left the bedroom for her office on the other side of the house where she'd sort through the papers for the next day's mail.

"Hi, baby!" Olivia's face brightened in anticipation.

"Olivia, I'm sorry to bother you, but I have to know something. Did you get in my house and leave me a note?"

Olivia glanced at the door closing behind Jan. "Why would I do a thing like that?"

"Someone did. You gave me back the key, didn't you?"

He meant the key to his place. They'd had a brilliant affair, so lusty and brawling it made her wet to remember. She had been hoping when he called that he wanted to renew their relationship and here he was asking if she still had the key. Steel slipped into her voice though she tried not to let it happen. How dare he?

"I gave it back, Karl. I don't have your fucking key. I wouldn't go into your house and leave you a note. If I wanted to leave you a note, I'd nail it to your goddamn forehead."

"Don't get that way, I just asked. I had some trouble last night and . . ."

"Well, I'm not the trouble you had and I'm pissed off you called me up thinking I was. Now I have to hang up. I'm shooting early in the morning."

"Olivia? Calm down, I didn't mean it that way."

"Fuck off, baby." Olivia slammed down the receiver, shaking all over in a sudden fury. She stood and the negligée fell open just as she caught sight of her reflection in the full-length mahogany mirror that stood in the corner. Her breasts needed some new work. Her neck . . . goddamnit . . . was already sagging again. She should have seen her surgeon before she took the part on Cam's movie. Those wrinkles in her neck might show up if they didn't get the lighting right. Fuck!

She tried to get hold of herself. If she let anger take over, she'd never get to sleep. She'd look like shit tomorrow. Everyone would notice.

She wished she had invited Jackie home with her tonight. A roll in the hay would have relaxed her. He was younger, of course he was. She didn't like to remember, but half of Hollywood was younger than Olivia Nyad. Although that had *never* mattered.

She pushed the intercom button on the wall and said to Jan, "You get in that shipment?"

"Sure. It came by courier yesterday."

"In my box? You put it in there?"

"Yes."

Olivia shut off the intercom and crossed the big, open room to her bedside table where the Goodie Box sat. It was an Indian-made box, a foot square, inlaid with mother of pearl and exotic woods. Inside she found the new stuff. Pills, the colors of the rainbow. She fondled the packages and felt her heart-rate diminish to a manageable pace. No one could tell her this was bad for her. They were wrong. Without a little chemical help, life was too raw to live. She found the plastic baggy she wanted and reached inside for two little white tablets.

She closed the box and walked into the adjoining bathroom for a glass of water.

Now she'd sleep despite Karl's phone call and the new regret he had stirred in her. That son of a bitch.

# 8

"People in Hollywood are always donating money to politics and causes. As if to expiate the sin of getting too rich and too famous too fast."

    Julia Phillips,
     *You'll Never Eat Lunch In This Town Again*

Robyn LaRosa wrote out a check for one thousand dollars and handed it to B.B. Bernie Bardacelli who owned one of LA's most stylish night clubs, the Universe, but his heart was in the redwood forest he came from on the Olympia peninsula. He hit his regular customers for donations to national parks, Greenpeace, whatever organization caught his fancy that week. This was the third such donation Robyn had made in a year.

"If that isn't enough, don't tell me," she said, flashing B.B. a grin.

"Yeah, I saw in the trades you sunk your money in one of Cam's projects." People jostled them, packing into the club. It was a Thursday night, but the Universe never had slow nights. Anyone who was anyone wanted to be seen there. From where they stood, Robyn spotted Travolta, girls hanging off him, and in another group, Wesley Snipes with his agent.

"It's going to make me enough profit to buy my own island if I want. You should have invested in it."

B.B. stuffed the check in his coat pocket. "If you'd marry me, I'd buy you an island. Which one you want? Cayman? Maui?"

Robyn snuggled up to B.B.'s huge chest. She ran long red nails down the front of his white starched shirt. "B.B., I'd wear you out in a week flat. You need to get in shape, you want me."

His laugh was deep and bear-like. He hugged her, then excused himself to handle club business. "I don't watch these guys, they rip me off, fucking gonzo motherfuckers."

Robyn doubted that. No one would screw over B.B., not even a bartender. He had been connected in Seattle and made enough from a string of espresso shops to move down into LA and open the Universe. If his size didn't scare you, his friends up in Washington state would.

Robyn looked around. She had to shove off, find a man. She was on the first level. The Universe was really three clubs in one. B.B. had gotten, as in *stolen,* the idea from a hot Atlanta club. The lower level was Hell. Down here were the heavy metal and punk rock bands. You couldn't hear yourself think. Not that people who came to drink, find bed partners, and gyrate to high-decibel music wanted to think.

Upstairs, on the second level, was Purgatory. Robyn didn't like that room. Country and western music was all the rage—dance instructors had made a killing off Californians giving lessons in the Cotton-eyed Joe and the cowboy two-step—but it sounded like twangy shit to her.

At the top, on the third level, was Heaven. That's where she headed now, threading her way up the wide carpeted stairs. All the new music was played in Heaven. Alternative. Smooth beat and singers with voices like honey.

Two men waylaid her on the way up, but they weren't her type. She knew she kept looking for another Karl, hunting his replacement, and hated herself for it but what could you do. They hadn't had a good marriage, but she kept looking for him in every man she met anyway, like she was *programmed* or maybe ruined for other men. It was sickening. Hell, she hadn't even taken back her maiden name. She had been LaRosa for seven years and figured there was no point in changing it. During those seven years she'd made all her connections in Hollywood and Burbank. People knew her, remembered her, as Robyn LaRosa. So now that's who she was.

A frail dark-haired girl was on the stage in Heaven, strumming a guitar and backed by a small combo. Robyn found an open stool at the bar and ordered vodka over ice. She wouldn't look around. Someone would spot her any minute. She knew how good she looked. "Like a doll," Karl used to say. She could pass for twenty-five, though she was ten years older than that. Ten years and ten months, to be precise. It was all due to bone structure, a personal masseur, salad bars and infrequent visits to health farms, but what the hell, wasn't it always?

She felt warm man flesh next to her bare arm and smelled the scent of a familiar spicy cologne just as her drink was served. She kept her gaze forward and said, "Hello. Yes, I'm alone. Yes, I want company. No, I can't give out my number until we have a few dances and drinks."

"I know."

"Karl!" She turned too fast and slopped her drink over the bar. "Jesus, what are you doing here?"

"Looking for you. How have you been, Robyn?" He leaned over and kissed her lightly on the lips.

She frowned. "I'm fine, Karl, but you could have found that out by picking up the phone. Not that you do that anymore. What's up? This isn't your kind of place."

53

"B.B.'s a friend of mine, too. We still have friends in common."

"But this isn't your kind of place," she repeated, undaunted. "What do you want?"

"Why do you have to be so hard?" He looked a little sad and disappointed. And nervous. Why was he nervous?

"I think we've had this conversation before. If I wasn't such a bitch, if I wasn't such a ballbreaker, if I wasn't so hard, you might have loved me more."

Karl winced and looked away into the crowd on the dance floor. "I still love you."

"Like hell."

He looked back at her and she felt her color rising. Every time she got around Karl, she got mad. He was her one failure. She had succeeded in everything but marriage, and it was like a canker, festering. It never went away, her failure to make him love her just the way she was. She couldn't have changed! Where would she be now if she'd been easy and good and sweet and . . . lovable?

"You still hate me, though, don't you?" he asked. He sipped a beer and stared right into her eyes.

She sighed and turned back to face the bar. "I don't hate you, Karl. I hate myself for fucking up, that's all."

"Have you been out to Malibu?"

She blinked, but didn't turn to him. "I live up in the hills, you know that."

"Someone got into my house, Robyn. Left me a note. Before that, someone tried to run me off the freeway."

She turned her head. Saw he wasn't kidding. Then her anger returned and her cheeks felt hot as griddles. "You think it was me?"

"You have a set of keys still, don't you?"

"You're accusing me of letting myself into the house

and—what?—leaving some kind of note? You think I tried to run you off the road? Karl, how much have you had to drink? I don't give a flying fuck about going back in that house. I couldn't fucking care less about writing you any notes!"

He glanced at the dancers again. "I called Sheinberg today and he put off our meeting. He's never done that before."

Robyn looked puzzled. "What's that supposed to mean?"

"And two of my newest clients called up to say they thought they wanted to think over signing with me."

"Wait." Robyn turned full around on the stool and took his arm. "You're trying to tell me something, but I think I'm missing exactly what it is. What in hell are you talking about?"

"I've got a bad feeling, Robyn. Someone's messing with my life and I . . . Well, I don't know who it is."

"It's someone who knows you," she said. "So you thought . . ."

"It's not you, is it, Robyn?" He put his beer on the bar and took her in his arms. He said against her ear, "Don't let it be you. Please. I meant what I said. I still love you."

Robyn felt her heart contract and her vision blur. Goddamnit, why wasn't it true? He thought he still loved her, but he never had, not really, not the kind of love that forgives faults and overlooks weaknesses. "It's not me," she said, weakly, her voice catching.

He pulled away abruptly. "I have to go."

"Don't. Can't you stay just a little . . ."

"I'm sorry, I really have to leave. I've got some stuff to do at the office before I can go home."

She watched him as he started down the stairs to Purgatory.

"Fuck," she whispered.

"Now?" someone asked from behind her. "Here?"

"What?" She turned to face a thin young man dressed in a loose brown jacket, sleeves rolled to the elbow. His hair was blond, his jaw shaded with a fine gold beard.

She smiled, at ease, her thoughts of Karl replaced with thoughts of her big king-size bed with this young man reclining naked on it. "Hi," she said. "I'm Robyn."

"Yes, you are," he said, moving into her sphere, an arm circling her small waist as he guided her out to the dance floor. "Robyn LaRosa. I've seen you around. You produce pictures. I know your credits."

"And you have a script you're shopping," she said, laughing at how he wasn't tying to hide his motivations. How refreshing.

"One or two," he said. "But they can wait."

She slipped into his embrace on the dance floor and closed her mind to everything but the music and the yearning building in her body. She'd always had a thing for writers, especially the brave, pretty ones.

# 9

"They love the scenes where people are running, screaming, naked through the halls. But they might just hate
themselves for liking them. This is no new process; it's
obvious that there is a vicarious thrill involved in seeing
the forbidden."

David Cronenberg

There was a concerted effort to hurt him and hurt him bad. But
why?

Karl stood just outside his office in Burbank with his employees. They looked like a group of shellshock victims—confused, angry, and more than a little afraid. They stared at him
as if he might wave a magic wand and make the whole mess
disappear. He was the boss, after all, he could fix this, couldn't
he? Harry, his media man, said, "Brace yourself, Karl."

Karl pushed open the cracked and splintered door with his
fingertips. He stood just over the threshold looking at the de-
tritus left by a mind deranged.

He winced, sucked in his breath. He looked over his
shoulder. "Have you called the police like I told you?"

His secretary, Lois, nodded her head in a jerky way. She
had tears in her eyes. One of her best charcoal suits she favored for work had a streak of blood down the front of the
skirt.

"I guess they'll be here soon. Did anyone touch anything?"

Harry said, "We just looked in. We haven't touched a thing. This is how we found it. And the security alarm wasn't on. Someone disabled it first."

As if they would or could go in and touch stuff, thought Karl. The place was covered with blood. It looked like someone had slaughtered a hog in the outer office. The upholstered sofa and deep cushioned chairs were slimed and wet with blood. The walls looked as if buckets of blood had been thrown at them. Great splashes shocked the wall and dripped long red teardrops toward the carpet. Lois' desk was slick, her computer terminal covered, the telephone sitting in a puddle of coagulated scarlet.

"Why would anyone . . . ?" Lois began, letting the question trail away.

"I've been having some trouble," Karl said. "My house. Someone trailing me on the freeway. Now this."

A patrol car pulled to the curb and Karl's people moved aside to let a uniformed officer pass. Karl spent the next hour sitting in the car with one of Burbank's finest answering questions. He detailed the other strange happenings recently. It was all dutifully recorded, the officer shaking his head. "We'll get a team out here to look for fingerprints. Breaking into your house and leaving a note is one thing, but trying to run you off the road and this—" his head tipped toward the sidewalk and the office—"this is enough to get an investigation started. It looks like you have someone serious on your case, Mr. LaRosa. We'll want a list of names of women you've gone out with for the last couple of years."

Karl rubbed the flesh over the ridge of his nose. "I've been checking with some of the women I dated. I can't rule out anyone, but I just can't see anyone I ever cared about doing this to me."

"People go off their nut. I've seen enough craziness to tell you plenty of people you'd think were straight as an arrow sometimes do things you'd think only a madman would do."

Karl sent his people home. He told them he'd call when the scene was checked out and he could get a cleaning crew in. They hugged him. They shook his hand. They patted his shoulder, and Lois gave him a little chaste kiss on the cheek. She was crying when she did it and he told her, "C'mon, no one got hurt, that's what matters. It'll be all right."

But he wasn't sure he believed that. He didn't expect the cops to find any fingerprints or evidence. The person who did this was too smart for making dumb mistakes like that.

Driving home again, calling from his car phone to reschedule appointments with clients, his fury began to grow. The shock was wearing off and the more phone calls he had to make, the angrier he got. It was one thing to slip into his house, but to wreck his office and scare his people—that was just about enough. Who the hell hated him that much?

On his last phone call he had to cut it short. His voice was getting too hard and the client thought he had done something wrong and Karl was upset with him. "Gotta go," he said. "I'll have Lois call you for a new time, okay?"

He punched off the phone and used it to bang against his right thigh as he drove one-handed. The investigating detective said he'd call his home when they were through at the Burbank office. Karl had to get hold of some outfit who could rip out the carpets and put in new, clean and paint the walls, replace the sofa and chairs . . .

"I'll get you, you piece of shit!" he yelled out loud. A driver in a Volkswagen in the next lane glanced over at him, probably hearing the shout, but not the actual words, frowned and dropped back a car length.

# 10

"I know what it is to feel lonely and helpless and to have the whole world against me, and those are things that no men or women ought to feel."

Richard Hannay in The 39 Steps

Cam watched the dailies with a weary sense of satisfaction. Getting Olivia through the scene where she had to haul the animal blood from the trunk of her car and splash it all over the office set was hell. She balked, complaining about using real blood. He'd had to threaten to replace her if she didn't do the goddamn scene and do it now. Didn't she know he couldn't use fake blood and get anything out of the scene? The actors kept forgetting this film was going to be shown through a new process and that the audience would spot fakery right off.

Then Jackie. That fucking half-wit over-rated moron! He'd had to do eighteen takes before he got the scene in the car right. His voice wouldn't work. Just wouldn't work. He sounded like a dispassionate stockbroker calling his clients, not a Hollywood personal manager trying to control his dread when he talked to them about a "little problem at the office" that meant they had to change their appointments.

Maybe Cam had made a bad decision hiring Jackie Landry

for the male lead. The man had done some good films, but they were lightweight. He was extremely handsome so he'd done a few romantic comedies and some dramas where not much was asked of his acting abilities. Cam thought he saw in Landry a spark of something that he could draw out on screen. A wildness the actor had never tapped before. There had been an early film starring Landry where he played a petty criminal type and he'd *almost* walked right over the line of acting the part into doing something honest.

Cam thought for sure he could push and prod Landry into giving that one superlative performance he'd detected lurking in the man in that early film.

But so far it was a washout. The man was stiff as starched Navy whites. The more Cam yelled at him, the more he bottled up and froze.

Still, the scene today hadn't gone so badly. It had taken them fourteen hours, but by God, they'd delivered what he wanted.

Maybe he could have a private talk with Landry before a scene where he would have to do anything really outstanding. Or he could pull that trick he'd done with Newman. Just walk off the set and leave him on his own. See if he'd perform when he wasn't under Cam's watchful eye. Knowing if he didn't, he'd not only disappoint his director, but the whole damn cast.

Cam shut off the machine and left the editing room. It was almost one in the morning, but he could still find a joint open where he could get a beer and a willing ear. How anyone shot a film without blowing steam was beyond him.

Maybe he'd go to the Universe and see if Robyn was there. She liked the fucking place, hanging with the Hollywood crowd, being seen, picking up dates. He'd ask her about Landry. Cam could force Olivia to do what he wanted. Or so

61

he hoped. There were some tough scenes upcoming . . .

But where was the key to Landry? Robyn might know. She knew all about how to handle difficult men.

# 11

"Like the gladiator games in ancient Rome, spectacle reduces empathy. Callousness sets in, indifference to suffering. More excitement is required. Dangerous to humanity."

Oliver Stone, Wired Auditorium,
*America Online*, August 16, 1994

The Body had made sure the sophisticated alarm system connected to the office was left destroyed, in tatters. The wiring had been disemboweled from where it snaked through the building walls, the connection box busted to plastic bits, wires torn.

The Body had done the job in the early morning. Wristwatch hands stood at three a.m. Not a soul on the street at this hour, few passing cars. It was a business district, upscale, not far from the studio where the *Tonight Show* was taped.

The Body returned to the car parked at the curb, right on the street, and lifted the trunk lid. Getting the blood was a difficult affair. Had to break into a stockyard way the hell out at the edge of LA and sacrifice a steer. What a mess. Took hours.

The blood had been kept in plastic containers with screw caps overnight in the refrigerator at The Body's house. The blood warmed from riding in the trunk. Warm and liquid.

The front office door was already open, yawning darkly

along the brick front wall. A crowbar was sufficient to jimmy the deadbolt, though it had torn up the wood doorframe.

The Body lifted the first five-gallon plastic container and carried it across the sidewalk and into the black gulf beyond the broken door. Carpet, thick and expensive, cushioned The Body's footsteps. One strip of pale light filtered in from a front window overlooking the street. With vision adjusted to the dim interior, The Body stepped quickly to the desk in the office and set down the container to screw off the cap. Turned. Threw the blood at the walls. Almost giggled at the splash it made and the destruction it caused.

Returning to the car, The Body removed another container. This blood was used on the desk and computer, with enough left over to soak one of the waiting chairs.

Again. A third container. Used for soaking the remaining chair and sofa.

And again, for the last retrieval, and the blood was used on two more walls.

It stunk, the air redolent with fresh blood. The Body gagged and backed away, pouring the remainder of the blood from the container in the footprint impressions left on the wet, red carpet.

Driving away, a sigh of relief, fulsome and noisy as wind in trees, filled the car. This kind of thing was so risky. A passing motorist or a patrol car might have stopped to see what was going on. Someone might have walked past the office and noticed the door wide open and the smell of blood.

Yet it had gone without a hitch as if the cosmos was working in concert with The Body to bring down Karl LaRosa.

It was all correct and good. It was meant to be.

If blood did not unnerve Karl, nothing would.

If blood did not put a crimp in his lifestyle and business

routine, there was little chance of ever putting Karl on edge.

Back at the house, The Body had to shower and dispose of the old clothes worn to dispense the blood. The containers were brought into the house and washed clean. The plastic sheet covering the driver's seat in the car was disposed of in the trash. If the murderer of Nicole Simpson and Ron Goldman could do away with a murder weapon, bloody clothing, and ruined shoes so that nothing was ever found by the police, then so could The Body. It was not as much trouble as one would suppose. Just about anyone could do it.

In the darkened nursery, sitting at the console, typing, The Body used up the hours until dawn when it was time to nap for half an hour before rising again to dress for the day on Cam's set.

Blood on the walls, the carpets, the furniture.

What a masterful idea the scriptwriter had created. What else might be in the script The Body could imitate? So far it had been the most fun in all the world. One day The Body would get the scriptwriter alone and talk about the movie. Cam had co-authored the script, the way he usually did these days on his films, but it had to have been the scriptwriter's baby, this blood scene.

Bringing fiction to life was exhilarating in the extreme. Playing the scenes before a camera paled in comparison to actually committing the scenes in reality.

It was doubtful Karl LaRosa would agree with The Body. Being on the receiving end of revenge couldn't be the most thrilling episode in Karl's life, something he'd been waiting for. And revenge was a cliché, wasn't it? However, revenge was wholly a human trait, a real oddity. No other animal took the trouble. It gave such satisfaction, revenge. Cliché or not, revenge was the anchor that held the planet in place in the solar system. People practiced it in large and small measure in all their daily routines. It was second nature to carry out revenge when wronged.

The Body moved to the bedroom and stood staring at the queen-size comfortable bed. No sleep to be had there. Sleep escaped from that mattress like steam from a kettle. Normal beds had ceased to work for sleep many years ago.

The Body turned away, leaving the bedroom behind, and entered the nursery again. The closet door was closed and now The Body opened it. Hanging from miniature coat hangers was . . . nothing.

There had been no time to buy baby clothes and that was in a way a blessing.

The Body dropped to its knees and crawled inside the closet and onto the four-inch foam rubber mattress pad. Plumped the pillow. Straightened the sheet. Reached up, grasped the doorknob, and first closed the door, shutting out all light, then reached for the switch low on the wall that turned on the small ceiling fan specially installed to circulate the air.

With eyes closed, sleep immediately tugged. Safe. In a cradle place, protected from all harm, shielded from all memory of the past. Safe from the world and the tumultuous trouble it held in reserve.

The Body tossed during the thirty minutes of deep sleep, wakened to the alarm set just at the head of the foam mattress on the floor, and sat up smiling in the close darkness.

Today a new scene would be handed out to the actors and crew to study. It could almost cause a person to clap both hands together in enthusiasm like a child with a big, gaily-wrapped box to unwrap.

No time for flights of fancy. Had to hurry. Make-up could camouflage the half-moons beneath the eyes and cover up the lack of sleep. Hurry, hurry.

Making movies was such child's play. Everything always taken care of by someone else on the payroll. You just had to show up on time, a warm body.

Orange juice from the fridge, gulped down. Toast, no margarine. A cup of yogurt, unflavored. Eat, eat, eat, must always remember to eat.

Showering took exactly two minutes. Scrubbing the head with herbal shampoo, the body with pure glycerin liquid soap.

Blow-dry the hair, thirty seconds of vigorous tooth brushing, a quick gargle, underarm deodorant applied liberally. Now to slip quickly into comfortable clothes easily removed to get into wardrobe on the set.

Keys to the house. Lock it up. Step lively to the car, retrieving the daily newspaper on the way. The Body was on. Another normal beginning of a normal day working in the Hollywood biz.

# 12

"The director is simply the audience. So the terrible burden of the director is to take the place of that yawning vacuum, to be the audience and to select from what happens during the day which movement shall be a disaster and which a gala night. His job is to preside over accidents."

Orson Welles, *Citizen Welles*

Cam started out the day yelling. Before he could get his loafers on the phone rang with the production manager's bad news. He was having trouble getting the permits to reroute traffic for one of the shoots and the scene would have to be put off for a couple of days.

"Couple of days? What do you think this is, a film bankrolled by the Shah of Iran?"

"Is there still a shah in Iran?" the PM asked facetiously.

"I ought to fire you for that." Voice and blood pressure rising. Putting off a shoot was no joke. Not in *anybody's* book.

"All right, I'm sorry. Listen, I'm working on it. I thought it was set, but someone at the courthouse fucked up, okay? I'll straighten it out as fast as I can. It's all I can do, Cam, don't start on me."

"Herb, I wouldn't start on you if you weren't so *goddamn incompetent, you skinny-assed motherfucker!*"

"I'm hanging up now, Cam. I'll see you on the set."

*"To do what? Watch the crew and cast twiddle their fucking thumbs?"*

A big sigh hissed through the phone line. "You can shoot around it, c'mon, stop now, already. I'm hanging up."

*"You hang up on me and I'll call Stickland, see if he wants you back!"*

Then there was silence. No sighing. No pleading for reasonableness.

Cam took the receiver and threw it on the floor of his bedroom. It bounced on the lush gray carpet like a ball. Then he picked it up again and threw it hard against the wall, cracking the plaster. The princess receiver set leaped up from the bedside table as if an electrical jolt had given it a pop. The third time he picked up the mouthpiece, he felt only a little better.

"Did you hang up?" he asked quietly, everything under control.

"No, I'm here." Another sigh.

Cam rubbed at his eyes with long, slim fingers. Then he reached for the crumpled pack of Camels next to the phone, shook one out and lit it. He drew in a deep puff of smoke before saying, "You're right, we can shoot around it. Get the fucker at city hall on the phone now and set it up for tomorrow. Not the next day. Tomorrow."

"Okay, Boss."

*"And don't fucking try to mollify me by calling me boss!"* This time Cam slammed down the phone in the cradle hoping the crash would bust the PM's eardrum.

Cam forgot to eat anything, forgot to brush his teeth, and forgot to comb his wild, crazy, and windblown hair. He arrived at the studio looking like a man about to blow a valve. As soon as the people involved with *Pure and Uncut* saw him, their glances fell or wandered elsewhere. Even Olivia carefully avoided looking at Cam straight on.

Catherine Rivers, as Cam's second-in-command, knew it was up to her to find out the problem and help handle it, whatever it was. She approached Cam the way a snake-handler went after a rattler. The stick and noose she used were her best traits: a cool exterior and iron constitution. She knew how to take abuse without making it personal.

"What happened?" she asked.

"We can't go to location. Fucking Herb fucking fucked up."

When Cam used three "fucks" in one sentence, it meant bad times ahead. Catherine looked out at the crew and nodded slightly to let them know the problem was going to be ironed out, just take it easy.

"How long do we have to postpone the scene?"

"I told him to get it fixed by tomorrow. I threatened him with Strickland."

"Ah." Herb used to work for another studio headed by John Strickland, a real ball-busting, back-stabbing son of a bitch nobody liked and just about everyone tolerated unless offered work elsewhere. Herb never wanted to have to go back to him. "Well, today what do you want to do?"

Catherine hadn't seen the script. She got the next scene Cam wanted shot just like everyone else. This put her at a distinct disadvantage in helping Cam over the bumps and rough spots. If she didn't know what came next in the line-up, there was no way she could help him pick a substitute scene. No day could be wasted. Sets couldn't be shut down for a day under any circumstances barring a classic, devastating, natural disaster. Hundreds of thousands of dollars couldn't be thrown away like that.

"Let me think!" Cam ran fingers through his disheveled hair. "I'm going to my office to find something. Keep everybody quiet. Don't let them get their pants twisted."

"You got it." Catherine walked off to have a conference with the actors. Next the crew. She'd tell them to sample the fresh strawberries catering had brought for breakfast snacking. Or the cantaloupe. Cantaloupe was high in vitamins C and A. Soothing food usually worked wonders on frayed nerves. Cam, for instance, needed about a truckload of the stuff.

Less than fifteen minutes passed and Cam literally burst from his closed office door. The door slammed and hit the wall, getting everyone's attention. You never knew when Cam was going to explode from his office or walk out like a regular human being. The explosions were enough to put everyone on fresh alert. Conversation stalled and the fresh fruit platters were forgotten. Cam looked like a mad locomotive as he swung his arms and barreled toward them.

"We were supposed to shoot out in the hills today, but that's been canceled until tomorrow. Here's the new scene. Keep the other one you studied last night and we'll play catch-up tomorrow. You've got forty-five minutes to study this one. Ad-lib if you have to, improvise, do a riff on the dialogue. We're getting it done today or we don't leave the lot."

He handed out the new batch of scene scripts, shooting them from his hands like throwing hot rocks. He consulted the big-faced Rolex on his wrist, clocking the readings.

Robyn called him over while the scripts were being read. The actors wandered to their dressing rooms. The crew went into various empty conference rooms that boasted long tables and comfortable chairs. No one mouthed a word of protest.

"Herb fucked up?" Robyn asked. "That's what Catherine told me, Herb fucked up."

"Royally. He's had months to get permits and work out all the legal stuff and now he tells me it's not done. I ought to slap the motherfucker into Sunday."

71

"You want some cereal? How about a slice of watermelon or some grapes?"

"What? Do I look hungry to you?" Cam twisted his mouth and frowned. He wore anger like a necklace, something big and gaudy and unmistakably expensive that lay in full view on his black hairy chest, glimpsed through the opening of his blue chambray shirt.

"You look like someone hauled you out of an alleyway. I hate to tell you this, Cam, but your hair could use a comb." She gave a small innocent smile.

Cam scowled at her, ready to blow like a volcano, but she smiled more brightly now, a fluorescent shine gleaming from her dark eyes. Then she reached out and smoothed down his ruffled black hair. When she did that, he grinned crookedly and all his anxiety fled. She was a rainbow and the storm was over.

"I been meaning to talk to you about Landry. I went to the Universe the other night hunting for you." He searched his back pockets for a comb.

"Yeah, what night was that? I'm not there every night of the week, Cam. Just most every night. Pick up a phone. They tell me the connections work real good these days."

Cam found what he was searching for in his back jeans pocket and combed his hair into a semblance of order. "Fuck what night, I didn't find you so let's move on. How do you stand that place? It's a freak show, the whole place is full of freaks. Never mind." He waved away her coming defense of the club. "See, Landry's not coming through. You know his stuff even better than I do. It was your fucking bright idea I give him the lead. If I remember right, you almost got on your knees and begged." His eyes twinkled, enjoying teasing her. But the anger returned, swift as sudden cloud cover. "Now how about you telling me why he ought to be doing this part

72

instead of his lookalike, the wooden Indian back in the Old West prop room."

Robyn laughed. "Aw, he's not that bad. I think he's nervous. You're intimidating him. You intimidate everybody. Except me. I think you're a pussycat."

"Shit, I'll show him intimidation if he doesn't break out of that daze he's in. You know what he looks like in dailies? Like Alec Guinness on tranks. I should have hired Hoffman even if I do hate that fucking egomaniacal dwarf. Or, hell, maybe I could have done something with Powers Boothe, has-been or not. I loved that guy as Jim Jones. I watch it every two years. Jesus, I don't know why I haven't used him yet, I need to write a note to myself."

"Landry's the right one for the job, Cam, and you know it. The names bring the wrong expectation for this part. We're not switching in mid-stream. I'll talk to him."

"You do that, okay? I've taken comedians and made them into dramatic actors, surprising not only the public, but myself. But I'm not so sure I can take a pretty-baby leading man and make him into the kind of star material I need for this. He doesn't have some cute little starlet here to hug and smooch on all day. I want him on the edge. Can you do something about putting him against a sharp razor, try to draw some blood? It's like some fucking vampire's already drained him dry."

"I said I'd try."

"No time like the present. He can't fuck this scene today because he's not in it, but he's in tomorrow's scene. Go after him now. Do what you got to do."

Robyn raised one perfect brow. "I don't think offering him a quickie would work."

"Like I say, do whatever you have to, but make him ready. Break that deadwood exterior or we're in big trouble, Robyn,

73

I'm not kidding you now, I'm serious. I don't have to tell you how important it is for everyone to pull out the best they've got in 'em."

Robyn patted Cam's arm, an unconscious motherly gesture, and headed for Jackie Landry's dressing room. It wouldn't take sex, that wasn't called for, not now, not for this. Not that she had any aversion to trying out one of the best-looking studs in Hollywood. But no, that's not what would turn the trick. She was going to appeal to his ego in other ways. Cam had to get him performing at top notch or *Pure* was going down the tubes. Robyn was prepared to lie or pray or get on her back for this movie, if it came to that, if she discovered that was what it took. That's how much it meant.

Just the future, that's all. The whole goddamn future. Ending up on some street corner hawking carnations didn't appeal to Robyn, and as far as she could see, that was the alternative.

# 13

"The thing about performance, even if it's only an illu-sion, is that it is a celebration of the fact that we do con-tain within ourselves infinite possibilities."

Daniel Day Lewis, *Rolling Stone*

"I don't have a part in this scene," Landry said as Robyn entered his dressing room after knocking. He looked confused and dis-appointed.

"You'll do your part tomorrow—the scene we were sup-posed to shoot today."

"Well, I don't know why Cam gave me this and told us all we had less than an hour to study it if I'm not in the scene."

"He didn't take time to remember who was in it and who wasn't. He's . . . a little flustered, what with the last-minute change and all." Robyn took a folding chair and dragged it over to the upholstered wing chair Jackie sat in, the script in his lap. "Look, we need to talk."

Jackie set aside the script, letting the pages fold closed. "You want something to drink?" he asked, beginning to rise from the chair. Robyn took his wrist and he sat down again.

"No, I don't want anything. I have to tell you something important."

"What is it?"

When he was puzzled his eyebrows drew together. He really was gorgeous. Redford as a young man had nothing on Jackie Landry. Robyn felt a sexual spin rush over her. Maybe she should . . . ask him out. She blinked away the thought for later. Stop this, she admonished herself. He looks nothing like Karl. He acts nothing like Karl. You won't like him in bed, you know you won't. And he's too young for you, at least too young for a serious relationship to develop. Get a grip, kiddo.

"I'm the one got you hired for the part," she said.

"You? Well, gee . . ." He smiled, his white teeth lighting up his face. Then the smile faded when she didn't return it. "Cam probably didn't want me. What's wrong? I'm fucking up, that's it, isn't it?" He hung his head, a little boy about to receive his punishment.

"Jackie, listen to me. What you've done in pictures is good work, you know that. People envy you and you're offered some of the best parts, you make big money. But until now you haven't been given a chance to really *act*. The closest you got to it was in that remake where you played the cheap hood—and even that was more romance than drama."

"I would have been better than Gere in *Breathless*. That's the cheap hood I *should* have gotten to play."

Robyn reached out and took his chin, lifting his broad, handsome face. "You would have been perfect in *Breathless*. But even in that you couldn't do what you can do in the picture we're filming now. Do you understand me? This is your shot, Jackie. You keep dancing around with Cam and missing the inflections and getting off mark and tightening up on camera, you're going to blow the one chance you've got to show the world what you're made of."

He jerked away his face from her hand and looked at the door as if he wanted to get up and run out of it. "I'm trying. Cam's pushing. He won't stop pushing me. If he'd slack . . ."

"Cam's not going to slack up. He's going to get harder, he's going to get so hard you'll think you have a hundred-pound anvil on the back of your neck. I think you can take it, Jackie. I'm the one who begged for your chance. I'm the one Cam's going to turn on if you don't come through on this. Not to mention what's going to happen to me if this picture takes a dive or it gets canned. I've never been involved in a film that got shelved, but things happen. Bad things. Don't let that happen to me, Jackie."

"I'm not deliberately letting anyone down."

He still wouldn't look at her. Her tone had been scolding. Now she rolled her head around on her shoulders to loosen up the muscles tensed and bunched there like gnarled tree roots. "Jackie?"

"What?" Sullen. She had to change it all around. Actors were all kids. More truth than lie. With a kid you reinforced with sincere flattery. Nine of out ten times it worked. She had nothing to lose because she was sincere in what she was going to say to him. It was always easier to be genuine.

"You're the only actor on this picture who has the least chance of being a star when the audiences flock to see it. Did you know that? If you go tell this to Olivia or any of the others, I'll deny I said it, I'll call you a goddamn liar to your face, but I'll tell you the truth in private. You can be bigger than Tom Cruise. You can be more sensitive and brilliant than Val Kilmer, more dynamic than Travolta was in *Pulp Fiction*, more sexually dangerous and attractive than Pacino in his early films, more moving and believable than DeNiro. You can reach the top with this one film. Only you."

His head came up slowly. He had recognized the honesty in her voice. It had touched him where he needed it most, she saw that in his eyes. He opened like a night-blooming flower, the understanding in his eyes widening slowly, circling his brain, settling into a comfortable place in his soul. Had no one ever told him this before? Didn't he know it? How could someone with such potential not know it?

There lay Jackie Landry's true innocence and his real strength. He had not bought into the Hollywood dream fully. He had not fallen for self-delusion. He had not inflated his worth until it was so large it engulfed a minor talent and rode it into the ground.

"You mean it," he said.

She nodded, biting her lip. She waited until the dawning of his understanding became full day. "You have to do this for me," she said, almost in a whisper as if this were a secret between them. "You have to do this for yourself."

She waited again while he stared at her, stared at her lips as if she might say more.

"I can't keep trying," he said, stating the truth he knew finally. "I can't try, I have to be what it is Cam wants. That's what you mean."

"Yes." Her heart leaped, rejoicing.

"I should have no fear, not of Cam, not of Olivia, not of myself."

"Yes, yes!"

"I have to be Perry Johns and no one else but Perry Johns. I have to be him more than I'm me. I have to let his suffering in."

"See? I knew you'd understand!"

He stood with her and they embraced, happy children, children who have forgiven one another past grievances and are willing to love again.

He said against her ear, "Thank you, Robyn. Even if you've lied to me, thank you. Don't worry any more, you don't have to worry about me."

She closed her eyes, basking in his maleness, secure in the

circle of his strong young arms. She whispered back to him, unable to stop herself, "Meet me at the Universe tonight. Dance with me then. Just one dance."

"All right," he said, releasing her and smiling down into her face.

He was radiant, an angel, and at that moment, God, how she loved him; every inch of him, every hair, every last masculine beautiful bit of him.

# 14

"Just like those other black holes from outer space, Hollywood is postmodern to this extent: it has no center, only a spreading dead zone of exhaustion, inertia, and brilliant decay."

Arthur Kroker, *Panic Hollywood*

Robyn melted in Jackie's arms during a slow dance in Heaven. The band sang old blues tunes made famous in the forties by Robert Johnson. The singer doing the cover version was black, male, and exceptionally talented, although not a rival for the throne of bluesman Johnson.

"I'll be good tomorrow," Jackie said next to her ear.

He was talking about the shooting of his scene the next day in the hills outside Hollywood. He had his arms around her waist, holding her tightly. She had her hands looped around his neck and hoped he'd do some dirty dancing before the singer finished his rendition of "When You Got a Good Friend."

"You'll be perfect," she said, meaning it. If he wasn't, Cam was going to give her real hell again.

She and Cam went back seven years, to the time when she first got into the business producing. They had done their first deal together, pitching a sweetheart western to Paramount. It hadn't gone over and was finally turned down by every studio they tried, but from then on Cam trusted her and knew her strengths. She could collect money men like other women collected diamond earrings. She was good at convincing them to risk it all.

But Cam would not spare her hell. If hell is what she deserved, he'd dish it out happily and serve up a side order of heavy suffering for good measure. That's what made him a genius. He might like you, but he wouldn't mind putting the screws to you to get his films right. All that mattered was the picture.

This time that's all that mattered to Robyn, too. That and good sex.

Jackie's body was lean and firm. Not a muscle-builder type, but still strong enough to make her heart skip beats. She had worn the blue dress, the one with the scooped neckline and mid-thigh skirt. Underneath, she wore sky blue stockings with blue and red splashed stiletto heels. Nothing else. Underwear wasn't necessary with the kinds of clothes Robyn chose to have designed for herself. The dresses all came with built-in bra bodices for the most elegant and natural uplift her breasts ever received. She might be small—all right, petite—but she made what she had go a long way. Anyway, it always surprised her how many men liked little women.

"Will you take me home?" she murmured, going crazy thinking about sex with Jackie.

They had shared dinner at the Beverly Wilshire, her treat, drinks in the bar there, his treat, and now a half hour rubbing bodies on the dance floor at the Universe. He had suggested Planet Hollywood and she said wait, let me show you the Universe, you'll like it better. And now it was time for the *pièce de resistance*. Show time!

"My pleasure," he said, maneuvering her from the floor before the bluesman finished his last guitar chord.

Robyn had hired a limo for the night to prove to Jackie how special he was. She'd dismiss it when they reached her place and she'd call it back if Jackie wanted to leave again. If not, if he stayed over, she'd drive him to location in the morning. Let everybody talk. It's what they did so well and she did have a reputation to uphold besides.

It was hardly ten o'clock. Neither wanted to stay up too late, not when the next day was the day Jackie meant to show her, show Cam, what he could do with his part.

Neither of them noticed they were being scrutinized from the shadows at one end of the bar as they gathered Robyn's light jacket and purse.

Both would have been surprised to know Cam sat there in the dark, nursing a draft while watching them all night.

On the other hand, if they had known he was watching, and thought it over a bit, they'd know they should have expected it. It was his biggest film. What Robyn did with Jackie to get him to act was of Cam's gravest concern. And if they'd known, they would have expected he was probably muttering to himself about how he hated the Universe, hated the alternative music, hated wasting his time in a Hollywood hot spot when he could have been down at some little stink-hole bar with real people.

But they did not know and Cam wasn't about to let them find out.

After dismissing the limo Robyn took Jackie's hand to lead him into the three-story, white stucco, two-million-dollar house in the Hollywood Hills earned from the profits on her last production deal. Once inside the elegant, but cold and austere house that she found too late she didn't like very much, she turned into Jackie's arms and kissed him long and thoroughly. He slid both hands down to cup her ass and she squirmed against him, china doll in the arms of a sun god. It was going to be a good night. He was as hard for her as anyone she'd ever fucked.

The telephone rang and they froze, tongues in mouths, hands full of body parts. The answering machine picked up and after an anonymous male voice asked the caller to leave a message, Robyn pulled away to listen more closely.

Jackie stood next to her in the shadowed foyer, waiting. They could hear the answering machine in another room off the foyer go click and then *beep* and then there was a two-second silence. Finally a heavy sigh floated toward them, amplified and weary.

Karl's voice suddenly echoed through the empty dark rooms of the spacious home.

"I've been calling all night, Robyn. I'm sorry to leave so many messages. They wouldn't let me talk to you on the set today, said you were busy, weren't taking calls."

Robyn stiffened. Jackie slumped.

"I have to get this," she said to him, moving away without turning on the lights, leaving him alone in the vast foyer.

Karl's voice continued. "The police have been called in now, but they don't have anything, really, it's half a joke to them . . ."

Robyn reached an extension and picked up. "What police?" she asked, sounding angrier and more put-out than she'd meant to sound.

"You're there! Oh, thank god."

"What is it, Karl? I have company."

"I'm sorry."

"What is it? You said you called the police."

"Robyn, you need to help me. Someone's . . . well, someone must be crazy. They broke into my office and threw . . . blood . . . all over everything. The walls, the desks, the . . ."

"Blood?" Blood, she thought? Did he say that?

She heard the front door close, a soft punctuation with a small echo. She said, "Wait a minute, I'll be right back." She dropped the receiver and let it dangle from the wall phone while she hurried to the foyer.

He had gone.

She opened the front door calling, "Jackie?" but he was gone. Not a trace of him on the walk leading to the street. No sign of him on the street either. He'd have a long walk to find somewhere to use a phone to call for a cab. What the hell was wrong with him?

"Well, shit."

She closed and locked the door, really angry now, and stalked back to the phone.

"Thanks a lot."

"What's wrong?"

"My company." She paused, hoping Karl would feel some twinge of jealousy. "Is no longer my company. He left."

"I'm sorry, Robyn, I said that. But this is important."

"Yeah, yeah. What about blood? I think you're losing your mind, Karl."

"I wish it were that simple," he said. And that's when she began to listen.

# 15

"Some people are addicts. If they don't act, they don't exist."

Jeanne Moreau, *International Herald Tribune*

"I had a call from my agent telling me I didn't need a publicity manager. I'm not big enough yet."

She sat across from Karl's desk wearing a prim gray suit that would have looked at home on a school teacher except for the fact she wore no blouse underneath. The jacket buttoned just above her waist so there was skin showing nearly to her navel. Flesh Girl. In his mind, that's what he'd nicknamed her. He was going to trade on that idea—nothing in the world skated as well as selling sex—but here she was leaving him when they'd hardly started a campaign for her.

"I think your agent's wrong. You're making a mistake," he said calmly.

She wrinkled her nose and glanced over at his closed office door as if she smelled something bad. She knew about the blood that had soaked the outer office. Karl didn't know how she and his other clients knew. It wasn't reported in the papers or trades. But word traveled in this town like an oil fire over still water.

"Whoever broke in the other night isn't anyone who knows you, Karleen. You don't have to be afraid."

"I'm not afraid," she said, straightening her shoulders and looking past him to the windows at his back. He wished she'd look at him. "I just don't need your services right now."

Karl glanced down at the pen in his hand. He'd been twirling it nervously and now he let it drop to the desk. He stood. "All right. If you've made up your mind, I guess that's it. I'm sorry to lose you. I had an interesting idea for your future, but . . ." He shrugged.

She stood and held out her hand. He saw half her left breast, a small suntanned moon peeking from the suit lapel. "It's got nothing to do with . . . you know." She gestured with her head toward the door.

"No, of course not."

"When I'm making more money, I'll probably be back."

"I hope you will," he said.

She wouldn't make a lot more money if she didn't use him, he thought. You didn't make it here by looking deliciously sexy in a gray suit or by having an agent. It took more than that, lots more. But she'd been scared off by the incident that had ruined his office and he had to let her go, what could he do?

After she'd left his office, he slumped in his chair. That was the fourth new client he'd lost in as many days. It couldn't just be the break-in. Someone was getting to them, warning them off. Karl wasn't much for conspiracy theories, but the actions taken against him were as plain as day. You didn't have to be paranoid to see the barren landscape lying in wait ahead of him. His stalker simply had to be the culprit, running off his clients.

Before Karleen Comodore had come to give him her regrets this morning, he had received in the day's mail a rejection for his request for a Gold Visa. He already had a Gold Mastercard, a Diner's Club card, American Express, and maybe half a dozen other credit cards. His secretary, Lois, must have filled out the Gold Visa request off one of the advertisements that came to the office periodically. She had been trying to handle things like that so he wouldn't be bothered. He, personally, didn't give a rat's ass about another gold card line of credit.

But that they had refused him made him sit with the rejection letter in his hand, puzzling. They turned him down? He was worth roughly a million plus, owned real estate in Malibu free and clear, took in a salary from his management business that consistently went over eight hundred grand even with two accountants trying to bury his profits from the IRS, and a bank somewhere in this country turned him down for a gold card? It was unbelievable.

First Karl called in Lois and asked if she was the one who had filled out the application for the card. She had, yes, was that wrong? She knew she didn't ask him, but . . .

No, he told her, it wasn't wrong, thanks. She went back to her desk, frowning slightly.

Then he called two credit bureaus. The one in LA and the one in Burbank. They would not discuss on the telephone his credit rating, but they'd send him copies of their reports for ten dollars a copy. He sent for them with the fees enclosed. Now it would be a few days before he could really find out what was going on. The rejection of his application for the gold card noted "outstanding credit obligations and payment record" as the reasons for turning him down.

Obviously someone had monkeyed with his credit rating. How could they do that? Computer hacking? A friend in the credit bureau?

Karl had heard of people being ruined by vindictive ex-spouses and envious business partners. There were ways to completely undermine a person's life since everything was digitally available. If you knew the codes and the under-handed tricks, the chains to yank, the people to bribe.

And somebody did.

A short rap sounded from the door and Sherry North-umberland peeked in. "Lunch?" she asked. "I have an hour free."

He smiled on seeing her sunny face. Sherry had been one of his first clients ten years before when he first started his business. He had been instrumental in getting her face known about town, introduced her to producers and direc-tors, took her to the right parties. She was doing okay now, chosen consistently for strong female leads. He remem-bered that he had bought the fine walnut desk he now sat behind from his commission on the Northumberland ac-count.

"Yeah. Lunch sounds great. Let me speak to Lois and meet you in the waiting room."

She shut the door but not before winking. He smiled, felt lighter than he had in days. Part of Sherry's success was due to the effect she had on people. She was like rain after a parched summer drought. He could use lunch with someone cheerful who might help chase away the clouds hanging over his head.

They sat across from one another at a little spaghetti place called Farrar's not far from his office. They wouldn't be both-ered here. And Sherry didn't need to be seen at Tuscany's in Brentwood to add to her allure. At least not today.

"So how's life, kid?" She slurped from a large Coke through a straw. She wore a dazzling buttercup-yellow dress that highlighted her dark looks. She favored the dress style of the fifties. Shirtwaists, pleated bodices, belts of the same fabric as the dress.

"Your account's doing okay. You don't need me much these days, Sherry."

She waved that away. "I didn't mean me. I meant you. I heard you had some trouble at the office. Who would do such an obscene thing?"

He sipped from his cup of coffee. His tenth since rising. He felt all jangled on the caffeine, but on the other hand he needed the lift. He thought if he didn't drink coffee down like water, he'd collapse in a tired little puddle.

He hadn't wanted to talk about his troubles. He wanted to hear about her picture and if she was happy with the new husband and the new baby. Tanya, they'd named her. "I guess everyone knows. I lost a new client this morning because of it. Rumors must make it sound worse than it was."

"Blood all over the place isn't bad?"

"It's some kook."

"I hear it might be a woman. I told you about loving them and leaving them." She grinned and pointed a finger at him. She could say things like that. They hadn't been involved. And he'd known her so long.

"I don't know who it is."

"But it could be a woman?"

He dug into his spaghetti. "I guess it could. I figure it has to be." He ate a mouthful, then put down his fork. "You're not leaving me too, are you, Sherry?"

"Hell no! You think I'd take you to a lunch this expensive to fire you?"

He had to smile. Farrar's was one of the most inexpensive cafés in the whole area. "I'm relieved to hear that. Even if you're doing fine, I want to keep track of your career."

"I'm not leaving you, Karl. Ease up. If you're losing new clients, they were kids you couldn't help anyway. You have to have balls for this business. They won't make it if a little

89

rumor and innuendo scare them off."

Though he secretly agreed with her, he knew there were other publicity companies they could turn to. He wasn't the only one in town. He was just the best.

"I know what you're thinking," she said, tackling a string of spaghetti that kept slipping off her fork. "There are other outfits they can go to, but no one like you, Karl. No one I'd trust my whole life to, but you."

He was touched and told her so.

"Don't thank me for the truth."

"What's the rumor?" he asked. "What are people saying?"

She motioned for the waitress to refill her glass of Coke. "It's nothing much."

"Tell me. If I don't know what's being said, I can't fight it."

She looked him in the eyes. He'd never noticed before how long her lashes were. She was a dove-like woman, soft and embraceable. He wondered why they'd never had an affair—and now it was too late. Maybe he wasn't her type. He didn't get to sleep with all his pretty clients. Didn't even make the effort. It got too messy combining business with pleasure, although that's how Hollywood worked, for the main. He just didn't like all the complications. Look how his marriage to Robyn had turned out for an example of how it could go wrong, he thought bitterly.

"They're saying you hurt someone. That someone's out to hurt you back."

"That's bullshit!"

"You told me to tell you the rumor. That's the rumor, Karl. I know it's a crock of shit and I said that to the person who told me. 'That's the biggest crock of shit I ever heard,' that's what I said."

"I've stepped on toes, but who in the business hasn't? But

I swear to you, Sherry, I've never deliberately fucked anyone over. Never. That's not how I operate."

"Singing to the choir, baby." She smiled again and he sat back, wiping his mouth, easy once more.

"So what are you going to do about it?" She took the refilled Coke from the waitress and gave her a smile as winning as the one she had given him.

"The police pulled out of it. They won't be a help so I'm on my own."

"Why did they do that?"

"They have a point system, sort of, in stalking cases. I don't have enough points."

"What's that mean?"

"It boils down to the fact I haven't been physically threatened or assaulted."

"Someone tried to run you off the freeway!"

He glanced up. "You know about that, too?"

She nodded. "I'm afraid I might know most everything. Like everyone else."

"The police said the freeway thing might not be connected. Until someone says they're going to kill me, put out a hit on me, or actually stick a knife in my back, they can't really get involved. There's something like four thousand stalkings going on in LA every year. Did you know that?" She shook her head. Shock at the high number caused her to frown, worried. Actresses were usually the target for stalkers. "And the numbers are rising. They don't have the manpower to get involved and they don't have the authority until there's been . . ."

"Blood."

He winced, remembering the office covered with sticky, stinking clots of the stuff. "Yeah," he said. "Until someone brings out the knife."

Sherry looked pained and pushed her plate aside. "I think my appetite just went to Caracas."

"Mine too."

He finished his coffee and she drank her Coke and they let silence hold them in the palm of its hand so they didn't have to talk anymore about what a toilet his life was turning into.

On the sidewalk when they parted, she gave him a big hug. "I'll spread the rumor that the rumor everyone's hearing is a lie. Maybe that'll help."

"You're fabulous, Sherry. I love you like a sister. Kiss little Tanya for me. We'll get together . . ."

She smacked him on the arm before walking away. He watched her yellow dress, the full skirt buoyed by petticoats, move and sway with the motion of her lithe legs.

She halted, turned around, shielded her eyes even though she wore dark sunglasses. "You'll be careful?"

"You betcha."

"All right." She waved. "All right," she said, "call me if you need me."

She left him on the sidewalk in the famous Californian golden sunlight, his worry heavier than it had been in his office, before the lunch.

Nasty rumors, horrible incidents, credit bureau snafus—what next, he wondered? Is there really a knife aimed at my back?

Who, who, who?

He needed to call Catherine. And Marilyn. And a few more women.

Sherry and the rumor mill were right. He had hurt someone and she was out to hurt him back. Hard.

# 16

"Immature love says: 'I love you because I need you.'
Mature love says: 'I need you because I love you.' "
                    Erich Fromm, *The Art of Loving*

Karl watched Lisa carefully as she removed her satin slip the color of cranberries and stood naked before him. He reached out and took her by the waist, drawing her close enough to press his face into her breasts. Lisa Golden's body could make him forget his name. He knew he shouldn't use her as a drug, but sometimes it was necessary to blot out the world just for a while. Lisa would forgive him if she knew. And she probably knew. Not only was Lisa smart, but she was perceptive beyond her years.

She ran the fingers of both hands through his hair, caressing his scalp and pulling his face over a few inches for him to take one of her nipples into his mouth.

His head swam and he groaned aloud. He moved from her nipple, kissing her breast as he went, rising from the edge of the mattress, kissing the hollow of her throat that smelled of a floral perfume and then to her chin, and finally her lips. He laid her on the bed, soaking in her heat.

She took a thatch of his hair and pulled his head away. He looked into her eyes, believing she would request something special.

"When can I move in?"

Oh god. Not that. Not now. He felt his ardor wane, turned from her, and lay on his back staring at the ceiling.

"Karl? Did I say something wrong? It's been a year of this aggravation where I have to dress and leave for my place or you dress and leave for yours."

He rolled his head from side to side. "It's not wrong, Lisa. It's just . . . inconvenient."

"You don't love me enough."

He shut his eyes. Of course he loved her, he loved them all. He just didn't love them enough, it was true, to marry, and that's where it always fell apart.

"You know the trouble I'm having," he said.

"I won't get in the way."

"I haven't lived with a woman since my divorce. It's better this way. Don't you know it's better?"

She sat up on an elbow and leaned over his chest. His hand automatically moved behind her and smoothed the velvety skin of her back. If they could just let this drop and return to making love, the night would be perfect again.

"Do we have to talk about this right now?" he asked.

"How many have there been, Karl? How many in this bed? A dozen, two?"

*Goddamnit.* The whole night ruined.

"I don't keep score," he said. "I've never seen you this way. Why would you ask me something like that?"

"I thought I was different for you. I thought, after this long . . ."

Now she was going to cry. She had put her head on his chest and she was limp as a rag doll. He felt moisture on his skin. He tightened his arms around her.

"Lisa, don't. You are different. You're important to me. I don't know what I'd do without you."

That wasn't what she wanted to hear, stupid lines all men

said to women. It wasn't enough and he knew it, but he couldn't help it, there was no more and that wasn't her fault, was it? She continued to silently cry. He lay there still, cold now, the sweat cooling on his body. He held her and waited, feeling like a bastard.

Lisa Golden had been a client for a couple of years, but nothing he'd tried to do to help her break out had worked. She was too ordinarily pretty and too moderately talented. She had nothing outstanding to offer Hollywood, nothing that would bring sparkle to the big screen, and the studios knew it without even giving her a screen test. Even Karl knew it, the first time he laid eyes on her, but you couldn't tell a young actress your misgivings and kill her dreams with such utter disregard. He had had to try despite the fact he'd be investing money in a losing proposition. This time, as he had expected, he failed.

Lisa left show business, coming to the conclusion her stars were not in alignment, her fate slated for another business. Besides, she was starving. Waitressing and studying acting at night kept her poverty-stricken. She had found work with a real estate broker, finally, as a representative. And excelled. Now she handled some of the biggest Beverly Hills and West Hollywood properties. Mega-million-dollar deals whose commissions allowed her to buy up a little condo here, a little cottage there. She was a dynamite businesswoman. She was already worth half as much as Karl, with no end in sight.

He admired Lisa's spunk. Pretty, cultured, and a go-getter. All rolled into one, the combination was irresistible to him. It was a plus, in his book, she wasn't involved in show business any longer.

But marry her? Let her move in with him or he with her? It was out of the question. He hadn't fallen in love with a woman but twice in his life. Once in college with a girl who went off to the Peace Corps and gotten a fatal tropical South African disease that killed her the year after he graduated. And one more time, years later, with Robyn. Oh hell, Robyn. It always came back to her. It was impossible she might be the one stalking him. It couldn't be.

As for love, he didn't think there was a third time left inside him. He's used up all his love, wasted and squandered it. The most he could feel for Lisa was deep affection and that was never enough, never enough, never. Savvy businesswoman or not, Lisa wanted the picket fence and the babies. She wanted a lifetime commitment. They all did and he didn't think that unreasonable. It just wasn't what he wanted.

Well, he did want that, why lie to himself? He turned his head to the side on the pillow and closed his eyes while Lisa cried.

He didn't know how to get it. Not again. Whenever he had tried for it before, the whole dream that was love had vanished before his eyes.

"It's dangerous enough you're here with me now," Karl said, stroking her hair. "I couldn't let you stay here."

"You really think someone might hurt you? Hurt me?"

They heard the front door crash shut and Karl was off the bed in a flash, his heart pounding. Lisa was right behind him, half falling from the bed and getting to her feet. He started from the bedroom, stopped and pushed her back roughly with his hand on the middle of her chest. "Don't come out here."

He realized only then he was naked and felt foolish, but not enough to stop going toward the front of the house. He snapped on lights as he went, dispelling shadows, his heart going crazy.

"Who the hell's there?"

The door was closed and no one was in the room. He hurried to the door and opened it, furious it wasn't locked. He had locked it earlier. He'd never go into the bedroom without the door locked.

He peered into the dark, down the brick walkway curving through red-blooming oleander and saw no one. He heard a car start somewhere on the street where he could not see. He turned, running through the house for the bedroom again. "I need my gun!" he said to Lisa. The shock had made white rings around her eyes so that she looked raccoonish in the dim bedroom lamplight. He reached in the bedside table drawer and took out a small Beretta.

He grabbed the bathrobe he'd discarded after his shower and threw it on. He ran back through the house again and to the front door, scampered down the walkway, looked up and down the street.

The car was gone. The street was empty save for a pair of taillights, dwindling red eyes that turned a far corner. He'd missed his chance to grab whoever had been in his house.

"Damnit," he said. His arms hung at his sides, the gun gripped tightly in the sweaty palm of his right hand. He felt defeated. It never worked the way it did in the movies. When Bruce Willis in the *Die Hard* movies needed to tackle someone, he never missed. When he landed a blow, it took the other guy down. But in real life going up against an enemy was more miss than hit. He wasn't a professional. He was just a man living on the edge, stumbling toward his own private Armageddon.

He trooped back to the front door and almost missed the creamy envelope stuck in the wood frame of the door facing. He reached out and took it, tore open the envelope and read:

*How can you sleep with women like her when you know*

*you love me? Your betrayal breaks my heart, Karl, it breaks my heart.*

He wandered through the house and found Lisa still standing in the bedroom where he'd left her. She was shivering and had put on her slip. "Gone," he said. "If I hadn't been naked I could have caught her."

"Her? It's a woman?"

He put the gun back into the drawer and sat on the bed. He handed the note to Lisa. As she read it he said, "It has to be a woman. A jealous woman. A crazy one."

"How'd she get into your house? I saw you lock the door."

"You tell me," he said. Did she have a key? He'd change the goddamn locks. "I'll change the locks tomorrow. I'm tired of this. I'm so pissed off I feel like punching holes in the wall. She was in the house. She must have been watching us." He glanced over at the bedroom door and tried to remember if he'd shut it before they undressed and couldn't remember if he had or not.

She sat down on the mattress edge, but didn't try to touch him. "My heart's beating so fast it might jump out."

"Yeah, mine too. Now do you see why you can't stay here? It's not safe. If I didn't have all my possessions here, I'd abandon the goddamn house."

"You can't do that. You can't let her scare you off, that's what she wants."

"Does she?" He wondered. What did she want, anyway? And how much of their conversation had she heard? She had been at the door, listening, he knew it. He couldn't have closed the door. Why close it, when they thought they were alone in the house? She'd wanted to scare them, slamming shut the front door as she'd fled. She'd wanted him to run through the house naked and scared. She had played him like a virtuoso on a twelve-string guitar.

"Why didn't your alarm system go off?" Lisa asked. She had risen from the bed and was now slipping on the rest of her clothes. She was leaving and he didn't want her to, but he wouldn't say that. It was probably best she left. He'd never be able to make love to her now. That's what the intruder had wanted, wasn't it? The bitch, the damned bitch.

"Whoever it is keeps disconnecting the alarm system. She did it the first time she got into the house and I had it rewired. Now she must have done it again.

"I hate these notes!" He threw it on the floor, knowing how childish that must look.

Lisa was dressed and holding her purse, her car keys in one hand. "I'd never do this to you, Karl. You know that, don't you?"

He looked up, surprised. "Of course you wouldn't do this."

"I mean if we . . . if we stopped seeing one another. If it didn't work out. I'd never do something like this. People who can't control themselves give me nightmares. Too many people just can't seem to control their urges anymore. It's like people have given themselves a license to go insane if things don't work out for them."

He crossed the room and took her into his arms. "I know, I know."

"And I won't bring up us living together again until . . . well, until this is over."

Afterward, you'll ask about it, though, he thought sadly. There will be no way you won't ask again. And that's when I'll lose you for good.

He kissed her gently and walked her to the garage door off the kitchen and out to her car, a little yellow Miata. He stood watching her back down the drive to the street. Once she was out of sight he still stood at the garage door, looking into the still, peaceful night. He could smell the night jasmine that grew over the fence. It reminded him of his youth in Santa Monica when he was out on the streets at night with his friends. They had always been surrounded by the sweet scent of jasmine offset by the salty sea breezes.

He lowered the garage door and turned off the light. He would burn the note. He would place chairs beneath the doorknobs again. Tomorrow he would have the locks replaced and the wiring for the alarm system repaired. Not that he thought any of it would do any good.

Preventative measures weren't solutions.

He just didn't know the solution.

# 17

"Hollywood's a place where they'll pay you a thousand dollars for a kiss, and fifty cents for your soul. I know, because I turned down the first offer often enough and held out for the fifty cents."

Marilyn Monroe,
*Marilyn Monroe in Her Own Words*

Marilyn Lori-Street hung up from talking with Karl. She sat scowling at the telephone handset on the coffee table a few seconds. Then she shrugged and let out a breath and went to the kitchen for cappuccino. A rich, dark, frothy cup would keep her awake too late, but she could take a sleeping tablet if it did.

She took the cup with her to the small studio area in her house. It was a small room done in pure white, with a wicker settee and little table, and a wicker rocker. The best thing about it was the exposure. Light flowed through the windows in three of the walls all day long. She loved her place in West Hollywood. She couldn't afford the rent in the better areas, not yet, but maybe after the release of Cam's film she might be able to. Still, she'd always remember this little house with the white rock garden and yucca plants. Besides, West Hollywood was particularly safe for a woman, she had been told. It was a gay community and women just weren't bothered in the neighborhood.

In the studio on an easel sat a watercolor pad of her latest little watercolor painting. Working on something would take her mind off Karl's veiled accusations. She painted oddities. Squatting men with their genitals excised, blood puddled between their knees. Bodies hung upside down on crosses on a dark field at night. Windmills with human arms that stroked the wind. Any horror that came into her mind, she painted. That way it was outside her, no longer inside where it festered and made her depressive.

She didn't try to understand what the paintings meant. They were hostile and demonic, that was easy enough to detect. They probably revealed the torture in her soul, but she couldn't interpret them beyond that. They just made her feel better, that's all, and sometimes one sold in a little gallery in LA where she let them be hung. She wondered what kind of people bought them. Crazies, no doubt. People as fucked up as she. The kind of people who used ice cream scoopers for marital aids and who went into their backyards at midnight to pray to Satan in the bowels of the earth.

She picked up a brush thick with scarlet watercolor paint and dipped it briefly in a cup of brown muddy water, then slashed a bold streak of the red across the sky of the painting on the easel. As she worked she tried to remember why she had come to Hollywood to pursue a life as an actress in the first place. She had been born Phillipa Lori Frankowitz and taken the name Marilyn Lori-Street when she hit town. Although Jews were in abundance in Hollywood society and many held powerful positions, she had the sense to know Frankowitz wouldn't do for onscreen credits. Lead actresses were once again beginning to use ethnic-sounding last names, but she didn't have the gumption. She also didn't have the time it would take to make a name like Frankowitz acceptable.

So she had named herself after her heroine, Marilyn Monroe—another woman with an unusable name when she came to this town. She had kept her own middle name, Lori. And she had added Street because . . .

She paused in her painting, the brush hovering inches from the wet canvas.

The street was bad. The street was hell on earth. She had been on the street a while, trying to make enough money to buy decent clothes and save enough for a safe place to live. The street had almost killed her before she even had a hundred bucks put back.

She had been beaten badly by a girl who believed Lori was stealing her street trade. Only a cop trolling past in a patrol car saved her from being marked ugly forever with a knife down her cheek.

She had slept on park benches, been thrown in jail for vagrancy, and shared beans from a can with a guy in rags who talked to her all night about how Jesus was a cunt and a liar.

It was no more than she had expected. Coming from Idaho where a third-rate high school drama teacher enthused about her talent on stage, thereby unwittingly sealing her fate, she had no reason to believe she'd land a part in a sitcom the moment she hit town. Hell, she couldn't even get in to read for a part for over a year. They took one look at her ragged nails and shoes that were run down at the heels and they showed her the door.

Luckily, she had met Karl in a little bistro in Brentwood where everyone was dressed in exercise gear and pristine white Nikes and Karl had saved her life. He took her from the street, helped with the rent for six months until he found her a small part in a thriller, and taught her how to behave and how to show gratitude other than by offering her body.

She owed him everything.

Which was why his phone call tonight made her angry enough to reinvent the new painting with a red, boiling sky.

She and Karl had had a thing. Like he said. A thing. He hadn't wanted to, but she had insisted and pressed herself on him until he couldn't refuse. Wherever Karl showed up, she was there. When he was alone, she latched onto him like an octopus, fearless and totally without inhibition. Had she not pursued him, she had explained back then, she'd have never been able to repay him and she couldn't stand being in debt, her pride was so great.

Yet she had been touched by her affair with Karl LaRosa deep down, so deep she had almost stopped painting altogether. She never thought that could happen. She had been painting as long as she had been acting. And she had been acting since she was a child, lying her way out of whatever small trouble foretold coming punishment.

When their affair took hold of her soul and she told him, he began to move away from her, a slow steamer making for the shipping channel. She saw it, almost from the corners of her eyes, his faithful tracking into the distance.

When she confronted him with her knowledge of what he was doing, he at first denied it and then said to her, "I never wanted this to happen in the first place, Lori. I was afraid it would come to this."

He was afraid!

It would come to this!

She quit him. Then and there, marching out of his office with her shoulders thrown back and her head lifted. She had seen one of his more luminous clients do that to him once and had determined if it ever came to it, that's exactly how she would exit. Haughty as hell. Cold as an ice storm. Expressionless and silent as a glacier.

Her agent found her work and she paid back every penny

Karl had lavished on her. She even sent back the heavy-link gold bracelet, though she thought it her good luck charm. At Christmas he gave all his clients nice gifts, so she packed up the bracelet and the crystal angel and the bronze elephant, all gifts from Christmases past, and mailed them to him.

She bought her own gold bracelet. And wore it to all try-outs and to the set each day, though she had to take it off for the scenes she played.

She put down the paintbrush and sipped from the cup of cappuccino. She brushed back the feathered blond bangs from her forehead and let air out of her lungs before breathing in deeply again. Was she in shape? Should she ride the stationary bike tonight?

She put down the coffee mug. Took up the paintbrush.

To hell with Karl LaRosa.

She would be a star soon, very soon, and Karl LaRosa could just go to hell for all she cared. Let him fucking go to hell.

# 18

" 'Too caustic?' To hell with the cost. If it's a good picture, we'll make it."

Samuel Goldwyn, *The Great Goldwyn*

"You let making movies kill it between us," Gary said. He was in the process of packing his bags. There was a betrayed, hang-dog look in his eyes. He accused Hollywood and everyone in it, said that show business was her lover, a thing he couldn't compete with. He'd been vying for her attention for three years and was at the end of his tether. He was right; Catherine Rivers loved Hollywood more.

She stood in the bedroom watching him, rather relieved to see he had made up his mind. The thought of divorce hurt her terribly, but not as much as the thought he might stay. All they did was ravage one another, their arguments so poisonous that they made her sick for days afterward.

"I'm sorry, Gary. I guess you're right."

He stopped packing to look at her. "You don't care, do you? You don't care that this place and this business killed our marriage. Three years down the drain!"

"I care but there's nothing I can do about it. I won't give up my job for you and that's the truth."

"Job?" He hawked out a sarcastic laugh. "It's your whole life. It consumes you. You haven't had a moment for me since you started this picture with Cam. *Pure and Uncut*, that's all I hear. Cam did this, the actors did that, the producer did the other."

"You're acting like a spoiled child. You knew it was my important break, Gary. It's my big chance to learn from the best director this town's ever seen. If you listened to me, you'd know why I'm all caught up in shooting this script."

"This is also your chance to lose me and good riddance, I suppose." He threw the rest of his things haphazardly into the suitcase and snapped it shut.

His hair was wiry with curls which, when they were damp, like now after a shower, gave him an angelic appearance. He was too soft for this town. He never should have moved here from the East Coast. He should have lived all his life in New York and married a nice Jewish girl.

"Are you sure you know what you're doing?" she asked when he brushed past her through the door.

"I'm absolutely certain. I don't hear you begging me to stay."

She let him go. Heard the front door shut.

She went to Barb's bedroom and looked in on her to see if she had woken. No, she lay asleep, arms flung out above her head, covers hiked down below her knees. Couldn't keep covers on the kid. Catherine used to worry about Barb getting cold, but unless she zipped her into a flannel pillowcase, she wasn't going to keep her under the covers.

Barb would miss Gary, but he wasn't her father so it wouldn't be as difficult as it might have been. Her father was a retired director, not a famous man, but not a failure at the game, either. He picked her up on weekends and took her for cotton candy and walks at the beach.

As Catherine stared at her little girl sleeping, she was reminded of the pregnancy before Barb, of how she had ended it. She thought then, when she did it, she'd never think of it again. But now that she had given birth to a child, the thought of the unborn came unbidden into her mind all the time. What if she'd had the babies? She had been carrying twins. Boys, girls, one of each? She didn't know. The pregnancy termination decision had been made too early to know the sexes of the fetuses and she hadn't wanted them to tell her, even if they'd known. At that time of her life, the pregnancy was just a nuisance. They'd been fathered by a man she did not love.

Still, regret struck at times, and she wished she could go back a few years and have a talk with her younger self. The decision might have been different. And would having children have really interfered with her career plans? Really? Maybe. Too late to know that for sure now.

Catherine closed Barb's door quietly and went to the kitchen for coffee. The house seemed empty with Gary gone, but it was a good emptiness. When he was here their voices were raised and they fought over her work. She had been so unlucky with men! If Gary had been in the business, it wouldn't have been that way. But he was a medical supply salesman, on the road a lot, and he didn't understand one iota what she was doing or why.

She poured the coffee and opened the door onto the patio. She sat down at a patio table just outside the kitchen. In the moonlight, with the kitchen light at her back, she might relax and forget. All gone, all the men in her life. The father of the unborn twins, Karl, Barb's father, and now Gary. She might as well admit it—she was a terrible risk as a mate. She was no good at it. Men came and went in her life like brief spring showers.

Tomorrow Cam had the location shooting and she had to pay attention. No one could get shots like Cam, no one could get a performance out of an actor like him. He was one of a kind and it was her great fortune he had asked her to be his assistant. It meant long hours and she didn't get to see Barb much. At least she had live-in help for when Barb was home after preschool and didn't have to worry, but she missed seeing her daughter.

A shadow flickered to Catherine's right and she flinched, staring in that direction. Nothing. Just a limb of a tree swaying in a breeze. She was on edge, that's all. What was it Karl LaRosa used to tell her? That she was too uptight? Wound up like a toy dog that walked and squawked and wagged its tail. He insisted she took too much to heart, said she made too many connections, she was water dancing in a hot pan. It was the reason they had split up. He hadn't done a damn thing for her career, either, to be truthful. In fact, her time with Karl was a real washout.

Face it, she told herself. All her time with the men of her life had been a washout.

Hair along the nape of her neck stiffened and a shiver ran over her arms though the breeze was warm. She looked again into the deep shadows. She felt watched. But in order to watch her, someone would have had to climb over the brick wall surrounding her property. That was ridiculous. No one would do that here in Beverly Hills. She was just nervous as water dancing in the hot pan again.

She'd go inside where she didn't have to see shadow play. Get some sleep, alone in her bed, the place on the other pillow empty again. No more thinking, no more regrets of the past or of the present. She was who and what she was, that wasn't going to change. And she was a good person. She would be a great director one day. Besides, though she might be losing her second husband, at least she had her little girl. That was what was important now. Her daughter and her career. It's all that she had ever really wanted.

109

# 19

"If you play a monster but don't touch on his humanity, he remains just a monster. If you can find his humanity, then I suppose that is the art of acting."

Gene Hackman, interviewed about his part in *The Quick and the Dead.*

This had nothing to do with the script. The Body felt lured to Catherine Rivers' home, pulled by an invisible leash.

Standing with an ear pressed to the door, listening to the argument between Catherine and her husband, had done wonders for The Body's morale. A few minutes earlier or later and the whole conversation would have been lost.

Minutes after Gary left the house with his packed suitcase, Catherine wandered into the kitchen and poured a mug of coffee. The Body backed from the door and found cover in the black shadow of an overgrown crepe myrtle tree. Blending into shadows had become second nature.

The door opened and out she stepped, beautiful in her royal blue dressing gown with the sash at her waist, her dark hair tied back with a barrette. She stared straight ahead, feeling herself alone, and then she sat at the glass patio table, both hands around the mug of coffee, looking down into the steam rising from the liquid.

The first time she glanced toward The Body, tension rode

the air like finely packed ozone particles. The Body drew in a single breath and held it. If she came to investigate she might get hurt. If she rose and moved into the shadows to investigate, she was lost.

She glanced away, shrugging off her sixth sense that warned her someone lurked nearby. She was heavy in thought, her brow puckered, hands still as death.

Then, after a while in contemplation, she looked again in The Body's direction and this time she took the creeping sense of being watched more seriously because she rose and entered the house.

Longing broke The Body's heart. It was necessary to lean against the tree, holding onto it to keep from falling. Hands held onto the bark so tightly that indentations pimpled The Body's palms.

Over the brick wall, onto the street, into the car and gone from Beverly Hills. Winding down toward the lights of the city, The Body reviewed the night's events. Karl in bed with that chunky high-toned bitch, Lisa Golden. How she begged to be taken in! Like a stray cat or dog, she wanted Karl to adopt her into his house, into his heart. Didn't she know Karl LaRosa had no heart? His feelings of love were like those of a king who had abdicated his throne. He didn't love women. He fucked them a few weeks or months and then he cast them off forever.

Slamming shut the door when exiting Karl's house felt like shooting off rockets on the Fourth of July. Let him know he had been watched. Let him know he had no privacy. His life was for shit. He no more had control of his destiny now than did the conductor on a runaway train screaming down a mountain slope.

Then driving over to Catherine's. Studying the layout of

the house and grounds, finding a way to slip past a neighbor's Rottweiller without arousing it, discovering the chink in the brick wall that protected the back area of Catherine's house, the chink that afforded a foothold so the wall could be climbed.

And listening in glee as Gary left his wife.

And watching with heartache a thoughtful Catherine sitting alone on her patio, coming to terms with the emptiness of her life.

But then it's what she deserved! She should have no husband. She should have no child either, but she did, she did, and The Body wanted it, but that was insane. Better not to think of the child. Not for a moment's time. Lapsing into that kind of thinking was more dangerous than anything in the world.

Karl would suspect Catherine of being his stalker soon enough. And when it all was said and done, perhaps The Body would consider doing something about the child then.

A pretty little girl, slim and blond and bright as sunlight reflecting off amber. Barbara was her name. A terrible name, a grown-up, prissy name, didn't fit the child at all. The Body could rename her anything. The name Michelle had always been nice. My belle, Michelle.

The Body had once had a sister named Michelle. A long, long time ago. Chubby little dark girl with dimples in her cheeks and stars caught in the depths of her eyes. Michelle loved to change her clothes all the time, exasperating their mother. She would leave a string of clothes throughout the house, discarding them as she went, donning other ones that might suit her for only ten minutes or so.

Michelle dead. Floating face down, arms hanging loose, in the sky blue swimming pool, hauled in with the long pole used for scooping up vagrant leaves that sometimes dotted the pool when the wind blew hard over the cottonwoods.

The Body parked and unlocked the door to the house. It was too hard tonight to go into the nursery and write thoughts on the computer.

Best to go into the sensory deprivation chamber and sit in the leather chair and wipe away all those old memories of Michelle before going to bed.

Try to forget everything. Just for a while.

# 20

"Talk to them about things they don't know. Try to give them an inferiority complex. If the actress is beautiful, screw her. If she isn't, present her with a valuable painting she will not understand. If they insist on being boring, kick their asses or twist their noses. And that's about all there is to it."

John Huston,
*Things I Did . . . and Things I Think I Did*

Georgie couldn't get the shot and he couldn't believe in the first place that Cam was going to make him try. Cam, livid as Georgie had ever seen him, screamed, "Do it over again, goddamnit, you're not listening to what I'm saying to you."

The problem was one of safety. And one of expense. A camera cost a lot of money, a lot, and even though this camera wasn't rented, but owned by Georgie himself (with help from Cam on their last film together), why would he want to bust it up? Georgie would do anything for Cam, but he wasn't keen on breaking his camera or his nose. Pain wasn't his bailiwick.

"I break my camera, you buying me a new one?" he asked Cam, only half joking, trying to get Cam to settle down to a serious burn rather than a raging cyclone.

"Don't worry about the camera, we're not talking about

the camera. I told you to do this shot this way and that's what I want you to fucking do. Olivia's character has gone wild and we're going to show it."

Georgie looked over at Robyn. The production company would be ponying up the costs if Cam got the cameras busted. She gave him a slight nod indicating it was all right, but he could see she was nervous about it by the way she fidgeted, rolling a pencil back and forth between the palms of her hands.

"Don't be staring off at Robyn," Cam said, almost in Georgie's face now. "Are you going to ram that wall or am I going to ram that fucking camera up your ass?"

The scene was set up on a soundstage. The day before they had filmed the location scene and it had come off pretty well. Now they were back on the studio lot and the scene involved Georgie, as first cameraman, being the point of view for Olivia as the stalker. He was her eyes while tearing up Landry's home. That took some skill, but Georgie had done point-of-view shots a hundred times and he knew how.

His camera told the tale. It took the viewer right into the madness of the character, showing all events as they happened through her eyes. Clothes ripped from hangers in a closet and sliced to shreds with a sharp, long-handled knife that flit in and out of the camera's eye, darting through the cloth, zippity-zip. Chairs overturned, tables pushed up against other furniture, cabinets flung open in the kitchen shot, and pans and dishes thrown around in a fury of breaking glass and banging metal.

It was cheesecake. All those scenes went fine. Georgie was huffing and puffing when he finished, but he got it right—or at least to Cam's satisfaction. But this. This was something else again.

This was where the character was supposed to fall into a

state of frenzy heretofore never seen on screen before. After taking her anger out on the set, she was supposed to take it out on herself by running and slamming head-first into walls and doors, falling down, getting up again—with shots of Olivia doing just that before the camera took over again in her place to show the physical abuse the character heaped upon herself. Cam wanted her to throw her body around the set of the living room as if she had become unattached to the flesh and was using it as a bludgeon.

She was great. She was better than great. With her hair streaming across her face and something in her eyes so wild that the crowd standing around fell stone cold silent, Olivia insisted on doing all the shots herself, no body double, no stunt woman. She banged and threw herself and grunted and growled. She had done her part so well that when the cameras stopped rolling, the place exploded in applause as if she had done her act on a Broadway stage. She had now left for the dressing room.

Cam began screaming. "*You didn't get it!* Georgie, are you listening to me? You slowed up just as you ran at the wall head-first. You've got the other shots right where you turn around, showing us the destruction of the room while Olivia's character slams a wall with her back, but you're not getting it head on! I want you to *hit the wall*."

Georgie was breathing hard and sweating. He moved back from the set's plaster wall and stared at it through his lens, lining it up. It wasn't going down easy, that wall. It wasn't going to fall over for him or explode apart with trickery. No zoom shots, no hydraulic tracks, no Steadicam. Not good enough for Cam. He wanted something else, something different. Oh lord god.

He sucked his bottom lip into his mouth and clamped down on it with his teeth. Had to do it, had to try. Cam wouldn't let him off the hook on this thing.

He took off in a sprint and went into a dead run, the same as Olivia had done and been filmed as she ran across the same living room toward the same wall. He let his lip go and his mouth fell open and . . .

Just before hitting the wall, he hesitated, sliding forward until he was only two inches from smashing into it. He lowered the camera in defeat. He thought his heartbeat could be heard all over the soundstage. It drummed loud in his ears.

"Cut! Cut!" Cam came stomping over, screaming again. "Hit it! Hit it, hit the goddamn wall, Georgie! Run into that motherfucker. I got to paint a picture for you? I want you to slam into that wall."

Georgie wiped the sweat from his forehead with a handkerchief he kept in his back pocket. "Cam, I hit the wall and this camera's gonna be ruined. It's lunchmeat."

"I told you already, I don't give a goddamn if you break the fucking camera, I want you to slam into the fucking wall! Do it again. Do it now. *Do it now.*"

Cam turned his back and moved out of range. He signaled for Georgie to begin. Georgie backed away, drew a breath, cursing the day he ever signed onto this project, then took off across the floor, aiming for the wall, the camera held steady as he could manage at eye level, his feet pounding the floor, his heart pumping hard, hard.

He saw the wall coming at him and something inside him cringed, yelling, *No, don't hit it, no, don't,* but he couldn't hesitate this time, he had to hit the damn thing running full blast, he had to . . .

The long front lens of the shouldered camera connected with the plaster with a sound so loud it hurt his ears. The sudden jolt rushed through his hands, arms, radiated through his shoulder blade and knocked him on his ass. He had broken his glasses. He sat with the camera in his lap and his glasses askew and cracked on the bridge of his nose. He should have taken them off. He didn't think. He hadn't given it a thought, nor had anyone else.

"Broke my glasses," he said, feeling the pain now in both shoulder and face. It was fire running through his bruised skin. If the insurance guys happened to walk onto the set and saw what he had done, they would have been aghast.

Cam ran over and grabbed the camera, checked the shot through the specially attached videocam that would not give him the proper frame or light, but would tell him if he got the shot he wanted. "No!"

Georgie heaved a sigh. He looked up. "I didn't get it?"

"Fuck *no!* It's all crooked, the impact isn't strong enough, it's not what I want. We have to do it again."

Georgie came to his knees and then to his feet, the glasses in one of his hands. He saw a knuckle was bleeding, droplets falling onto the floor. He must have scraped it against the rough plaster. He glanced over at the silent crew standing around the set. Everyone mesmerized. Olivia had returned to the set, legs crossed, the script lying open in her lap. Her look was impassive. Landry stood nearby, frowning. One of the extras, a girl, covered her face with shaking hands. Georgie knew before the day was out, she'd quit.

He looked up at Cam again. "I can't do this," he said calmly.

"What do you mean you can't do it? Of course you can do it."

"I'm not doing it. Is my camera broke?"

Cam turned it around and looked at the lens. "It's got a crack. We'll get another one for you to use. I'll buy you new glasses. I want it shot again, okay, and this time you have to really do it."

Georgie reached out to take the camera as if he were willing to comply with Cam's wishes. Once he had it in his possession, he looked at Cam, his vision blurring without his glasses, and said, "Get someone else. You're crazy if you think I'm trying that stunt again."

"You're stalling on me, Georgie? All these years together and you're fucking walking off a set when I need you to do something for me?"

"You've asked a lot of me, Cam, but this is too much. I'm not doing it."

Georgie squared his shoulders and lugged his camera with him as he walked away. Mutters ran through the others on the set and he decided he wouldn't look them in the eyes. He was right on this one. He didn't have to be bullied into half killing himself. Not for one lousy shot.

Behind him an ominous silence issued from Cam. By the time Georgie got to the bathroom to wash his hand and check out the damage to his face, he heard Cam's loud voice raised, calling for the second cameraman to take over. Fine. Let Masters get his face shoved in.

After he had cleaned his hand and found a Band-Aid to slap over it, he returned to the set to watch from the sidelines. If Cam didn't see him, he'd be all right. He had to watch this scene shot. He wanted to see someone dumb enough to run into the freaking wall with a heavy camera worth thousands of dollars.

Cam stood in a huddle with Masters, giving instructions. He was animated, moving his hands around, pointing, grimacing. He was talking low now, not shouting. Maybe he thought he should use a new method on the troops. He did that for contrast. He did anything to get what he wanted. Shout one moment, hug you the next. It might make him a genius, but it was also manipulative and sometimes cruel.

Georgie had been with Cam for years and he had accepted Cam's rages until now. It was the first time he'd crossed him and he didn't care if he got canned for it. He wasn't going to pull a crazy stunt like that.

Cam walked away from the cameraman, turned, put his hands on his hips. Masters shouldered the new camera with the rigged video so Cam could check the shot. Georgie couldn't see his face without glasses, but he knew Masters must be making some kind of fierce face, trying to muster up the courage to do what he had to do. The crowd watching took a collective breath and no one moved a muscle. Movie making was supposed to be high art and illusion. People weren't called on to risk themselves this way. The very thought put everyone into a grip of silence and worry.

Masters started running across the set. He ran faster and there was the wall right there, right there, and wham! Masters hit it full throttle. The concussion of camera against plaster sounded like a thunderclap. Masters bounced back and landed in one direction while his camera flew out of his hands in another.

Cam ran over to the camera first and checked the shot. He turned around, grinning, and put out one hand to help Masters up off the floor. Georgie heard Masters say, "I think I broke my hand. I can't move my fingers. Jesus Christ, my fingers are broken."

Cam patted him on the back, still grinning like a crazy-in-love baboon. "It's great. You got it. You got the shot I wanted. You're a good man, Masters, you're a most excellent man."

Cam gestured someone over. "Take him to see the doctor, get his hand looked after."

Georgie stood in awe of the other cameraman as he was led away. He'd actually done it, actually run right into the wall with the camera to his face like some suicidal air pilot taking out a tanker. It was amazing what Cam could inspire people to do for him.

The crowd began to talk and Cam went on setting up the next shot. He was on the third cameraman now and none of it had slowed him down for a minute.

Despite himself and his personal feelings about how he'd been hurt trying to get what Cam wanted on film, Georgie had to admit a grudging admiration for both the director and the cameraman. Cam might be relentless, but he was right about how that shot would look on screen. It would make an audience suck in their gut in pure wondrous shock.

It was going to be one hell of a movie. "Pure and Uncut" described it correctly, no false advertising there.

# 21

"Where does one go from a world of insanity? Somewhere on the other side of despair."

T. S. Eliot, "Harry, Lord Monchensey"

Go slow, go easy, baby, take it easy. Slip in, destroy everything not nailed down, slip out. Don't let it get away from you.

That's what The Body tried as a control mechanism, knowing with one part of the mind that advice to the self wasn't going to work.

Karl LaRosa wasn't home yet from his office in Burbank. There were two free hours before he could be expected back.

Two hours to mangle and crush.

The scene filmed by Cam was brilliant, nothing short of brilliant. If The Body could create the same kind of massive devastation, Karl would come into his home, take one look, and have a heart attack.

First the kitchen, make it methodical. Neighbors weren't going to hear anything. Karl's house was set too far away from neighbors, all the wealthy on Malibu Beach believing that privacy was of the utmost importance. Stupid overpaid fuckers.

Breaking the first dish, a saucer, was the sprinkle before the deluge, the stream before the gullywasher. The glass sprayed out across the floor, shards of pure white splinters thin as toothpicks. Beautiful.

More dishes followed, crashing into the wall, the stovetop, the refrigerator door, the floor, until there were nests of splinters lying all about.

The Body felt blood pumping through the extended veins of arms and legs and forehead. Fury was coming. It hovered like a shy lover at the edge of the shadows, waiting to be lovingly called forward into embrace.

Slow down, control it, control it.

Pans had to come out from hiding in their shelves, foodstuffs had to tumble from cabinet doors, fresh food had to emerge from refrigerator shelves, frozen food from the freezer. All of it thrown, not just dumped, but *thrown* around the room, swinging the arms like windmills. And laughing, laughing to beat the band, what fun it all was!

The kitchen was done. Premium work. Much better than what had been carefully arranged on the set today. You couldn't arrange chaos. You had to become a part of it and let it possess you. Movie making was magic, was artifice. The real thing was so much more invigorating.

Steady, slow down, take a step back, survey.

But still the blood pumped and the veins stood out blue and pulsing and the heart thump-thumped crazily. It was all building and The Body knew in the deepest core of being that there was no turning back now. There was no human control on earth that could stop what was coming.

Hurrying into the living room, The Body let the frenzy take over though all the while the mind advised against it by crooning, *Slow down, take it easy, do it right, don't let it bear you away.*

Remembering the scene on the soundstage, The Body took up sofa pillows and ripped them with a knife lifted from a kitchen drawer. The phone and attached answering machine were ripped from the wall and thrown across the room. The sliding glass patio door took a chair to the midsection and crackled into a spiderweb of safety glass. Break the coffee table's legs off, smash it, stomp it!

It was too late, too late to hold back now.

A spare bedroom for guests, turned into garbage, the bed cut open and leaking stuffing. The drawers pulled out and broken into pieces. The blinds left hanging like Medusa snakes from the windows.

Then into the bath where everything in the medicine cabinet was thrown so hard, jar by container by bottle, that noxious liquids and salves gushed and split open and sprayed across the wide mirror. A roll of toilet paper was stuffed and stomped into the toilet, which was then flushed so that water ran over onto the floor.

In a small study the books were ripped from shelves and their pages torn and thrown like confetti into the air while The Body laughed hysterically, having now given in to the rage, and become lost totally to the rush of destruction.

Karl's bedroom saved for last, his clothes taken from their hangers in the closet and ripped into streamers with the kitchen knife. His drawers torn out and dumped in the center of the floor, the mattress wrenched off the box springs. The Body threw itself onto the leaning mattress and, accompanied by a growling that sounded like an animal about to rip open a new asshole for an enemy, the knife flashed into the stuffing, slashing at it, slashing it into deep volcanic crevices of darkness.

The Body rolled from the mattress and got upright again. There were tears on The Body's face. The mind was gone, having given in to the sheer exhilarating horror of physical violence. Unlike the scene shot on Cam's film set, this was no movie, this was no script, this was no idle entertainment, oh no.

It was death in the making. It was the sign pointing toward the coming of death splendiferous.

Black hatred infused The Body with the strength of Goliath. There was a big chair to overturn, a heavy-framed picture to rip down from its perch and send sailing into a wall.

And then the ultimate release of pent-up passion.

The Body dropped the knife from a gloved fist and shivered for a moment in ecstasy. With eyes closed and teeth gritted, The Body felt the first wave of urgency. Eyes flew open and the legs moved The Body faster and faster from the bedroom to the living room, tripping over downed furniture that lay spread-eagled and dead and broken. Then the legs helped The Body lurch into the wall.

The shock of contact shook The Body's bones and rattled the teeth.

Again. Backing up, running at the wall, just as the cameraman had done, running like a fullback for the goal, head down to chest and . . .

The Body found itself on the floor and crawled to bruised knees. Felt the tiny stream of blood coming from somewhere on the scalp. Took the blood and smeared it over the cheekbones and lips, yes, over the lips now, so as to taste the thrill of madness.

Up again, shakily, head pounding with pain, flinging the body forward to the wall once more, slamming into it, crashing from the side with the arms bent and held together so that the wall cracked and gave, plaster crumbling to the carpet.

Backing away, stumbling backwards, ramming the wall with the back so hard that the head snapped forward.

Finally, it was upon The Body, attendant to it; the demon

of lunacy everlasting so that all thought fled the brain and there was nothing in the world but the walls; the walls, and the body slamming into them, bouncing off them, falling and getting up and slamming into them again.

And again.

And again.

When the heat of fury sighed into the realization of physical limits, The Body stopped abruptly, seeing for the first time not only the ruined house, but the ruined person who stood in the house.

That's when The Body left, shaking all over as if from palsy, and drove away, satisfied the scene had been played exactly right. More perfect than any actor pretending madness on a painted set, with false props and breakaway boards and glass that would not cut.

If only Cam could have seen it. If only a cameraman had filmed it.

Blood dripped from The Body's forehead and there were red scrapes on the arms, but otherwise, nothing too harsh had been done to alter the health of the flesh.

Bruises could be covered and they would heal.

Not so easily the rents in Karl LaRosa's life. Those would never heal. They would only split further to reveal the putridness and the unspeakable emptiness behind the veneer of a normal man leading a normal life.

The Body licked sore lips and swept back bloodied hair from the forehead. The drive home was long and served to cool the blood, calm the system.

The evening had been more exciting than any before it. How could this be topped in the script?

Easy now, slow down, take it way down. Squelch all the noise and listen to your own advice, The Body thought.

Get home first, safe and sound, take a long hot bath, with

the head resting on the cool white rim of the tub. Review the scene in quiet contemplation. Give yourself a rest. A pat on the back. You did so well. You were not controlled, but you completed the scene with Oscar-winning zeal.

You deserve a rest.

# 22

"The passion for destruction is also a creative passion."
Mikhail Bakunin, *Reaction in Germany*

Karl stood at the door leading into the kitchen from the garage. He stared dumbfounded at what had been done to his home. First anger came at the sense of invasion and total destruction. This was followed by a deep, compelling sadness that the human race could be so vengeful, that it knew no bounds when it came to retribution for perceived wrongs—whether that perception might be based in fact or not.

He stepped over shards of glass, picking his way gingerly around cans of pinto beans and corn, through spilled Golden Grahams cereal, over dented pans and pots, melting ice cream cartons, thawing packages of fish, vegetables, and meats.

There was ketchup everywhere, like globules of darkening blood, streaks and spots of mustard on the stove top, grape juice splattered over cabinet doors and milk souring on the pale yellow walls.

In the living room it was worse. Stuffing lay about like drifts of snow over the broken tables and chairs. Moonlight spread across the fractured and webbed glass of the sliding doors like molten silver patterns of crocheted lace.

Karl made his way through all the other rooms, taking big

deep breaths, sighing to himself, grieving for his possessions. A self-pity came over him, knowing that his beautiful things could be ruined so easily. His home was a shambles. He wished he could leave the house, re-enter it, and find everything perfect again.

He picked up a small glass paperweight in his study. It wasn't broken, but the bottom had a chip missing. He set it on the scarred desktop where it fell over and rolled until he caught it and mindlessly slipped it into the pocket of his slacks. The heavy round weight of it knocked against his thigh as he finished up seeing the mess in the bathroom. He lowered the toilet lid and sat down. He stared at the floor between his feet, at the unrolled toilet paper lying in ribbons there.

He should get up and try to do something about all this. He should unclog the toilet, clean up the smeared remains of mouthwash and toothpaste and liquid soap puddled over the countertop. He should pick up the food in the kitchen and mop the floor.

He should move out. Leave town. And never come back.

The courage to go on had to be found. Something to rattle him from his depression. He stood and walked through the rooms again, facing what he had to do. And where was the note? She always left him a note.

He made his way again to the study and looked around, thinking the note might be there. But there were too many papers, ripped books, sheets of the yellow pages. If the note was here, he would never find it.

In the bedroom, that's the most likely place it would be, he thought, and picked his way through the rubble there again. He scanned the room, eyeing everything carefully. Then he saw it. A creamy square of stationery lying on the floor at the foot of the bed. He might have overlooked it amid the clutter if he had not been searching for it.

He picked up the folded paper and gently opened it. *Do you like it?* the note read.

"What do you want?" Karl shouted as if the person who had written the note was present and could hear him. "What in the hell do you want with me?"

*Why did you throw me away like garbage? You see the state of your house? That's how you left me, torn to pieces.*

*It's going to get worse for you. Much worse. You should have loved me better.*

The note ended with the puerile Xs and Os, the kisses and hugs of a warped personality. Karl strained to understand. He must have inadvertently hurt someone horribly. He didn't remember hurting anyone that badly, but it must be true. If only he could remember who. And when. All this time he had tried to decipher the actions taken against him to determine who might be doing it, but he just couldn't.

Earlier in the day he had gotten copies of his credit reports from two different credit agencies. He discovered many of his bills had been paid late, putting him into a category of credit abusers. But he had never been late paying his bills. Not that he knew about. He even drove to the agencies and talked to the people there. They insisted the reports were valid. He had not paid on his accounts with various creditors for months.

Karl made the agencies take a statement he signed stating he felt the reports were incorrect and that he had never made late payments in his life.

It would do no good, his statement. His credit was in the dumper. He didn't know how it was done. Any number of ways could have been used to ruin his credit rating.

Someone could have stolen his outgoing mail so his payments were never sent. That theory was the least believable since most of his bills were paid from the office in Burbank. Another way could have been found by someone hacking into the agencies' computers and altering information. This seemed possible. In a generation where computers handled all the information and records, a computer expert could easily do what he wished once he got through to a company's computer database, connected through a modem from his home computer. Or someone inside the agencies had been paid to falsify the information. That didn't seem feasible either, not at two major credit-reporting agencies.

It was all done electronically, he imagined. You couldn't get the agencies to believe such a thing. It meant admitting their computer systems had been broached. Rather than think themselves vulnerable, they would consider his idea to be just an accusation made by a bad credit risk.

His credit was ruined now. Nothing he could do to repair it. There was no way he could prove his files had been electronically changed.

His house all in ruins around him.

His clients leaving him right and left. Two more had ended their contracts with him today.

His office broken into and covered in blood. His employees nervous and jumpy.

Did this person who had done all these things to him want to make him crawl?

That was a good supposition. If he lost his credit and his clients, he would soon go out of business. Once a downward spiral started, how was Karl to stop it?

If he could only find out who was doing it. None of the women he had contacted seemed to even know what he was talking about, much less appear guilty of the acts. How far back in time should he go? How many women should he question? Five years, ten? Back to his college days or high school?

The worst of it was he suspected whoever could go to this much trouble was someone who would fool him if questioned face to face about it anyway. Anyone this determined could look him straight in the eyes and commiserate with him, even, and he wouldn't be able to tell. He'd never ferret out the culprit.

Yet he had to.

He looked around at the house with its contents torn and scattered and knew he had to. His life, his future, his peace of mind; everything depended on it.

He refolded the note and took it with him to the kitchen. He almost slipped in a puddle of melted vanilla ice cream, but caught the edge of the counter in time to stay his fall. He took up the wall telephone receiver and dialed a number. When the man answered, Karl said, "My house has been vandalized. It's in complete ruin."

Jimmy Watz, Karl's longtime friend said, "Shit, Karl, you need to call the cops."

"It won't do any good."

"I'll come over."

"Okay."

Under the blazing overhead lights that threw the broken furniture into vivid relief, Karl sank down onto the torn sofa in the living room and he waited for help to arrive. This just seemed too big to handle alone. He hadn't the energy to tackle it without backup. He needed one other sane voice to tell him it could all be straightened up, it could be set right again. Without that, Karl might sit all night long on the sofa holding the folded note, depressed to the bone.

Karl had known Jimmy Watz since college days when they roomed together at UCLA. It was Jimmy, a drama major with hopes of breaking into Hollywood, who pointed out to Karl where his greatest talents lay. Once they graduated, Karl had taken on the task of finding Jimmy a venue through the labyrinth that was Hollywood. Getting to the right people was something Karl could do quickly and with ease, mainly because he wasn't doing it for himself—he was on a quest for a friend. He could take the No sir, you can't see him today, and the No way you're getting in to his office, and the lies and subterfuges and delays without letting it bother him. Or deter him. It wasn't his whole life that was on the line. Rejections held no power over him. That made him relentless and it made him successful.

Karl got into studios that Jimmy never could have penetrated. He set up meetings with producers and directors that most would-be actors would have killed to attend. He convinced pretty secretaries to give him appointments with their high-power bosses, showed up looking cool and intelligent in his best clothes, and he talked up Jimmy Watz as if Jimmy were the second coming.

By the time Jimmy had his first bit-part, he was encouraging Karl to take on pumping up actors' careers as a full-time job. "Karl, man, you've got it, you know? You ought to be an agent."

But Karl didn't really want to be an agent. He couldn't see himself working in a mailroom for two years and trying to wangle his first assistant position. He didn't really want to handle the contracts between actors and studios. No, he told Jimmy, that's not for me.

"Then start your own business. Be a . . . be a publicity maven!"

"A what?"

"Start a publicity company. Take young actors like me and get them in, just the way you've done for me. Teach them how to handle themselves. Publicize them. Get them press, get them into meetings, get them agents . . ."

So that's how it had started. With Jimmy playing a street punk part in a low-budget crime flick. Karl never looked back. He found Jimmy a good agent, worked out subtle but effective publicity campaigns, and Jimmy was more than happy to pay him for those services.

It wasn't long before Karl rented a small office, not in a good part of town, but he found a couple more young actors with talent who didn't know how to break in and he helped them get to where they were going. The business boomed. Within five years, Karl took care of fifty clients and had moved to his Burbank office. He'd hired a secretary and later had to take on assistants. His client base swelled to almost two hundred and fifty.

Jimmy was right. Karl was good at it. He had no wish at all to enter the business himself so that freed him to work on behalf of his clients. The more Karl did for the young actors and actresses, the more his business grew.

Not that Karl took on everyone who walked through his door. Some of them he had to turn away, so many came to his office looking for some kind of foothold into show business. Many of them just didn't have the right attitude or they didn't have the God-given graces or looks to make it. Most of all, too many of them had no training and no aptitude for acting. He couldn't push someone who had little chance of making it.

The word spread through Hollywood circles. If you've got what it takes, Karl LaRosa can help you find the right agent, he can get your name noticed, and start you on the road to success. But if you don't have what it takes, Karl's not going to take your money and run. He just won't take you at all.

Thanks to Jimmy, Karl had found a direction for his life.

He had never known in college what he wanted to do. He took a smattering of courses that gave him two majors, neither of which directed him to a point on the compass where he could spend his energies in something he loved doing. But when he got Jimmy started out in the business and saw him move forward, Karl felt genuine satisfaction. He had been the maker of the dream come true. He had been instrumental in helping a friend get what he had always wanted. It thrilled Karl and made him work even harder on Jimmy's behalf, and then for the other clients he took on.

It had been a good life, a successful, fulfilling life. Until now, when trouble dogged his every step and all his years of work were about to go down the drain.

Jimmy came through the garage and into the kitchen. He stopped there and cursed at what he saw. He glanced at Karl sitting with his hands in his lap on the living room sofa. "Karl, what's going on here?"

"I don't know," Karl said, his voice full of defeat. "Here's the latest note." He held up the paper and waved it in the air. His friend had been told about the others.

Jimmy picked his way into the destroyed living room and took the paper from Karl's hand. He read it and cursed again. "You need the police to handle this," he said.

"I told you already. They don't have the time to get involved when it's just property being destroyed. They'll come out and take a report, but they can't put a watch on my place or follow me around every day. There's no point in calling them and wasting their time. That's the impression I got the last time I called them."

"You must have some inkling about who's doing this," Jimmy said.

Karl looked around the room. He reached out and picked up one of the shattered legs from the broken coffee table.

"I've talked to some of the women I dated."

"Yeah?"

"Hell, I don't know who it is!" Karl exploded, rising from the sofa and kicking at the table in front of him. He threw the busted table leg down and turned, stomping through the rooms, Jimmy behind him. "I don't think I'd know if I talked to her."

"But how many women could hate you this much, Karl?"

Karl turned around and his face was pale with anger. "None of them could hate me this much. I've never done anything to anyone to make her hate me like this."

"Don't get pissed off at me. Just listen, okay? We need to figure out something. You can't just keep going in circles, wondering, while this continues."

"Someone fixed my credit rating," Karl said.

"Fixed it?"

"As in they fucked it up. I couldn't buy a loaf of bread on credit now. I'm down for late pay on every loan I owe."

"That's impossible."

"It may be impossible, but it's reality. I went to the credit agencies to see what was happening when I got turned down for a credit card. Whoever tore up my house monkeyed with my credit rating. I don't know how. You can do anything you want if you have a little computer knowledge, you know that. How does this person disarm my alarm system over and over again? How did she get into my office? She just did it. She won't quit doing it. She's like a force of nature coming at me."

"The credit thing may be a more serious blow than your house getting slummed."

Karl leaned against the wall in the bedroom while Jimmy surveyed the damage. Jimmy whistled. "This is gonna be costly," he said.

"Very."

"I'll help you clean it up. We'll haul out the broken stuff and put it in the garage for now."

"It's not your mess, you don't have to," Karl said.

"Yes I do have to. Now shut up and lend a hand. We better start with the kitchen. You'll have stuff growing in there if we don't get it cleaned up soon."

Karl followed his friend to the kitchen and mechanically helped to take up the food cartons. They found sponges and towels to clean up the floors, cabinets, and appliances. All the time he worked in silence, listening to Jimmy trying to cheer him up, while his heart grew heavier. His world was slap-ass crazy now. There was no making sense of it.

There was no way out.

# 23

"The truth is really an ambition which is beyond us."
Peter Ustinov, *International Herald Tribune*

"Something funny's going on."

Cam gave Robyn a look and replied, "Something funny's always going on. Who's into the nose candy this time?"

"That's not what I mean. We may have a minor drug problem with one or two of the cast and don't we always? But this is about something else."

"Well, what's it about?"

They sat together hunched over a table at the House of Blues, just about the hottest nightspot in Hollywood. One of the phrases you heard in this town above all others was, "You like the blues?" It was as if you couldn't really be part of the showbiz scene if you didn't love blues music. Robyn could take it or leave it. Cam cared little about music, except for maybe old Jefferson Airplane tunes, Mick Jagger, and the Beatles.

"Can we get outta here and go some place quieter?" Robyn asked. She liked the club all right, but not enough to try to have a private conversation over the noise of the crowd. She saw famous faces peering through the subdued light and was afraid one of them might overhear what she had to tell Cam.

"Sure, c'mon, I'll take you somewhere. We never should have met here in the first place. You know how I hate being seen. And *don't* ask me if I like the blues."

Cam led her through the mass of nightclubbers, but it took them ten minutes to reach the door. Stars and gutsy wannabes, agents, producers, and directors had to say hello to them, had to kiss the air around their faces, had to shake their hands. No opportunity to hobnob with the powerful and famous could be allowed to pass.

Cam drove her a few miles away to one of his favorite hangouts, a bar called the Roost. A movie star wouldn't be caught dead in it. As they entered, he said, "Look, no one to maul us! Isn't this joint a beauty?"

Robyn didn't like Cam's low-class dives. They always made her nervous enough to slip off her jewelry and stuff it into her purse. But at least this place would afford them anonymity and that's just what they needed tonight.

After they had ordered their drinks and were ensconced in a back booth that sported curling gray duct tape over the rips in the plastic, Robyn said, "Something weird's happening, Cam."

"Okay, tell Papa." He took a slug of his beer straight from the bottle. Robyn watched his throat work as he swallowed. She had to admit he fit into this kind of bar much better than he did at the House of Blues.

"You know my ex-husband, Karl?"

"Don't think I've had the pleasure. He must be one crazy son of a bitch to divorce you." Cam grinned widely.

"I divorced him, but that's not the point." She gave him a wolfish smile. "Karl runs a company over in Burbank. He works with new actors, getting them good press, helping them find agents who will take them on, that sort of thing."

"Yeah?"

"Well, he's having a big problem now."

"What's that, too much pussy?"

Robyn frowned. "Sometimes you're too crude to live."

"I'm sorry, I shouldn't have said that. Not about a husband of yours."

"He's not my husband and I don't care how much he gets laid, but this is serious, Cam, I want you to listen to me."

Cam bobbed his head. He drank again from the beer bottle, then said, "Go on, I'm listening."

"Karl started having a problem in his life about the same time we started filming the movie. First someone got into his house and left a mash note. The same night he was almost run off the freeway, someone playing tag with him. Then his office was broken into and . . ." Here she hesitated because until this point Cam wouldn't have made the connection. She paused to give weight to the matter and to have Cam's complete attention . . . "they threw blood all over his front waiting room."

Cam's eyes opened a little wider. "No shit," he said.

"That's not all. Every single scene we've shot so far has happened to Karl."

"What the hell."

"Last night he came home to find his house vandalized. It was torn up good and proper. Everything, just like we shot yesterday. Right down to the note left behind for him."

Now Cam looked shocked. He clutched the beer bottle in one hand, but had forgotten all about drinking from it. "Who's doing it?" he asked. "Someone trying to sabotage my film? What asshole's doing some harebrained fucking thing like this? I'll fire the motherfucker first thing in the morning!"

"Karl doesn't know who it is."

"What do you mean he doesn't know who it is? He must know. It has to be someone on the set who gets a copy of the daily script scene. It could be any one of them . . ."

"Cam, listen. Karl doesn't know about *Pure and Uncut*. No one knows about it but us, the crew, the actors. Remember?"

Realization hit. "Oh shit. That's right. It's not in the trades. And you haven't told Karl about it?"

She shook her head. "If I do that, he's going to come around. He's going to disrupt shooting. He might even bring the police."

"No fucking way. Not on my set."

"I told you. We have a problem."

"You're not going to tell him, are you? It'll fuck up everything we're doing. You tell him, we'll get shut down. Why would anyone take the goddamn script and use it for a roadmap to stalk your ex? What kind of wacko would do such a stupid-ass thing? It's a fucking script! It's . . . it's tinsel and cheap celluloid . . ." He was spluttering.

"I know. I think someone's lost it. Someone has a grudge against Karl and she's using the script scenes to get at him."

"It's a woman? Like in the script?"

Robyn shrugged. She pushed aside her screwdriver. The orange juice was making her sick. The bartender hadn't used good vodka. "Karl had a few affairs. Before and after our marriage. Not during, or at least I don't think so. But he's been involved with a few women. Some of them work for us on this picture."

"Who? I'll talk to them."

"You can't do that."

"I, by God, can do that. I'll threaten them or fire them. I'll stop this right now before it goes any further."

Robyn looked at her hands on the table. "He dated Olivia once."

"Olivia! Jesus Christ, I can't fire Olivia. I can't even threaten to fire Olivia. I need her."

"That's right, you do. We do."

Cam ran both hands through his hair. It now stuck up and out from his head, a black halo. "Who else? Go ahead and tell me everything."

"Catherine had an affair with him. It was right after we split up. He was on the rebound and she was there to catch him. I think it lasted a few months before they broke it off."

"Not Catherine."

"And Marilyn was a client of his at one time. It was a while ago. I heard she put the make on him and I'm not sure if he took her to bed, but he probably did. She left soon after I heard the rumors about them being an item."

Each name Robyn gave out caused Cam to shrink back. He now sat completely against the booth, his mouth hanging slightly open. These women were the backbone of his film. His assistant director, his actresses.

"There might be more," Robyn said, hurrying to get all the bad news out before she lost her nerve. "Karl is . . . well, he's a good-looking man, and he's got a lot of power to help actors. You know how women swarm to men in this town with a little bit of authority. I don't know if even some of our extras or bit players might not have had a thing with him."

Cam jerked toward the table and leaned across to her. "That's it, then. We don't say anything. We're not fucking private investigators, we can't be responsible for ex-husbands and people who go off their nut. We start sniffing around our people, they're going to find out why. The news will leave the set and travel. The nondisclosure form won't stop something like this from spreading. The cops will get called in and we'll find our schedule loused up. You understand?"

"I was afraid you'd say that."

You never saw it coming when Cam exploded. His temper was like lightning striking from out of a clear blue sky. "You can't tell him about this! If you do then everything we've worked for goes down the drain. If you really suspect someone, if you get a direct line on this, you can try to talk to the person privately, but you better be goddamn sure of yourself before you do it. If you're the one who burns down this project, we both get scorched. I'm not letting anything stop my production, you got that? Nothing!"

"You're right, Cam. We can't let this out. We can't endanger the film."

"Okay, we agree on this. If you tell Karl what's happening, if you clue in people involved with the film, it's all over for us. I don't know what loony's out there running around mimicking our scenes, but there's really nothing we can do about it."

"There's just one more thing, Cam." She could see from the red blush creeping over his face that his blood pressure was up, but she had to tell him. If he blew a heart valve and collapsed right in front of her, then she'd know she had gone too far.

"What is it?"

"The end of the script. Remember how it ends?"

He sat back again, slumping into the booth. It was as if she'd taken a two by four and knocked the wind out of him. *The end of the script.*

Murder. Bloody, chilling, and violent.

The stalker killed the main character. Olivia killed Landry.

Which meant someone probably meant to do the same to Karl LaRosa.

Robyn knew that neither she nor Cam might be able to live with that. Making a movie was one thing, but standing by while a real crime was committed was another entirely.

Robyn had always loved Karl.

# 24

"Alcohol is barren. The words a man speaks in the night of drunkenness fade like the darkness itself at the coming of day."

Marguerite Duras, *Alcohol*

When Robyn left him, Cam sat for a while alone in the booth of the Roost, drinking beer and bemoaning the risks involved in the life he had chosen to follow. Wasn't it enough he had scraped by in this town when he was trying to get his first film off the landing pad? He must have walked off two layers of shoe leather and pulled half his hair out. He had to grow a whole new persona to deal with the assholes with the money in this fucking town. He had to play the same brand of hardball. He had sacrificed everything to get started as a writer and director.

Now this.

If what was happening to Karl LaRosa found its way to the trades, his film would be notorious. Not only that, but everyone and his brother would read the whole plot of his movie before it ever got canned or distributed. Hell, before it ever even finished shooting. Down the rathole of failure, that's where his project would go. Sliding down into the crud where failed films dropped off the face of the earth. The studio wouldn't just shelve it. They'd destroy every copy.

"Mind if I sit with you, baby?"

She was his age, not young, and overdressed for the joint, a little black skimpy number that clung to her ripe body like a banana peel.

The eye shadow was blue and made her look like a kewpie doll. The lipstick was pink, dime store variety. The jewelry was fake and glittery. She reminded him of a jungle predator, one of the fast toothy ones, maybe a jaguar or a black leopard and he liked her immediately.

"No, I don't mind," he said, knowing she was just what the doctor ordered. "Have a seat."

She slid in across from him, where Robyn had sat earlier. She smiled, showing a row of crooked, lightly stained bottom teeth. Nicotine. She took out a cigarette now from a small gold lamé purse. She waited for him to light it for her. He didn't have a lighter, didn't smoke. He shrugged and said sorry, but he took her lighter from where it peeked from out of her purse flap and flicked it, holding the flame to the end of the tobacco.

"I make movies," he said while she inhaled.

"Yeah, ain't everyone doing that? I happen to have been in a few movies myself. Once upon a time."

"*Sunset Boulevard*?" It was a joke and not a nice one. It was a film about a faded, old, really old, movie star losing her mind.

"You trying to be funny?"

Oh, she knew her movies now, didn't she? She couldn't be fooled. He was sorry to have said something so cruel. She was too smart to put down that way. Sometimes his mean spirit found itself abashed when confronted with the human results of his loose, killing mouth.

"I'm sorry," he said, "you obviously don't deserve that. So what kind of movies were you in? I don't remember seeing you, I'm sorry to say. I bet you were a knockout."

Her shoulders rose a little, then fell. "I don't want to name them. They weren't much."

Porno then, Cam thought. Actresses always reeled off their credits, no matter how bad the movies, unless they had played in porno. Then they didn't.

"What's your name? I'm Cam."

"Rhonda."

"What you drinking, Rhonda? And will you go home with me after we lift a few?" He gave her the full grin, the one the women seemed to always fall for.

Her wide eyes lowered in schoolgirl fashion, trying to say to him, "I'm shy, don't treat me ugly," but nevertheless she nodded. Surprising himself, Cam found her sweet and vulnerable. Nothing like how she looked. Imagine finding a sweet girl beneath an older woman in too much make-up and too little fashion taste. Life was a wonder, it really was.

"Rhonda, I need to talk to someone about my movie, you mind listening a while?"

She took a puff from the cigarette. "No, I don't mind. I'd like that. Maybe I can help."

She would help him all right, she would keep him warm in his bed later, and she might even be a good lay. He would tell her he had serious problems on his set, but he wouldn't tell her exactly what. He had to be circumspect in these places sometimes. The women he romanced all knew how to pick up a phone and dial in news to the columnists. There was a little money in it. Too tempting not to spill secrets.

He ordered her a drink, rum and Coke, and they sat in the booth with him talking and her listening until he felt better. And then he took her to a motel where he treated her gently, with gentlemanly concern.

Her skin, beneath the clothes, was smooth as satin, and she kissed him with the abandon of a young schoolgirl. He loved her smell—damp and musky, the intimate scent of a woman on the verge of losing her looks and a reason to go on. He even loved the blue eye shadow glinting at him from her closed lids while he mounted her. He made love to her the way a husband of many years might, taking his time, relishing the long, slow moments that he took to make her trust him, love him, really love him.

She was a treasure hidden behind tacky packaging. He told her how wonderful she was. She moaned and planted a trail of hot kisses along his neck then she took one of his hard nipples into her mouth to tongue. An exquisite thrill ran down his chest to his groin.

"Do that again," he told her.

He threw back his head and allowed the sensation to take over his mind. Nothing in the world existed but the woman named Rhonda with her hands behind his back and her mouth on his nipple and her soft sweetness lying open beneath him.

This would be one of the best nights he had experienced in ages.

Sometimes he got lucky that way.

# 25

" 'For your own good' is a persuasive argument that will
eventually make a man agree to his own destruction."

Janet Frame, *Faces in the Water*

Olivia Nyad hurried up the walk to Karl's front door. Tired and
worn from her day on the set, she looked her age. Fine spidery
wrinkles radiated from the corners of her eyes. Her mouth
drooped and her movements, usually swift and youthful, tonight
were sluggish.

She rang the bell, then stood nervously putting a cigarette
out on the brick at her feet. When Karl opened the door, she
swept into his arms, a dramatic heroine. She could see
herself, as if she stood back watching a scene being shot.
That's how she lived her life, viewing it from the outside to
see if it passed muster. She thought everyone else did the
same. Calculating gestures and actions, she believed, were
part of being human.

He gave her a brief hug then took her by the shoulders to
move her back so he could see her.

"What are you doing here, Olivia?"

"I heard about your house. I couldn't believe it and had to
come by to see for myself." She pushed past him to the interior of the house and stopped, surveying the dregs of the
damage that had not been cleaned up. The living room was

empty of furniture, the walls had dents in the plaster, the sliding glass door opening to the outside was still a starred wide sheet of safety glass.

"The glazier can't show up until tomorrow," Karl said, noticing how she stared at the glass.

She turned around to Karl who had followed her inside. "Where's your furniture?"

"It had to be taken away. It was all broken and ruined. I haven't been anywhere to order new yet."

"Who the hell did this to you?"

"Someone who must hate me with all her heart."

Olivia didn't like the way he had said that. She didn't like he way he was looking at her. She felt defensive, as if he were making a silent accusation. "Karl, I told you once already that I'm not responsible for what's happening to you. I don't know why you keep suggesting I have something to do with it. You really think I'd come in your house and do . . . this?" She swept her hand around at the empty, desolate room.

"I guess not," he said softly, moving around her to the kitchen. "Do you want something to drink? I just laid in new stock. Everything in the cabinets had been busted and spilled on the floors and walls."

"You have scotch?"

"Sure."

She stood at the end of the counter and watched him pour it over ice cubes. He knew she took it over the rocks.

"I hope you don't mind the plastic cup. I haven't had time to buy dishes either."

She looked around. There was a dent on the front of the refrigerator door as if someone had kicked it. There were holes in the walls and streaks of rust and yellow that must have been made from splattered food. One cabinet door below the sink hung from the hinges.

She took the clear plastic cup and said, "I don't mind what I drink from."

A silence fell between them while they both sipped from their drinks. Finally Olivia blurted, "Karl, I wouldn't hurt you for the world, you know that, don't you? I loved you once and I was hurt when we broke up, but you can't believe I'd get in here and do this thing, do you?"

He rubbed a hand over his eyes. He looked older, weary unto death. There were new lines on his face and a darkness of surrender in his eyes she had never seen there before. She almost moved into his arms again to hold him. He had always brought out her maternal instinct. She wanted to baby him, to rock and soothe his furrowed brow and tell him everything was going to be all right.

He said, "I don't know what to think anymore, Olivia. I don't think it's you. No, I don't think that."

Even though he tried to sound sure of himself, Olivia detected the hesitation. He really did think she might be the guilty party? She felt something inside her shrink. Tears formed in her eyes and she turned away from him.

"Is there anything I can do to help?" she asked.

"Tell me who's doing this," he said.

"I wish I could."

"Look, I've got something to show you." He had raised his voice and then he walked around her from the kitchen, across the empty living room. He was headed for his bedroom where they had spent many a lovely, long night in one another's arms. She could hardly follow him, her legs had suddenly grown so weak. The memory of being in Karl's arms, having him inside her, feeling his breath against her face, his lips upon hers . . . It was enough to cause her to grab the edge of the counter to keep her steady.

Goddamnit, she wasn't over him yet. She'd never get over

him. Being in the same room with him made her want to fling herself against his chest, tear off his clothes, and tell him what a mistake he had made to leave her. No other man in her life had caused her to feel so deserted, so alone. She had taken lovers since her affair with Karl and none of them filled the empty hole in her heart left behind by him. She was a torch carrier. Just like the woman who must be trying to destroy him. And Karl knew that about her. No wonder she was a suspect.

He returned carrying a slip of notepaper. He thrust it at her. She put down the plastic cup and took it. She read the words inscribed there. She understood why he thought she might have written it. She did have a reputation for vengeance in her affairs, business and personal. They called her "Killer" as a joke. People feared going up against her or incurring her wrath. She never forgot a grievance or forgave it. She found a way sooner or later to repay her enemies and detractors two-fold.

She read the note over again before handing it back. "I didn't write that," she said, hoping he would believe her.

He stood holding the note, staring down at it. His face was caught in a grimace, as if he held something toxic and he had forgotten to don protective gloves. "Whoever this is, she's going to bring me down." He glanced up and looked her in the eyes. "The whole process is in motion. I just found out someone tinkered with my credit rating. Someone is getting word to my clients, new and old, warning them off me. I'm losing business every single day. I don't know how to fight it. This woman is invisible and it seems she's also invincible. I changed my locks. She found a way past them. I had my security system checked and fixed and rechecked. She disables it whenever she wants in. It's like I'm a soft target, Olivia. I'm wide open and nothing I do covers me."

She wanted to tell him that what was happening to him was from the script. From *Pure and Uncut.* But she couldn't do that, no matter how much she wished she could. Cam would drop her, hire a new lead, and re-film all her scenes. She knew Cam. His threats weren't idle when he had them sign the nondisclosure. She couldn't lose this part. Even for Karl.

Realizing her ambitions and career were more important than Karl's future made her flinch. She ought to hate herself, but she couldn't change, could she? She was Olivia Nyad, Hollywood star. Aging, losing her looks, and soon her screen appeal. This movie was the best thing that had come along in her entire career; she wouldn't give it up. She was Killer. She was one tough, determined broad, hallelujah. Unless Karl was about to be murdered, she didn't think she could confide to him the connection between the script and his troubles.

Naturally this meant someone involved with the picture was after him. Just as, in the film, she stalked the character Landry was playing. Despite how horrible the reality of it was, she had to admit the scheme was a clever one. If she knew who on the set might be doing it, she'd go to her and do something. But she had no more idea than did Karl.

The doorbell chimed and they both turned in that direction. Karl put the note on the counter and went to answer the door.

Olivia stood still, finishing off her scotch. She heard Robyn LaRosa's voice and knew it was time to go. She took up her car keys and walked toward them in the hall.

"I have to be on my way, Karl." She didn't mean to sound so cold, but now Karl had his ex here, she was superfluous. Even though Robyn was the film's producer and main investor, she didn't like her worth shit. She expected the feeling was mutual. Hiring her for the lead was a business decision.

Nothing in Hollywood was personal when it came to money and making a success of a project.

"Oh, hi, Olivia." Robyn gave her a worried look. Olivia wanted to say, *No, I didn't tell him he's living out the script,* but she couldn't say that, of course. She said hello, thanks for the drink, Karl, and fled from his house, her cheeks burning.

She was still jealous. She had had nothing good to say about Karl's ex-wife when she and Karl had been lovers. She had nothing better to say for her now, despite Cam's project. She had to get out of here. She never should have come at all.

"What was Olivia after?"

Karl returned to the kitchen counter for the scotch bottle. He poured himself another and found a new cup for Robyn. It seemed tonight every woman he'd ever been with might drop by his house. "She heard my place had been torn up. She came by to tell me how sorry she was. That's what you're here for, isn't it? To tell me how sorry you are?"

"Do I hear you getting into a mood?" She took the scotch from him and looked around the empty living room.

"Oh, I'm in a mood, all right. I'll get over it, of course, just as soon as my stalker dies and goes to hell."

"Oh Karl."

"Well, what kind of mood did you expect to see me in, Robyn? Am I supposed to be throwing an open house party?"

He stood at the broken sliding glass doors with his back to her. He still felt jangled by Olivia's visit. He never knew when Olivia was 'natural' or acting. It was the reason they had split up. He had never really gotten close to Olivia, not the real Olivia, not the one who was naked and maskless.

Come to think of it, he hadn't much more insight into Robyn. He'd been married to her seven years and knew as little about her real self as he did Olivia's. Not that Robyn

153

acted all the time, but she was closed off to him in all her deep vital places she kept secret. When he had brought it up, she hadn't understood what he meant. Or pretended she didn't. Their marriage, especially toward the end, had felt like ten miles of rough road. And he drove down it in a Model-T. Alone.

"Why don't I take you out to dinner?" she said from behind him.

"I'm not hungry. I ate a late lunch."

"Won't you even look at me, Karl? You're making me feel . . ."

He whirled. "What? Guilty? Are you guilty, Robyn? Have you begun haunting my life to try to drive me crazy, or what? Just what is the deal anyway?"

When he had first turned she looked shocked, but now her features had all changed to stony surfaces. She might be a flat rock on a river bed. An immovable mountain. He could never get through to her and this time was no exception.

"Thanks for reminding me why I left you," she said, setting her plastic cup on the counter and adjusting her shoulder bag. "I don't know why I bother giving a damn about what happens to you anymore."

She was halfway to the door before he fell apart. He went after her and grabbed one arm, swinging her around to face him. "You don't know what it's like," he said. "I don't have a life anymore. I feel like a goddamned puppet manipulated by invisible strings. Whoever is doing all this to me just blithely goes ahead from one tactic to another and I'm helpless against her."

"You don't have to take it out on me."

"I know, I know I shouldn't, but it just comes boiling up. I can't seem to stop it. If I didn't vent once in a while I don't know what . . ." He let his sentence go unspoken. He let go of her arm and looked back to the starry planes of the shattered glass doors that now reflected moonlight.

This had been such a nice, comfortable home. Now it was a shattered and eerily empty mausoleum.

"I didn't go in to my office today," he said finally. "I had to be here to direct a crew I hired to take out the damaged furniture. Every piece they hauled off the premises made me angrier. By the time they were finished, I must have looked like an enraged bull. The guy collecting the money for the work was Hispanic, could hardly speak English. Two of his workers had to actually give him a little push from behind before he'd come up to me to take the cash. I guess they thought I was going to blow up at them and scream or go nuts or something."

"I'm sorry, Karl. I'm trying to imagine how bad this is for you. I really do want to help if I can."

"But how?" he asked. "How can anyone help me?"

"For one thing, you have to tell me who you suspect. Maybe going over a list of the women you . . ."

"With you?"

"Yes, with me. Look, we've been divorced a long time. I'm not going to get jealous at this late date over your affairs. That's all over. I'm trying to be your friend. If you'll let me."

If he had had a chair nearby, he would have sagged into it. He had drunk too much scotch without eating anything. His stomach was on fire and the inside of his head felt fuzzy, as if moss had grown over the lobes of his brain while he wasn't paying attention.

He slowly shook his head. "I can't do it tonight. I'm too whipped out. Maybe we can meet for lunch or dinner or something. I could use some help, I know that."

"All right, Karl." She patted his arm. "All right, not tonight. You should go to bed early, get some rest. Do it for your own good. I'll call you, set up a time we can meet. I'm on the set every day, but maybe one night we'll have dinner or you can come over to my place."

"Thanks, Robyn. I'm sorry about what I said before. You just happened to be around at the wrong time. Olivia didn't help things."

After he shut the door on Robyn, he leaned against it, forehead touching wood. No point in locking it, he thought. He had nothing left to steal and as for the stalker, he couldn't keep her out when she wanted in anyway. Let her, by God, come in while he was sleeping! He'd use his gun on her. He'd drill her full of holes! He put his index finger to his lips and blew, then laughed aloud. He'd seen too many movies. He couldn't drill straight holes in a board with a drill, much less kill someone with a gun.

Jimmy Watz had brought over a folding cot for him to sleep on until he could find time to order a new bed. Tonight he wouldn't even shower first, he'd just strip down and lie in the cot drinking scotch until he fell asleep. Surely tomorrow would be a brighter day. At least the woman screwing with his life hadn't yet really tried to physically harm him. There had been that early instance of bumper tag on the freeway, but it wasn't so serious. More of a playful game, that's all it had been.

He must be grateful for small favors.

He staggered toward the bedroom, surprised he couldn't walk straight, then laughed at himself again, remembering he had to rescue the bottle of scotch from the kitchen counter first. He turned and retraced his steps, found the bottle, and swung it by the neck as he made his way toward the cot through the shadow-pooled rooms.

It was for his own good that he go to sleep. Robyn was right. For his own good . . .

He sat on the side of the cot, downing one more drink before lying back on the pillow. It was the last he knew. Oblivion took him before he had time to undress.

# 26

"I have spent more than half a lifetime trying to express the tragic moment."

Marcel Marceau, *The Guardian*, London

This was a series of scenes that Cam knew would really give a theater audience a chance to gasp and scream. He wanted it done right. Everything must be executed perfectly.

Four cameramen from different angles were filming the action. The stunt car drivers for Olivia and Jackie were buckled into their seats and revving the motors. They were filming on a closed section of the freeway just after sunrise for the best light. The other cars' drivers were in position on the track and ready. Cam had instructed each one individually on what he wanted from the shots. He didn't want to have to film it ten different times and have to use up too many extra crash vehicles.

This wouldn't be a car chase the likes of which every movie-goer had seen ad nauseam a million times. Cam wanted this in extraordinary close-up, zooming in on the car crashes, a few overhead helicopter shots for wide view, and a choreographed chase that in 3-D would make the audience grab hold of their seats and press make-believe brake pedals on the floor.

He took a breath, raised his hand, and when he dropped it he yelled, "Go!"

It was a ballet in speed, screeching brakes, spin-outs, skewed guardrails, and crunching metal. He was going to get it in one! Just one take! He began to jiggle around like a man needing to go to the bathroom, watching it go down. The stuntman driving Olivia's car came up behind the Mercedes that Jackie was supposed to be in and rammed it so hard it left the middle lane and shot like a bullet into the far right lane. The traffic in the two crossed lanes stuttered, swerved, crashed, all on cue.

Cam began to clap his hands with each impact until he was literally swaying and cheering as the chase progressed. He sat in a chair raised twenty feet above the ground by a hydraulic arm so that he could see the action unreel down the highway. He had no idea if the trailing cameramen were getting the best shots, but the drivers were doing stupendous jobs.

Olivia's driver caught up with the Mercedes, rammed it again, this time from the side. Once more. Then the Mercedes leapt ahead and spun around cars in the way, passing them at eighty-ninety miles an hour. Now it was tricky. Both cars had to weave in and out of lane traffic like working out a maze. They hadn't rehearsed it. Model cars had been set up on a table to show how Cam wanted it filmed. The drivers carried it all in their heads and if just one of them fucked up, the whole shot was cooked.

It went beautifully. Cam grinned so hard his face hurt. When at last the car with Jackie's driver in it spun out, doing a three-sixty, and slammed into the guardrail before breaking through and racheting down an incline onto another feeder road before straightening out, Cam felt like spreading out his arms and flying right out of the chair into sunny sky.

The cars all slowed and turned, heading back toward the beginning of the highway where the production crew was set up. Cam motioned for his director's chair to be lowered to ground level.

Robyn came over, her hand over her eyes in order to block the sun. "That was a good one, right?"

"It was spectacular! It was moonlight and roses. It was caviar! It was sex all night with a goddess." He turned and waved at the vehicles so the drivers could tell he was pleased.

"Oh, I wouldn't go that far," Robyn said.

Catherine came to them, a clipboard in her hands. "I've got Olivia and Jackie ready to film the inside car scenes. Is it a go? You think the freeway shots worked?"

Robyn said, "He's ecstatic. He thinks it went better than sex with a goddess." She smirked at Cam, but he wasn't listening. He was on the walkie-talkie with his cameramen.

"Great," Catherine said. She stood by, waiting for Cam to instruct her on the interior car shots with the actors. She was surprised when Robyn leaned over and whispered, "Have you seen Karl lately?"

She wondered what the hell Karl had to do with today's shooting. They were too busy to gossip about an old shared lover. "Not lately, why?"

"I was just wondering."

"But why?" Catherine frowned.

Cam moved off from them, involved in technical aspects he had to attend to. Catherine knew she'd just have to wait until he was ready for the actors. Then he'd come back to her and together they'd set it up.

"You haven't talked to him then, not at all?" Robyn asked.

"No. What's going on, Robyn? Why are you bringing up personal matters like this on the set?"

Robyn shrugged and looked off at the stunt drivers getting out of the cars, taking off their helmets and wriggling out of their fireproof suits. "It's nothing," she said. "Karl's had a stretch of trouble . . ." She looked straight at Catherine again. ". . . And you haven't heard about it, huh?"

Catherine shook her head.

"Never mind, then. I just thought since you two were together a while, he might have called you."

"Well, now you've got me worried about him. What kind of trouble has he had?"

"Never mind, I said. If Karl wants you to know, he'll get in touch with you."

"Yeah, right." Catherine tried not to let the sarcasm creep into her tone, but Robyn had a bossy, icy quality about her that often caused Catherine to act distant and sulky herself.

Robyn walked off without a by-your-leave. Catherine stood holding the clipboard and a pen, watching the other woman's sexy walk. How she could look like someone who stepped out of a *Playboy* centerfold shoot while being on location in this early morning heat, Catherine couldn't understand. There were packets of sweat under her own arms and her hair had frizzed in the morning damp into tight little wiry balls. She knew she must look like an unkempt poodle.

Jesus, *nobody* ever looked that good off camera. And Robyn wasn't even an actress. It was a crying shame she didn't wear jeans and running shoes like the rest of the folks on the set and at location shoots. It had to be absolute murder staying cool in silk slacks.

Catherine chewed on the top of her ballpoint pen while she waited for Cam to return. She bit down hard on the plastic cap, thinking over what Robyn had said about Karl. Maybe she should call him. See how he was holding up. He probably had a new girlfriend who was putting him through the wringer.

He always had a new girlfriend.

# 27

"Death is a shadow that always follows the body."

English Proverb

Karl spent two more days away from the office trying to oversee the repairs to his home and the installation of new furniture. He spent half of one day consulting with a different home security company who guaranteed no one would be able to disable the new system. "For this kind of dough," Karl said, "my house better be impregnable."

After he wrote out all the checks and sent home the workmen and delivery people, he sat down on the new, dark, paisley-printed sofa, put his feet up on the new coffee table, and smiled at the makeover. Hell, it had been a few years since he'd refurbished the house anyway. It was due for an overhaul. Not that he could forgive the woman who cost him so much anguish and money. But there were up sides to everything, even vandalism. You just had to look at it properly, he told himself.

Now it was early morning, close to seven a.m. and he had to get back to his office in Burbank to see how many more clients had walked out on him. His secretary Lois was getting worried. His assistant showed signs of deep stress. The mood at the office was downbeat and spiraling toward sullen. He'd stop off at a florist on the way in and buy huge sprays of fresh flowers. Lois could place them all over the office and maybe that would cheer everyone up a little. And he'd order in lunch from the Italian spaghetti place he liked. A treat for everyone—deep-dish pizza or maybe the delicious spinach lasagna. He had to let his people know things were going to be all right.

And they were. He'd make it all right. He'd go back through all his old affairs again and speak to the women. He'd ferret out which one had gone off the deep end and see that she stopped this harassment. Surely he would be able to tell from looking in a woman's eyes how mad she was. Anyone capable of the damage his house had sustained had to be walking the razor's edge.

He was on the freeway, traffic beginning to thicken the closer he got to the Burbank exit. He hadn't been watching his rearview mirror when the jolt came. The Jaguar lurched forward a car length and the steering wheel literally flew out of his hands. His head was whipped back. He let out a gasp. He grabbed the wheel just before ramming the lane separator wall.

"God almighty," he said beneath his breath. He looked in the rearview and side mirrors. Behind him, perhaps three car lengths away, was a white Ford, older model, large, maybe a Continental. It was gaining again. He tried to see the driver, but the sunlight sheeted the windshield of the other car with opaque gold. Hell, it might be a demon or a gargoyle driving instead of a woman, for all he knew.

He stomped the gas pedal and began looking in the lanes to his right for space to move over. He'd get off the freeway at the next exit. He'd call the cops at the first service station he found.

The Ford rammed him again, but this time Karl was ready for it. His hands gripped the laced leather covering on the

163

Jaguar's steering wheel so hard they felt glued down. He had tried to hit a burst of speed in order to avoid the collision from behind, but it was too late.

Suddenly he was slammed forward again, his head banging the headrest with a popping sound. His vision went all out of focus and he couldn't tell if he was in his lane or not. When he could see straight again, he realized he was swerving into the lane next to him and the car there taking up the space screeched its brakes trying to avoid being hit.

Now Karl screamed out, believing he was about to die in a fiery crash. He swung the wheel hard left, avoiding the other car by millimeters.

He looked in the rearview. The white Ford was gaining for the third time. The front end of the car was smashed up pretty good, which made Karl realize his own car must look like a crushed tin can in the rear.

Upping his speed to over a hundred miles an hour, Karl passed the car in the right lane, the one he'd almost hit, and swerved in front of it. He saw the next two lanes over to the right were pretty busy—cars, pickup trucks, a semi. He couldn't get over yet. He pressed the accelerator and the speedometer inched up to one hundred twenty. He had passed the wolf pack of vehicles and found a little area of empty lanes.

Sweat rolled down his face. He could feel his heart rocketing around like a loose pinball. He passed over into the next lane right. He saw the Ford, two, four, then five cars behind, doing the same. Shifting lanes. Relentless.

"Oh god," Karl whispered, so scared he thought he might black out. "Get me out of this," he prayed. "Ohgodgetmeoutofthis."

He had one more lane to cross over so he could reach an exit and a feeder lane. There was a farm truck with an old tin camper on the back in his way. If he sped up to pass it, he'd be blocked by another wolf pack.

He dropped back, hoping to scoot over behind the farm truck. Then the white Ford was behind him. He still couldn't see the driver. They were headed east, the sun square in front of them, lancing off the other car's windshield, making the driver invisible.

Opening! Karl quickly changed lanes, saw an exit up ahead. It didn't look more than a quarter mile distant. If only he could . . . The Ford rammed him and the wheel again flew from his fingers like a startled bird winging away to freedom. The Jaguar angled to the left into the left lane's traffic just coming up on him. Cars hit their brakes, swerved and hit other cars in lanes next to them. Before Karl could straighten out the Jag, he heard metal bending and the sound of explosions as half a dozen cars and trucks slammed into one another.

Now the Ford was in the lane left of Karl. He looked over, waiting for the front end of the Ford to clear his midsection, trying to see the driver. Before the big front grill came even with his door, Karl saw it shift like a gear clicking into place. It was going to sideswipe him.

Karl didn't know what to do, step on the gas or the brake. He didn't have time to do anything. The Jag flew from the lane onto the emergency stopping pavement, hit the gravel lining, and went airborne over a short ditch. It landed hard on the incline, the tires digging in, and spun onto the feeder road that was mercifully empty. Karl hit the brakes so hard his foot slammed into the carpet. The Jag burned rubber on the feeder, the back end whipping around until the car had done a full circle and shuddered to a stop. The engine stalled.

Karl hung over the wheel, breathless. "Goddamn," he muttered. "Oh shit."

He craned his head to look for the white Ford but it had vanished. The driver must have gone on down the freeway. It was already out of sight. Karl hadn't even had a chance to watch for the license plate.

Cars had slowed and stopped behind Karl on the feeder. They took turns honking their horns at him. Karl reached with trembling fingers to the key in the ignition and started the car.

He didn't realize his head had bumped the front windshield and that he was bleeding from the front of his scalp.

He didn't know he'd even been hurt until one side of his face felt wet and he reached up to wipe off what he thought was sweat and brought his fingers away blood red.

# 28

"The insane are always mere guests on earth, eternal strangers carrying around broken decalogues that they cannot read."

F. Scott Fitzgerald, *The Letters of F. Scott Fitzgerald*

The Body made it to the studio gate just fifteen minutes late. Cam was going to throttle him, but no matter what degree of rant he got into—and he could get into some good ones—he'd get over it.

The effort on the freeway from Malibu to Burbank had taken time, it was so out of the way. Waiting not far from Karl's house, The Body had followed him from his block right onto the entrance ramp. This meant the day started before dawn. A full day's excitement and work and danger had been used up in mere hours.

Then after the rear bumper ramming and the last slam into the side of the Jag, The Body had to drop off the smoking, wrecked Ford in an alley in Hollywood where the other car was parked.

It all took time. It took finesse. It took such careful planning and a cunning performance.

And it involved courage. The Body might have been hurt trying to ram the Jag at those speeds. Or another car might have gone out of control and totaled out the Ford.

The Body quaked at the thought. It was as if a chill crept up the spine, ending with an electric shock at the base of the neck.

Working on the set after the long, hard hours of setting up Karl on the freeway was child's play, but it did demand attention. First to deal with Cam for being late, then with the other crew members who didn't seem quite with-it for some reason. Everything had to be shot over several times. A boom mike didn't work, one of the cameramen was off with a rampaging case of the flu, no one hit their marks, the lighting director argued with the prop people.

The day wore on endlessly, winding down finally like a battery-operated toy going on the blink. The Body said good-bye to everyone and left the studio lot as fast as possible.

Once safe at home, The Body went directly to the sensory deprivation room and locked the door. Felt in the dark for the leather chair. Sat and reclined with feet raised.

Breathed deeply of sin and covetousness and retribution. Luxuriated in replaying the early morning chase step-by-step, scene-by-scene. It was almost the way it had been filmed the day before. Very few differences, save for the lack of cameras, pacing vehicles, and little or no chance of harm.

Had Karl been hurt when he went hurtling down the embankment to the feeder lane? Had someone crashed into him or had the Jag landed on another car that happened to be passing by?

The Body hadn't been able to slow down enough to get a glimpse of the aftermath. Maybe The Body should have turned on the car radio on the way home to check for news of Karl LaRosa's death. If he'd died, they would have surely reported it. Karl was a man of power behind the scenes; he was a puppet master. He had groomed enough stars over the past ten years to make him newsworthy.

Well, The Body didn't turn on the radio, therefore there was no way to know if Karl were alive or dead or hospitalized. It was too early for him to be dead, but The Body had to take into consideration that any action mimicking the script of *Pure and Uncut* could result in murder. At any time. Things could always go wrong. They weren't being as carefully choreographed as they were on soundstages and location shootings. It was all up to chance whether Karl survived to the end of the script or not.

It would be a pity if he succumbed too soon, but it was his demise The Body meant to achieve, early in the game or late. It really didn't matter all that much.

The effect of the silence and impenetrable dark served to ease The Body from a frenzied state to one resembling peace. The face relaxed once the mask was tossed aside. The limbs fell loose. The eyes rolled back in the head, and visions of blood and destruction were let from out of the cage in the back hallway of the brain to go dancing down the synapses and neuron networks.

For another hour, until the timer signaled The Body must leave the deprivation room, madness reigned, gleeful and faceless as a mime on a street corner.

# 29

"Scratch a lover, and find a foe."
Dorothy Parker, *Ballade of a Great Weariness*

When Catherine Rivers called Karl's house after work on the set was finished for the night, Jimmy Watz answered the phone.

"Can I speak to Karl, Jimmy?"

"Who is this? Catherine?"

"Yeah."

"I'm sorry to have to tell you this, but Karl's having to stay overnight in the hospital. He was in a wreck and wound up with some stitches in his head."

"He was in a wreck?"

"Right. He said some joker ran him off the freeway this morning going in to work. He went down an embankment and onto a feeder lane. Luckily the feeder was empty at the spot where he ended up or he'd probably be dead."

"Oh, Jesus, Jimmy. Where is he? Is he going to be all right?"

"He's in General. They're keeping him for observation, but he's going to be all right. Had a long cut on his scalp and some bruises, that's about it. He's pretty shook up."

"Robyn told me Karl's been having a rough time. Could you fill me in?"

Jimmy hesitated a couple of moments and that made

Catherine frown. "Jimmy? What's been going on? I want to know."

"Too much to tell you about over the phone." Jimmy was evasive. "Let's just say someone's got it out for him."

"Who?"

Another pause. Jimmy finally said, "Karl doesn't know yet. Some damn nut, if you ask me. Tore up his house just a few days ago. Now tried to run him off the road."

"Thanks, Jimmy. I'm going to the hospital to see Karl. I'll talk to you later."

Catherine picked up her car keys from where she'd dropped them next to the phone. She called to her housekeeper to watch after Barb, she had to go out again. On the way to the hospital she couldn't help but notice the similarities between Karl's house being roughed up and his accident on the freeway today to the scenes they had recently filmed for *Pure and Uncut.* Some coincidence. It gave her a prickly feeling of foreboding. It was just too coincidental, wasn't it?

She found out from the hospital information desk where Karl's room was and took the elevator up. The door to 221 was closed. She pushed it open slowly, wondering if she might accidentally intrude on some kind of medical procedure or maybe an aide giving Karl a sponge bath. She was relieved to see it was a private room and Karl was alone.

"Hi there," she called cheerfully, having steeled herself for the worst. Karl's head looked like a bandaged melon. Both his eyes were blackened and an angry lump the color and size of a red rose swelled his left cheek.

He was sitting up in bed, propped by two pillows. He immediately muted the television set where the evening news was playing. He turned toward her as if his head were made of thin, fragile glass that might roll off his shoulders and break.

"Catherine. Who told you?"

"I called your house and Jimmy answered. He told me. I wanted to see for myself how you were." She approached the bedside and laid a hand over his on the mattress. He withdrew his hand from beneath hers. She gave him a slightly puzzled look. "You look beat up, I'm afraid."

"Everything from my neck up hurts," he said. "I was bleeding like a slaughtered hog when they brought me in. How are my eyes? Last I looked, I thought I had turned into a raccoon."

She shrugged and tried to smile. "Looks like you took a few too many one-two punches from a heavyweight contender. Did the doctors say you're going to be okay?"

He shifted on the sheets, trying to sit straighter. She automatically put her hands under his arm and lifted to help him. She could feel him stiffen and draw away a little. Maybe his ribs were bruised too. Just what was his problem with being touched by her?

"I can go home tomorrow. They're just keeping me to see if I'm going to fall into a coma and die or something." He grinned a little to show he was making a brave joke. "It's not a bad head wound. Got some stitches . . . oh, about fifty-two of them." He reached up and gingerly touched the bandage on his head. "These bruises are from being knocked around in the car, slamming my head into the windshield. No big deal. I'll live."

"Before I knew this happened," Catherine said, "Robyn told me you'd been having trouble and asked if I'd talked to you. Jimmy wouldn't tell me much about what's been going on. What's this about somebody busting up your house?"

Now he turned to face her, wincing as he did so. His color was the dull, washed gray of concrete so that the black eyes and raised red knob on his cheekbone stood out like garish blobs of paint. "You're pretending you don't know about this, right?"

"I'm not pretending anything, Karl. I didn't know anything until Robyn said something today."

"You know, you're the one who might have made my life work out. If we'd given it a chance," he added.

"Well, that was a long time ago. Why don't you tell me about the things going on in your life now?"

"That's just it, Cat. Someone from the past is out to gut me like a fish. And doing a damn good job of it, I might add."

"The person who ran you off the road today, you mean? Did you see him?"

His eyes narrowed down so there was no light at all reflected from them. It looked as if empty black eye sockets were trained on her.

"Sun kept me from seeing who tried to kill me today. But it's a her, not a him. Right, Cat? It's a *her*."

"A woman? Who do you know crazy enough to play tag on a freeway during rush hour?"

"You drive pretty good, as I remember."

She had felt that coming since she'd walked into the room. He was holding back, he wasn't his old self, and it had nothing to do with his injuries. "You think I tried to run you down? Karl, why would I do that?" Maybe he was suffering from some kind of mental lapse from hitting his head. She had heard of head injury patients acting out of character. This wasn't at all like Karl to be paranoid and accuse people of crazy things.

Now he glanced away and his mouth was set in hard lines. "Just come out and tell me if it's you, Catherine. Whatever you've got against me, we need to work it out."

"Karl? What's wrong with you? I didn't run you off the road this morning."

"Do you blame me for losing the babies? You got rid of them because of me, didn't you?" He sat straight up and grabbed her by the arms, pulling her in close. She shuddered, looking into his eyes. She saw rage there, enough for him to tear her head off if he wanted.

He said, low and threatening, "How can you think it was my fault? I didn't even know about the pregnancy. If you'd asked me to choose between our relationship and the lives of the unborn, I wouldn't have hesitated a second. I would have told you to spare the twins."

His words were a kick in the stomach that caused her to pull free his hands and step back from the bed in shock. "What are you talking about, Karl?"

"You didn't know I found out about the abortion? You had it two days before our second date. You must have thought I wouldn't want anything to do with a woman pregnant by another man, but would have been wrong. You didn't even say anything to me. Did you even bother to tell the father? Did he want to abort them too?"

Tears cascaded down Catherine's cheeks. She tried to bury her sorrow and the vile sickness that had risen in her to form a hard knot in her throat by pushing her head down, down, forcing her chin toward her chest.

"I have to get out of here . . ."

She whirled around and stumbled into the food stand, knocking a Styrofoam pitcher of ice water to the floor.

"*You* did it, Cat. I didn't do it. I didn't even know. Is that why you want to hurt me now? To get me back for something I didn't really do? Don't you see how unfair that is? Cat, talk to me!"

She stepped over the ice and the puddle of water, grabbed the door handle and pulled the heavy door toward her. Everything in her vision was clouded by a veil of tears. She heard

Karl pleading with her at her back, but she was out the door now and away down the hall, stumbling, crying, wiping the wetness from her face, and furious now, pinwheeling down the hallway. She ran past the nurses' station to the elevator door.

She did hate him now. She hated him for making her remember, for making her rehash the morality of her decision. For making her feel like a hard and cruel woman who had no heart at all.

In the elevator, alone, she wiped the last of the tears from her face. She thought of Barbara, her little girl, of how much she loved her to distraction, would do anything for her, sacrifice anything.

She sucked in breath, hurried out of the elevator on the ground floor, and rushed from the building.

What he had said hurt because it pointed to the truth she didn't want to think about. She could have sacrificed one affair with a man, with Karl, for the twin children she had been carrying in her body. She had acted selfishly and without honor. She had aborted the fetuses for the worst reason of all—for the hope of a love that never materialized. She had lost all around.

Done it to herself.

But Karl was wrong. She didn't blame him for anything.

She had absolutely done it to herself.

# 30

"Hollywood money isn't money. It's congealed snow, melts in your hand, and there you are."

Dorothy Parker, *Writers at Work*

Karl looked straight ahead through the windshield of Lisa's car. She had taken the day off to pick him up from the hospital. She had been with him a few minutes when they'd brought him into emergency the day before. His face wasn't as black and purpled with bruises then. She flinched on seeing him this morning. He had to hold her close and reassure her before she stopped her anxious fidgeting around the room, gathering his things.

"Karl, why don't you let me drive you to my house? I don't think you should stay at your place until this gets resolved."

He tried to shake his head, but it hurt too much. "No, I'm going home. No one's going to run me out of my house. Whoever this is, she's not going to win. Not an inch."

Lisa turned left onto his road. "If she kills you, I guess that means she wins."

"No one's going to kill me. I'm going to start carrying my gun."

"That won't help much when you're in your car being bumped off the freeway."

"It'll help." Karl felt stubborn enough to hold out against any logic she might try on him. He wasn't moving out. He wasn't running. He wasn't going to give up his life or his career or his future over this.

He turned in the seat so he could see Lisa. "Have you talked to the garage that towed my Jag?"

"They left a message at your office. It's going to cost about six grand to repair the body damage. You wound up with two flats on the rear, too."

Karl kept silent, seething. He loved that car so much. It wasn't worth all sorts of body work, really, except for a sentimental old fool like himself. He'd rather have the older Jag than a new one. He'd have to pay the money for repair. If he said anything about this right now, he was afraid he'd start yelling and that would scare Lisa, the way he had scared and hurt Catherine last night. Unlike Catherine, who he suspected might be his stalker because it seemed to him she had the most motivation—as wrongheaded as it was—he really didn't want to upset Lisa any more than he had to.

"I'll need a loaner."

"I already handled that for you." She turned into his driveway and parked next to a blue Chevy Caprice.

"That?" he asked, indicating the Chevy.

"It's all they had."

"But it's so big and *American* looking."

She grinned over at him. "It's a Chevrolet, Karl, it's supposed to look like an American car."

"Well, I guess it might be more protection in freeway mishaps," he said, not quite kidding. "It was great of you to go to this much trouble to get me wheels."

She reached into her purse and produced the keys. He took them and held onto her hand, drawing her over to kiss her. For just a few moments the pain in his head went away and he felt at peace. "Thanks," he said. "Without you and Jimmy, I don't know what I'd do."

"Jimmy said he'd come by later, see how you are. He's working on the lot at Universal."

Karl kissed her again and opened the car door.

"You sure you should stay here, Karl? You won't reconsider?"

"You worry too much. I'll be fine." He didn't know if he believed that, but people had to lie sometimes just to keep everything square.

He let himself into the house before Lisa left the driveway. He shut and locked the door, engaged the alarm system.

His head hurt again and he needed to take one of the Tylenol 3 tablets prescribed by the doctor he'd picked up at the hospital pharmacy. He needed to call Lois and see how the office was doing. There would be a lot of calls to make.

And he needed a nap. He hadn't slept worth a damn in the hospital bed, nurses checking on him all through the night.

He touched the bandage around his forehead and then gently probed the swelling on his cheek.

He had to be so careful now. He had to watch his back at all times.

This must be what it felt like to be a foot soldier in a guerrilla war. You had to notice every leaf movement, the sound of every breaking twig. An enemy might hide in the shadow. Your life depended on being observant.

He had never been a soldier. He had never before been under attack. But he was learning fast what it took to survive.

When he went to open the cabinet in the kitchen to get a glass for water so he could take a pill, he saw the note.

He withdrew it and stood reading the words, heavy apprehension seeping into his bones.

*I hear you survived. I'm so glad. I don't want to hurt you,*

*Karl. You're my life. If something happens to you, I might as well be dead too.*

*Will you take me back now? Can you honestly tell me you're sorry for past transgressions and love me again?*

*Think about this before you answer. I'll be in touch to let you know what to do.*

Karl ran his thumb over the string of Xs and Os that ended the note.

Perhaps this was his chance. If she let him meet with her or if he could leave a message somewhere, then he could watch to see her pick it up.

He'd have her. He'd have her good.

# 31

"In love, unlike most other passions, the recollection of what you have had and lost is always better than what you can hope for in the future."

Stendhal, *De l'Amour*

Robyn made reservations at the Phoenix restaurant in the Algonquin Hotel on Sunset for a party of four. The Phoenix used to be the hot spot for Hollywood stars, but these days it had been supplanted by trendier places like the House of Blues, Planet Hollywood, and the Universe. The Phoenix's lack of notoriety meant they could talk without a lot of interruption.

She wasn't sure she knew what she was doing, calling this meeting. But she owed it to Karl. She still loved him, though she couldn't live with him; no, of course not, never again. She needed to investigate how the others felt about him to see if she could ascertain a clue as to who was doing the stalking. She owed him that much.

As she drove through Hollywood, she thought of the time when she and Karl talked about the pressures on a person trying to make a career in show business. He had said, "Half my clients can't take it. They go a little batty. They can't take the discipline and the dedication it requires to make something of themselves in this town. Either that, or their dream is bigger than anything they might reasonably hope to come true. I don't have to tell you how many thousands come out here every year just to get disappointed. Some of them become eccentric or distant. They divorce themselves from reality in order to live with the rejection. It's why I'm in this business. To save as many of them as I can from that kind of black nothing of failure."

She had admired him so much for his belief in the possibility he might be a savior. But now she remembered what he'd meant when he'd talked about how rejection and despair turned some seekers after fame into ruined individuals. "What happens to them," she had asked Karl, "when they don't make it, say they've tried for years and they still don't get a break? What do they do?" This was her naive question before she herself tried to put together her first film project. Afterward, she knew all the answers.

"It's back to the salt mines," he had said. "If their dream was strong, losing it might kill whatever happiness in life they had hoped for. They'll go back home and nurse their wounds the rest of their lives. They're our Could've Beens and some of them are Should've Beens. But once they're off the treadmill and they've given up, it's over."

"No more hope for their names in lights," she had mused.

"No more hope, in some cases, for anything meaningful ever again."

Perhaps that was what had happened to Karl's stalker. Maybe it was someone on the set besides the women she had invited tonight to the Algonquin. Someone who never really made it. It could be a grip or a gofer or a light director. It could be one of the cinematographers, editors, sound people. Women did many of those jobs on the set of *Pure and Uncut*. One of them might be a discarded lover Karl hardly remembered now. Most of them got copies of the script scenes. And the ones who didn't could have stolen one somewhere. A

nondisclosure form didn't keep the script completely inviolate from the curious eyes of people working on the picture.
She suspected even a few of the extras had found a way to
weasel a look at the script.

She arrived at eight p.m. and took a table more or less out
of the route of foot traffic. She was the first arrival. The Algonquin was a tiny place with a white exterior and not a lot
going for it. The Phoenix was quiet and nearly empty on this
weeknight. She ordered a pink Russian, just for the hell of it,
and sipped while waiting for the others.

Olivia was the first to arrive. She was made up too heavily
so that even the dim lights couldn't disguise that she was an
older woman trying to pass for a younger version of herself.
She wore an unflattering magenta-colored pants suit with
wide legs and a plunging bodice jacket. She didn't look very
pleased when she took a seat across from Robyn.

"I need to be getting ready for bed. Tomorrow's going to
be a rough scene."

"I know and I appreciate you coming. I'll try not to keep
you long." Robyn motioned for the waiter to take Olivia's
drink order.

Marilyn and Catherine came in together, probably having
arrived at same time in the lobby. They took their seats and
gave their orders to the waiter who still stood around in a
slight daze, recognizing Olivia's famous face.

"I haven't been here in ages," Catherine said.

"Well, I've never been here." Marilyn looked around ap-
preciatively. "It's nice. Small. Quiet, but nice."

After they were seated and settled in, Robyn said, "I don't
know how much all of you know about what's been happening to Karl, but I thought we needed to get together and
talk about it." She decided it was best to launch right into the
reason she'd called them together. They all really did need to

get home to make it an early night. There was not much energy left over after working on the set from five in the morning until sundown.

"I know he's been getting notes and stuff," Marilyn said.

Olivia cleared her voice and said, "His house was broken into and everything in it torn up."

"Really?" Marilyn turned to her. "I didn't know about that. Poor Karl's got a crazy on his hands."

"Catherine, have you talked with Karl yet?" Robyn asked.

She sat staring down at the napkin in her lap. "I didn't want to come here," she said. "Karl isn't a part of my life anymore."

"Well, he's not part of any of our lives as far as I know, but the circumstances surrounding what has happened to him force this meeting," Robyn said, pausing to look around at the other three women. "You know someone's following the script, stalking Karl."

Catherine now glanced up and her face was stony. "I noticed it. I went to see him in the hospital, thinking I could let him know I was sorry about his car accident, but I didn't know I'd have to stand there while he accused me for it. How many of you think I'm harassing Karl LaRosa?"

Her question was a challenge. Her voice had risen as she spoke and the others were staring at her.

"Look," Robyn said, "let's not get into a hissy fit about what Karl does or does not think. He's working without all the facts, isn't he? He doesn't know the stuff happening to him follows the script almost to the letter. He doesn't know the four of us, women who used to be in his life, are working on that movie."

"Someone has to tell him," Marilyn said. She was about to say more, but their drinks were delivered. She drank from her glass of beer before continuing. "I hadn't heard about his house. Why was he in the hospital?"

Robyn looked at her uneasily. "You don't know he was run off the road and almost killed?"

"Well, god, no, I didn't know that! How bad was he hurt?"

The other three women exchanged glances.

"Hey, you don't think I'm the one doing stuff to Karl, do you? I swear I didn't even know all of it."

"I didn't call us together to throw blame. I was hoping to be reassured that none of us would do these horrible things to Karl. He could have been killed in that wreck." Robyn didn't want this to turn into a guilt fest.

"Then why did you call us together?" Olivia asked. "It wasn't to treat us to dinner, I imagine. Although I'm starving. That handsome waiter making googoo-eyes at me comes back over here, I'm ordering hors d'oeuvres. Who likes stuffed mushrooms?"

"I wanted to discuss what we're going to do about it," Robyn said, directing the conversation back to Karl and ignoring the mention of food.

"About what?" Catherine asked. "He acted like I was the one who ran him off the road. And I didn't do it!"

"Now calm down, don't get excited," Robyn said. "I didn't want us to sit here and accuse one another. I just want to know what you think's going on. It has to be someone working on the film. Someone who gets a copy of the script scenes every day."

"I don't know what's going on, but I say we have to tell him." Marilyn lifted her head, ready to argue about it. "Are you sure it's following the script? You mean his house was torn up just like we filmed? And he was chased and run off a freeway, just like in the script?"

Robyn sighed and twirled her glass on the table. "That's exactly what is going on, Marilyn. Every time we film a scene, it happens to Karl. Or maybe sometimes it happens *before* we film it, but soon after the scene is handed out. And we can't tell him. I don't see how we can do that. I just don't think we can. We have to think of something else."

"Why can't we tell him?" Marilyn turned to Catherine, sitting next to her.

"Leave me out of it. He made me into the bad guy, remember?"

"Don't you think we have to tell him? He might even need a copy of the whole script so maybe he could stop this." She turned back to Robyn. "You have the whole script. You've seen it and we haven't. You could give it to him."

Olivia said, "Cam would kill us if we let the script out. We signed those nondisclosures. We'd be breaking contracts."

"That's why we can't tell him. You do see that, don't you, Marilyn? Cam would never forgive us. I've already talked to him about it and he said no way do we tell Karl," Robyn said.

Marilyn protested, "But what's wrong with you? Is Cam nuts? Karl might wind up murdered if we let this go. He has to be told. It's not like we're giving it to the gossip columnists. Karl's not going to tell anyone about the movie."

"Maybe not," Robyn said, having thought this out previously. "But he might have to tell the police. There was a report filed when his office was broken into . . ."

"All that blood," Olivia added.

Robyn continued, "Or he might tell Jimmy. Jimmy's his best friend. Or he might tell his girlfriend, what's her name . . ."

"Lisa," Catherine said.

She bit her lip and Robyn saw it. Marilyn and Olivia were both surprised, watching her.

"You know his girlfriend?" Robyn asked.

Catherine shrugged. "My husband bought our house from

185

her. He told me she was dating my old . . . that she was dating Karl."

"Nevertheless," Marilyn said, "Karl wouldn't let the script out. He just wouldn't do that and you all know it. We have to tell him, no matter what Cam says. I mean, we're not going to sit around and let Karl go through this, are we?"

Robyn thought about her years with Karl, about how much she had adored him. She finally nodded. "I guess you're right. He can't be kept in the dark. This kind of secret could get him killed. One of us has to tell him what's going on so he can protect himself."

"I'll tell him then." Marilyn, satisfied now, drank down the rest of her beer and waved for the waiter for a refill.

"That doesn't solve the problem of who it is connected with the film doing this," Olivia said. "Once Karl knows what's going on, he'll be in a better position to save himself from whoever this asshole is, but that doesn't stop it, does it?"

Robyn ordered another Russian from the waiter and after he'd departed she said, "Who else but the four of us might be playing this dangerous game?"

"Well, it has to be somebody else. I know it's not me," Olivia said.

"Or me," Marilyn chimed in.

"It's definitely not me," Catherine said harshly. "I guarantee you. It's not me."

# 32

"Forsake not an old friend; for the new is not comparable to him."

Ecclesiastes 9:10.

Marilyn didn't have time to make a trip to Karl's house to talk to him about his troubles. She called from her house instead, the moment she returned home from the Phoenix.

She hadn't turned on many lights in the house, being in a rush. It scared her to be alone when too many rooms were in darkness. She turned her back on the doorway leading from her studio to the rest of the house, trying to ignore it. She stared at the painting she was in the process of finishing. As Karl's phone rang, she picked up a dry brush and went over some of the brush strokes in the paint, smoothing them out in her mind.

Karl's answering machine switched on and she frowned. She was saying, "Karl, it's Marilyn, I have to talk to you, it's impor—" when Karl picked up the phone.

"I'm here," he said. "Just monitoring the calls. What's up, Marilyn?"

"I wanted to come over and tell you this, but I don't have time tonight. We have to be on the set early tomorrow so I have to get some sleep. Why do you live so damn far out of the way?"

He laughed. "I might ask you the same thing."

"Anyway, I've just come from the Algonquin. Robyn, Olivia, Catherine, and I had drinks together."

"Yeah?" He sounded interested.

"They told me about your house and the wreck. I was really shocked. We all decided we had to tell you."

"Tell me what?"

"Karl, everything that's been happening to you is from the script we're shooting. It's called *Pure and Uncut*, you know, Cam's special film processing that will make the movie sort of 3-D?"

"Wait, what do you mean, it's in the script?"

"Well, the script's about a man being stalked by a woman. Olivia's playing the part and Jackie Landry's the lead. The man in the movie works in the entertainment business and the stalker, Olivia, is a former actress."

"Okay."

"Everything we film seems to be happening to you. You know how your office was broken into and blood thrown all over the place? We filmed that already."

"Oh, that's just great . . ."

"Wait, there's more. You're getting notes, love notes, and the man in the movie's getting the same kind of notes. His house was broken into and all his furniture destroyed, just like your house. And Karl?"

"Yeah?" His voice was hardly audible.

"The last scene we shot was out on the freeway. Jackie's character was run off the road. Just like what happened to you."

"Unbelievable. Who's doing this, Marilyn?"

"God, Karl, if I knew don't you think I'd tell you? I was the one who lobbied to tell you about the script. Cam made us sign nondisclosure contracts and he might even dump me from the project for telling you this. But I insisted we had to tell. You have to know."

"I want a copy of the script."

"I don't have it."

"You don't have it? How can you not have it, you're acting in the picture, aren't you?"

"Sure, but Cam doesn't give us the whole script. We get our scenes that are supposed to be shot the next day. We don't even get much time to rehearse. It's really a hush-hush project. Everything about it is a secret. It gets out to the trades, it ruins it for Cam. You won't mention it, will you? Not even to Jimmy? Or your girlfriend? And you can't tell the police, oh god, don't go to the cops. Cam would be sure to fire me then."

"So you only get the next scene."

"Right."

"So what's the next one? You can tell me that much at least."

She told him the bare outline of the action sequence they would be working on the next day. He promised he wouldn't tell anyone. He further promised he wouldn't go to Cam unless he had to. He understood what kind of chance she was taking, he didn't want her to get hurt or to lose her job.

"Take care of yourself, Karl," she said.

"Don't worry, I will. You might have saved my life. I owe you, sweetheart."

"Don't be hurt no one has told you before now. You know what a tyrant Cam is. He doesn't take any of this seriously, what's been happening to you. All he thinks about is *Pure and Uncut*. Don't blame the others for not coming to you sooner."

"I'll try. It's going to be hard, but I'll try."

After she had hung up, feeling lighter than air because she had done a very good deed for a good man, she squeezed out a tube of yellow color onto her palette and swirled her brush in it. She would paint the sky in her painting with sunshine. The image of the bodies hanging from the windmills out on the desert was disturbing, but the sunny sky behind them would cause a startling effect. She might sell this one for several hundred at the gallery.

She'd title it *Plan Gone Awry* in Karl's honor. He'd like that.

When the phone rang, she jumped, having become immersed in artwork. She picked up the phone and heard a voice say, "Don't tell him. You tell him, you're dead." Then a click and a dial tone.

She stood holding the phone in one hand and the brush of yellow paint in the other. Her eyes unfocused as she stared into the depths of the canvas past the figures hanging dead, nailed to the windmills in killing sunlight so bright it seared the eyes.

She finally took a deep breath and returned the phone to the cradle of the receiver. "Too late," she said, trying on a grim smile.

# 33

"Murder in the murderer is no such ruinous thought as poets and romancers will have it; it does not unsettle him, or fright him from his ordinary notice of trifles; it is an act quite easy to be contemplated."

Ralph Waldo Emerson, *Experience*

The Body paced through the house, front to back, going in circles, busy grasping at the air as if there was something there to grab hold of and wring to death.

Marilyn couldn't tell Karl about the script. She couldn't do it, she couldn't.

This was a disaster in the making. It would ruin everything. Karl would be put on notice. The Body couldn't surprise him if he knew what was coming. *Goddamn* Marilyn.

Call her, tell her what will happen if she tells.

The Body snatched up the phone and dialed Marilyn's home number. After issuing the warning some peace of mind should have descended, but it was not to be. The frenzy only increased. Marilyn might not be someone who could be dissuaded by a phone call.

Cursing, The Body hurried into the silent room with the padding and locked the door. Couldn't sit down. Couldn't relax. It was all getting out of hand. How could that have happened? It was planned so meticulously. The Body hadn't believed any of the women involved on the set would tell Karl— at least not until it was too late to save him. They were all ambitious, selfish bitches and The Body had counted on that. They wanted their positions. Every one of them lusted for fame. They wanted this movie more than life itself. It would make them all stars, make them rich, make them immortal if what Cam expected at the box office panned out. This movie might be studied in film classes a hundred years from now because it would be the first commercial success in a new medium. Millions of dollars were invested in it.

How could they let Marilyn tell and chance getting the picture shut down, cops crawling all over the place? How were they going to insure Karl didn't call in someone and sabotage the entire film?

The Body prowled the dark room, the black room. The complete lack of light suited The Body's mood. Blackness, darkness, nothingness. Hate was black. The heart of the darkness lay in wait for hatred to bloom and so it did.

Forgetting that the chair stood in the room's center, The Body ran into it and nearly toppled over it to the floor.

"I'll kill her," The Body mumbled, kicking at the leather chair, then kicking it again.

The refrain rose and fell in the room's confines, the words absorbed into the thick walls. "I'll kill her. I'll kill her for this. She needs killing for doing this. I have to kill her. I have to stop her."

The dark room wasn't having the calming effect it should have. The Body left it and moved through the empty house, footsteps echoing, to the nursery where the computer monitor sat on the white child's desk. The word processing software was open and a blank page for the diary glared pristine blue, a blue all-knowing eye, shining into the baby's room.

For what might have been hours, The Body sat before the monitor typing over and over again:

*Hate, hate, hate, kill her kill her kill her hatehatehate . . .*

# 34

"In all chaos there is a cosmos, in all disorder a secret order."

Carl Jung, *Archetypes of the Collective Unconscious*

Karl could hardly contain himself, his mind on how to prepare for assault from his nameless stalker. He needed to handle a lot of stacked-up business on his desk in the office, but every time he tried, he'd catch himself sitting, daydreaming, staring at the wall.

Lois tried to make the bad news palatable. He had lost two more clients. Someone had sent them updates on his company claiming it was in financial trouble and not to be trusted to handle their affairs. One of the clients, a man who had come to him straight from a hit play, someone Karl had found a high-powered representative in the best talent agency in town, brought his letter to the office and threw it on Lois' desk before telling her he didn't need LaRosa's help from now on.

Karl scanned the letter and before he had finished reading the lies, crumpled it in his fist and threw it across the room. Lies. Innuendoes. Gossip.

But it was losing him clients. Karl wondered how many of his people had received the unsigned letter. He needed to call everyone, reassure them the letter was from an enemy and it was all scurrilous lies, please don't believe a word of it.

Yet all he could do half the day so far, rather than attend to his clients' affairs, was work out in his mind how to fend off the coming attack Marilyn had told him about from the script of *Pure and Uncut*.

The stalker would attach a bomb to the underside of his car.

He'd had Jimmy drive him into work. He would have to get the loaner, the Caprice, checked out before he drove it. He wasn't going to be blown to smithereens today. He was going to discover who was involved in this crazy thing and put a stop to it, permanently.

After lunch and a brisk walk in the air, he returned to the office and did some of the calling around he had put off. He couldn't find all his clients at home so he'd have to try later. The ones he did get to talk to assured him they would ignore the letter if it came.

At five p.m. he left the office and took a cab to Malibu. He had an appointment to meet with a mechanic at his house. This man always did the work on the Jag and was repairing it now. He'd know a bomb device when he saw one. He couldn't get away from work until after six, but he'd be there, he told Karl.

Karl was going to get him to explain what to look for and where to look. After this visit, Karl would be the one checking out whatever vehicle he meant to drive. Once he found a device attached to his car, he'd call the police in. This was a direct assault on his life. Now maybe they'd take his stalker case seriously. Sooner or later they had to.

# 35

"I do not believe that any man fears to be dead, but only the stroke of death."

Francis Bacon, *An Essay on Death*

It had been a very long day. Marilyn played Olivia's best friend in the film and the scene they had just shot entailed Marilyn listening in horror to a tirade Olivia went into about the man she loved and hated, the man she would destroy given half the chance.

It was an emotionally draining scene to shoot and Cam was hard on her. He was harder on Olivia, but the whole scene was a study in despair and lack of control. Olivia raved. Marilyn, as her friend, stood by, shocked at the vehemence displayed, and afraid that her friend really meant what her character was saying. Marilyn had to try to dissuade her, talk sense into her. Cam made her do the scene over and over, different angles, different lighting. It took forever.

They never even got to the bomb scene and what a relief that was. Although Marilyn wasn't featured in that scene, she didn't even want to be present when they shot it. Not after she knew how someone on the set was stalking Karl, using the script scenes. At least she had warned him. She wouldn't have his death on her conscience.

She went straight home from the studio lot and let herself

in the front door. She didn't immediately know she was not alone. She flicked on the living room light, dropped her carrying bag she always took to the studio, and, stooping, untied and pulled off the size-too-small Nikes she never should have bought.

On the way to the bathroom to shower, she began to unbutton the blue painter's smock she had worn that day to work.

In the hall between the living room and bath she realized someone was in the house. She halted, breath catching in her throat. She had heard a door ease closed behind her. She twirled around, ready to scream. Saw nothing in the shadowy hallway.

"Who's there?"

A shadow slipped across the hall, a human silhouette falling from the light in the living room. Someone had been in there when she came in.

She was supposed to be safe here. It wasn't fair someone had come into her home and waited for her. She'd never believed that could happen. She should have taken a lover or a roommate to live with her. She should have had an alarm system installed, but who could afford it?

She was trembling all over and underneath the smock her skin had slicked down with a sheen of sweat that now chilled her. She might paint the most appalling visions of death and disorder, but the thought of it actually encroaching and invading her own life had always been the farthest thing from her mind. What she worked out in her studio was art, torturous artscapes from a timid, frightened mind. Real life horror, not the kind in movies or her paintings, was two steps beyond any of her real experience. Even in those days on the streets, she'd never been in mortal danger.

She began to call out again, but her voice was a croak and

she didn't recognize it. She swallowed hard and tried once more.

"What do you want? If you're here to rob me . . ."

She hadn't seen the shadows flicker again, nor had she heard any sounds. It might all be her vivid imagination. It's true she was easily spooked. Sometimes at night she'd be sound asleep and wake up startled at some sound from the house settling. She'd creep from bed and search out the house before she could sleep again.

She might not have seen the human shadow at all, really, or heard a door closing at her back . . .

The horror that she drew, the horror that she imagined so well on canvas, but did not believe might ever come close to her, leapt from behind, strangling her and lifting her off her feet. She kicked wildly, gasping for air, beating at the arm around her neck which shut off her wind so that she could not scream, could not even speak.

She was flipped around to face the bathroom door that stood slightly ajar. Her kicking stockinged feet knocked it open and she was bodily carried into the bath. She thought she caught a glimpse of her attacker in the counter-length mirrors above the sink, but the image was a blur of black cloth, black ski mask, and then she was turned to the right, toward the shower and tub stall. Her head was forced forward with a jerk and her forehead banged into the frosted glass of the shower door, cracking it.

Marilyn saw stars and prayed not to pass out. She squirmed and gouged and kicked for her life, but she hadn't a chance to divert or stop the unseen big blade of a knife that drove between her third and fourth ribs on the left side, angling up toward her heart and lung.

Her screams, loud and echoing with abandon off the tiled walls, went higher and higher as her head hit the glass again and the knife plunged again and the blood ran down her side to her waist, her hips, her thighs, and down her jeans soaking them black, pooling on the floor where her white socks were quickly soaked red. She slipped and slid until finally her legs gave out from under her and she collapsed down, down in a heap, dying with her eyes open, staring at how incredibly red was her blood, more red than any paint she had ever seen, redder than a fiery sky shining down over a field of the crucified windmill dead.

The Body stood panting over the corpse for what seemed an eternity. Finally when breathing was regulated to an even flow of air in and out of the lungs, and the flooded fury of combat eased to a trickle, The Body leaned over and carefully removed the clothes from Marilyn Lori-Street. Blood was everywhere, but there was time, all night in fact, to take care of that.

Once the corpse was nude, The Body lifted it onto the lip of the tub and tipped it over into the purity of the white porcelain. Her neck was crooked, perhaps broken now. The legs lay cocked up against the tiled wall. Something about the vulnerability of the naked feet gave The Body pause. They were small, blood-smeared and high arched; beautiful in the way only perfect appendages could be. Marilyn's hands were not nearly so nice as her feet.

The Body looked at the large knife lying in the pooled violet-red blood on the floor. It was sharp, having just been sharpened for this specific job of murder. How hard could it be to dismember the body in the tub?

The Body had all night.

# 36

"Every murder turns on a bright hot light, and a lot of people . . . have to walk out of the shadows."

Mark Hellinger, *The Naked City*

Officers Dorian Lepski and Shane Miller patrolled the street past the famous Garden Palm Restaurant and Bar during the eleven-to-seven shift. Dorian drove, idly glancing along the sidewalk to his left as Shane monitored the buildings to the right of the car. He was tired and his back ached. He should get one of those wooden car seat covers purported to massage the driver's back during long hours at the wheel. He'd seen them for sale at the drug store for less than ten bucks. Cheap investment.

It was a quarter to six when he came up on the Garden Palm and noticed something not right.

"You see that?" he asked his partner. "What the hell is that?"

It looked like something hanging on the door. It wasn't a package. It looked like . . .

"Looks like a leg, for cripes' sake," Shane said. "Pull over there."

Dorian did a U-turn in the empty street and pulled the cruiser up at the curb in front of the Garden Palm. From his vantage point nearest the curb, Shane said, "I'll be god-damned. It's somebody's fuckin' leg."

Dorian climbed from his seat, his back creaking. Shane was at the door before him. They stood back two feet and stared incredulously at the body part dangling from the door handle of the restaurant. A wire—looked like an unwound clothes hanger—was wound around the ankle and the other end was wrapped round the door handle. Blood had dripped from the jagged thigh to the concrete step.

"I ain't ever seen anything like it," Dorian said.

"And in this area," Shane agreed.

"Wonder where the rest of it is?"

"Guess we better call the lieutenant to handle this. I sure as hell am not going to touch that thing." Shane returned to the patrol car to call for help.

Dorian Lepski rubbed at the small of his back and stood gazing at the hanging leg. He'd bet it was from a woman. Small delicate foot. Smooth skin, hairless leg. Had to be a woman. Damned nasty way to go.

He shivered and rolled his shoulders. Sometimes being a cop made him want to run off to an Amazon forest and build a hut out of leaves and never see another human being again. Especially dead ones.

Pan didn't think of himself as a homeless person. He was just a guy down on his luck and in need of funds. He'd be on top again when he could get a handle on this terrible floating anxiety that came out of the blue to make it impossible to function some days.

He didn't know how he had gotten himself from his usual haunts onto Rodeo Drive, Los Angeles' high-priced shopping district. He'd been walking all night, not feeling sleepy. He could sleep in the day, in the park, when it was warmer. And safer. Never knew what might sneak up on you in the dark. So he kept moving and noticed around dawn that he was way out of his neighborhood. If he didn't get off Rodeo before the shops opened, they'd call the cops on him and get him thrown in the hoosegow for vagrancy.

He hurried down the block meaning to take the next street corner that would lead him away from the area. He almost missed it. Not the corner. The arm.

He was past it before the sight registered on his brain. He stopped in the middle of the sidewalk and looked around, all around, up and down the street, behind him, up at the blank-faced windows on the expensive buildings.

There was no one around. A car drove past, but the driver didn't even look at him.

Down at the corner the stoplight blinked red.

Slowly, Pan turned around and walked back to the Rodeo Drive boutique where he had seen the arm.

It hung from a wire attached to the shop's polished brass doorknob. It was really an arm. It wasn't his imagination. He reached out tentatively and touched the wrinkled flesh of the elbow, then jerked back his finger. Cold. Around the wrist there was bruising and discoloration where the wire was wrapped. The fingers stood straight up as if thrown out in alarm. A woman. It was a woman's arm. Nice manicured nails, young tight skin, no rings.

The arm had been cut off at the shoulder socket. A too-white knob of bone stuck out from the end of the raggedly cut flesh.

Pan looked around wildly again, hoping no one had seen him near the arm. He looked at the picture window of the shop. Marvin's Fine Leather. Handbags and suitcases and portfolios crowded the window arrangement.

Marvin sure would be surprised when he came to open up.

Pan stumbled backward, away from the atrocity, ashamed that he had touched it. He turned and ran for the corner, took it going so fast he almost fell down. Four blocks distant he found a phone booth and called 911 to report anonymously, "There's a cut-off arm hanging on the door of Marvin's Fine Leather on Rodeo Drive," he said, then hung up abruptly before they could ask him his name.

He felt the black cloud of fear descend over him again and he began to make gibbering sounds as he hurried toward his neighborhood. He just couldn't stop being scared. Scared of cars on the street, scared of houses full of quarreling families, scared of shelters and strangers and cats and dogs. Scared of thunderstorms and Santa Ana winds.

Now he would be scared of losing his arms and having them hang from the doors of exclusive shops. He wrapped his hands around himself and hugged tightly, hurrying, hurrying away from the horror that would stay with him the rest of his days.

Cam came out to his Cadillac sedan, his arms laden with papers and the notebooks he took with him to the set every day. He got the back door open and dropped the burden on the back seat.

He opened the front driver's door and was fumbling with his car keys to get the ignition key in his grip so he almost bent down and slipped into the seat before he noticed it was occupied.

He drew back in terror when he saw the head sitting on the white leather.

He let out a yelp and backpedaled from the open car door.

He was hyperventilating. He couldn't get enough air. Maybe he was going to have a heart attack. He clutched his chest and stared at the head. He knew who it was. He knew who that head belonged to.

He turned in the driveway and vomited, bent over, eyes

squeezed closed. After heaving up his breakfast of coffee and cinnamon buns, he wiped the back of his mouth with his hand.

It was Marilyn. Someone had decapitated her and left the head in Cam's car. He forced himself to look at her again. Her blond hair was streaked rusty with blood. Her eyes were open and covered with a glassy film. Her neck looked as if it had been sawed and hacked. There were slice wounds above the fatal cut that severed her head from her body.

Cam turned away again, feeling his stomach lurch. Nothing else to come up. He heaved dryly.

"Fuck," he murmured. "Fuck, fuck, fuck." Two emotions warred for his attention. His sadness that Marilyn was dead. And his worry about how this would affect *Pure and Uncut.*

Already his mind was working on the problem. He could have her written out, edit out her scenes. Or he could have Olivia's character turn on her best friend and kill her. The scene could be shot really dark so anyone in a blond wig could be Marilyn filmed from the rear. He'd have to do that, then. Kill her off. Her murder might even bring some tabloid publicity to the movie when it was shown. The morbid curiosity roused by her death during filming could only help the film. Besides, it was too hard to rewrite some of the already filmed scenes and then reshoot.

When he called the police . . .

He drew himself up straight and ran a hand down over his belly, hoping it would settle down now.

Hell, if he called the police, they'd be all over the set. Add in Karl LaRosa's problems and now this death of one of his actresses and he might as well shut down the project. Cops would interfere. They'd investigate *everybody connected to the film*, most particularly the man who found Marilyn's head on the seat of his car.

"Fuck," he said again. What was he supposed to do? Just throw away millions of dollars invested and forget making his film when it was going to be the one that superseded anything he had ever directed? The one movie that would catapult filmgoers from the dark ages into the future of film technology? He could be the first. The leader, the innovator.

The revered.

Or he could call the cops to come get poor Marilyn's head off the Cadillac's seat and seal his own failure. No investor would ever trust him again to try the new techniques. Why, they already had the equipment ordered for the theaters across the country, they had already backed more than a hundred theater owners to expand their screens for overhead and wraparound projection!

Too many people would go down the drain. Hollywood would never forgive him. If *Pure and Uncut* failed, it would make the *Heaven's Gate* debacle look like a minor setback.

He knew what he had to do. He wasn't proud of it, but he had to do it. There wasn't anything he could do for Marilyn now. She was dead; she couldn't accuse him.

He ran back into the house and found a pair of leather driving gloves someone had given him as a gift last Christmas. He lifted them from the box they had come in and slipped them on. Nice fit.

Then he found a black Hefty garbage bag in the kitchen pantry. He brought it out to the car and flapped open the bag. He reached into the driver's seat and put his fingers into Marilyn's matted hair. He cringed and his stomach flopped around like a fish in his midsection, but he managed to lift the head and drop it into the garbage bag without going into the dry heaves again.

He opened the rear door and deposited the bag on the

floorboard. Oh God, if she rolled around back here while he was driving . . .

He slammed the door shut and returned to the house for a soapy wet washcloth to clean down the white leather seat. While washing the blood off, he turned his head to his left and stared at the dash. He held his breath. This was awful, this was worse than anything he'd had happen to him since Nam. If he ever found out the motherfucker who did this, he'd break the son of a bitch's fingers one by one, then he'd break his fucking neck. He'd do that before he ever called the cops.

He checked to see if the leather was clean and when he was satisfied, he took the cloth indoors, rinsed it out in the kitchen sink, and draped it over the counter edge to dry. The scent of blood was in his nostrils and he didn't know if it would ever leave. He should find something to deodorize his car, but . . .

He had to hurry. He was holding up the production already. He was late. Catherine or Robyn would be calling any minute to see what was wrong. When he got to the studio, he'd tell them he'd overslept. He would act as if he had a hangover. They'd believe that. He often had hangovers.

He drove away from his house and out of Beverly Hills. He passed a stretch of undeveloped woods and slowed. He parked, leaving the car running, waited for cars to thin out until no car was visible on the road, then he opened the back door and withdrew the garbage bag. He walked quickly to the edge of the road and looked down at the overgrown ravine. He hauled back and swung the bag the way he would a baseball, giving it his all, and saw the round object lift, bump a limb, fall and tumble down the ravine out of sight.

In the car again he put it into gear and drove away carefully, not wishing to leave his tire tracks behind in the gravel lining the road.

Done, he thought. I'm sorry, Marilyn, but the picture means more to me than you do. The cops will find the bastard who did this later. Right now you just have to understand what I'm working against.

He came onto the set flushed and angry. Everyone stayed out of his way, which worked to his advantage. He had a feeling his day was all uphill from here if he didn't think too much about what he had done. But he didn't want to fuck with anybody and he didn't want to look anyone in the eyes. One of them probably cut off Marilyn's head. Filming a movie about a killer and dealing with a real one weren't the same thing at all.

A few people asked about Marilyn, wondering why she wasn't in her dressing room. Catherine called her house and reported no answer.

Luckily she wasn't due to be in the scene today. They'd discover soon enough she was missing and would begin to shoot around her until Cam could finally write her out of the rest of the picture without drawing any protest. If she didn't show up, how could they use her?

He didn't give himself time to worry why the killer had put Marilyn's head in his car. Not until much later, after he had gone home for the day and he had stopped by one of his hang-outs to drink beer with construction workers, did it occur to him to wonder why that had been done.

Maybe the killer knew him so well he or she knew he would dispose of the head and not call in the police? Had he been used? Manipulated?

"Fuck," he said to his bar companion, a man with a fifth-grade education and biceps the size of a wrestler's. "I'm having a lot of problems doing this film. A lot of really serious problems."

"Tell me about it," the other man said, hefting a can of

Bud to his mouth. "I like movies."

But Cam couldn't. Not this, he couldn't tell. He would never tell this to anyone, ever. His shameful act would be buried in his psyche until he died.

# 37

"Cinema, radio, television, magazines are a school of in-
attention: people look without seeing, listen in without
hearing."

Robert Bresson, 1950–1958: Exercises

The whole office was buzzing with speculation about the latest
grisly Hollywood crime. Not since the murders of Nicole Brown
and Ronald Goldman had any Hollywood death caused such a
sensation.

In some ways, Karl thought, reading the account in the
front pages of the newspaper, this crime was more frightening
than the ones involving Simpson's ex-wife. The body parts of
the unidentified female victim had been strewn all over the
city. The Garden Palm restaurant had to close when the press
swamped it, shooting film for the television news stations
and taking pictures for the newspapers.

On the other hand, the owner of the shop on Rodeo Drive
kept his doors open and became a minor media celebrity by
giving lurid accounts of how the dismembered arm looked
hanging by wire from his door.

A teenage boy, interviewed on *Current Affair* about reporting the leg he found lying on the star-studded sidewalk in
front of Grauman's Theater, was offered a part as a Power
Ranger on the TV Saturday Series because he looked so fresh

and handsome on the tube.

The second arm was discovered sticking out from a Dumpster at an all-night restaurant on Sunset and the torso, armless, headless, legless, was reportedly sitting propped upright on a bus-stop bench not more than four blocks away. An old woman called in to report it, complaining the elderly couldn't even depend on mass transportation in this city because of the crime problems and what they might find waiting for them at bus stops.

The authorities, without having possession of the head, had no way of determining the identity of the corpse, but the county coroner, a man who had handled both the Marilyn Monroe case and the notorious Brown-Goldman case, told reporters all the parts belonged to one woman.

Karl shook his head at the cruelty involved in such a crime. It didn't do much good for his business. It didn't do much for Hollywood. The finding of body parts all over the place had effectively rid the streets of hookers, afraid the casualty came from their ranks, but it had also dampened the enthusiasm of shoppers along Rodeo Drive and Sunset Boulevard. You couldn't turn on a radio or television without being bombarded with the harrowing facts from the media.

Lois knocked on his private office door and then slipped inside, shutting the door behind her. She held a secretarial notebook and pen to her chest.

"Can I talk to you?" she asked.

Lois, even more than his assistant, was his right hand. Most of the work carried on at LaRosa Enterprise was conducted by her.

"Sure," he said, nodding and pointing to the chair before his desk. "What's up?"

"Well, I got a call from your accountant the other day when you weren't in the office."

Karl felt bad news coming. He sat up in his chair and leaned on his elbows on the desk. "Go on."

"He said the IRS had been in touch with him concerning your last quarterly. I'm afraid it's not good news, Karl."

"I owe money," he said, wondering why he was not surprised. If someone had been able to put the screws to the credit reporting agencies, why not the IRS?

Lois looked down at the pad in her lap. "A lot," she said.

"A lot? How much?"

"The accountant said they're doing an audit. They're claiming you owe a hundred and twenty thousand in back taxes to the government. Employee taxes that were miscalculated or unpaid or something. Or maybe he said it was taxes on unreported earnings. I can't remember now, it upset me so much."

"Jesus." Karl swiveled away from the desk, turning his chair so he could look out the window at the street.

"The accountant says they're wrong, but he sounded worried. He wants all our files. All the way back for six years."

Karl didn't say anything. He entertained no doubt this latest round of bad luck was generated by his stalker. Before this his dealings with the federal government had been pristine. It was a nuisance case, plain and simple. Numbers were scrambled in his file some way. How in the hell did someone do that?

"Don't worry, Lois." He turned back to her. "You're worrying. You look like you just came from your best friend's funeral. This stuff is just temporary glitches, all right? It'll get worked out. I know it's more work for you, getting the files out of storage, but I don't want you to worry about me."

"It seems . . ." She had tears in her eyes and looked down at her pad again.

"What is it?" he prodded gently.

"It seems too much that's bad is happening to you. I don't understand it. The office broken into, your house ransacked, the . . . wreck."

She didn't know the half of it. His people in the office didn't know all about the notes he got or the way someone had manipulated his credit reports. They didn't know someone in the business who was involved with the shooting of a new film was using the script as a roadmap. Still, if he could, he needed to reassure his secretary. The rest of the office took cues from her. If they saw her upset and worried about him, it put everyone in the doldrums.

He stood up and circled the desk between them. When Lois rose he put his arm around her shoulder and turned her toward the door. He spoke softly. "It's going to be okay. Everything's under control. This IRS thing is just an aggravation. I don't owe that kind of money for back taxes. They made a mistake, that's all. Why don't you order a few pizzas for lunch to be delivered? Let's cheer the office up. You want to do that?"

She smiled up at him. "With anchovies?"

"Oh, god, no."

She grinned prettily. "I was just kidding. I know anchovies make you sick."

She was a good person, efficient, understanding, and, when she wasn't worried about his affairs, she could be a great little tease.

"Get outta here," he said, aiming her out the door. "I have to call some people."

He shut the door and stood with his back to it for a few moments. *A hundred and twenty thousand.* Someone was very good with computers. Someone was extremely intelligent and competent in finding ways to ruin him. At least with Marilyn telling him each day's shooting script, he wouldn't have to be so afraid of being caught unawares. He now had his own inside information. He wasn't blundering around blindly now, waiting like a clay pigeon to be shot out of the air.

Things could be worse.

# 38

"How does one kill fear, I wonder? How do you shoot a spectre through the heart, slash off its spectral head, take it by its spectral throat?"

Joseph Conrad, *Lord Jim*

The Body did a remarkable job at that day's shooting despite the air of distress that hung over the crew about the woman's dismembered parts found all over Hollywood.

They'd never identify her without the head. And Cam must have taken care of that since he came to the set and never said a word about it when the reports started coming in. Just what The Body had counted on. If there was one person who wouldn't want to get involved in a murder investigation, it was Cambridge Hill. Not when his movie was at stake.

The Body wondered all day how Cam had reacted when he found Marilyn's head on the seat of his fancy Cadillac. And what he did with it before he came to the studio lot. He couldn't have just put it in the trunk to dispose of later, could he? No, he would have already done that. The Body just hoped he hadn't stuffed it into his curbside garbage pail. It might be found too soon if he had.

Too bad about Marilyn. She had a scene coming up with Olivia tomorrow and that's when everyone would begin to worry when she didn't show up. Eventually they'd all begin to theorize about how she came up missing at the same time as the news was full of reports of a woman's body parts being found all over the city, but by then it would be too late to worry about it interfering with The Body's plans.

If only she hadn't been so insistent in the Phoenix that night that they must tell Karl about the script. Looking at her from behind a potted palm, The Body's vantage point at the bar, it had been almost more than The Body could do to keep from strangling her in front of everyone.

At day's end, The Body drove past Karl's house just in time to see him exiting a yellow taxicab and paying the driver.

He wasn't driving the loaner car!

The Body rolled on past, eyes straight ahead. It was twilight and the car's headlights beamed white, unforgiving light on the tall, skinny palms and fragile crepe myrtles. They looked washed out, not green enough to be real. Nearby the sea hissed along the private stretches of beach adjoining the Malibu enclaves.

The Body turned around and drove past Karl's house again, noticing the lights on inside. Parking at a distance, The Body jogged back to the driveway and crept to the far side of the Chevrolet Caprice. Hunkered down. Looked beneath the car to the exhaust system, hunting for the simple bomb device put there the day before.

As suspected, it was gone.

Marilyn had called him. She'd told him. Before The Body had gotten to her and despite the warning phone call, she had told him about the script and the very next scene.

Scrabbling back away from the car and moving stealthily down the drive, The Body fumed. If Marilyn weren't already dead, she'd die in a different fashion. Not from a knife through the heart this time. She'd be alive while having her limbs taken off, one by one. She'd know what was being done to her beautiful young body before she expired. She'd witness her own desecration.

On the way home, The Body stopped at a phone booth set away from a gas station and dialed Karl's number.

Karl jerked up the phone on the second ring before the answering machine could engage. "Yeah?" He was dripping water, just out of the shower and not yet dried off. The towel hung from his free hand and he saw that his wet footprints looked dark gray against the carpet leading from the bath.

"I'm going to kill you," a voice said.

Karl pressed the receiver hard against his ear. "Who is this? You're not going to kill anybody. You're a coward, a slithering, snake-bellied coward and I'm not afraid of you."

"The pieces of that body they found?"

The voice was muffled and of indeterminable gender. Karl wouldn't have made out the words had he not been concentrating and listening carefully. Now he bit down on his lip at the mention of the crime that was all over the news. He knew, *knew* suddenly, what the caller was going to say and it made his legs rubbery so that he had to collapse onto the side of the bed. He pressed the receiver so hard to his head that it hurt.

"What are you talking about?" he whispered.

"You know what I'm talking about. The arms and legs, the torso. They don't know who it is. But we know, don't we? It was that lying, big-mouth bitch Marilyn. She told you about the bomb. You had it removed."

There was a pause and Karl could hear the caller breathing.

"You can't stop me now. You're a dead man."

Before Karl could say anything, the call was disconnected. He sat naked, bewildered and grieving, droplets of water from his hair sliding down his forehead and the back of his neck, chilling him.

Marilyn had been killed because of him, because she'd tried to save him. Oh God in heaven. Oh dear God. Because of him. The foul evil that had been aimed at him had found another target for just a little while and Marilyn had been sacrificed in the furnace of that hatred.

He had to call the police. He had to tell them he knew who those scattered limbs belonged to. He had to let them know there was a killer on the loose. An insane murderer.

The phone rang again and Karl jerked up the receiver.

"I forgot to tell you something."

"You . . . !"

"You call the cops? That's what you were just thinking, isn't it? You call the cops, though, and I make you a promise. Another old girlfriend loses her head over you."

The cackling laughter rung in Karl's ears long after the caller had hung up and the dial tone buzzed monotonously. Karl sat with the receiver lying in his lap and he could still hear the sexless, maniacal laughter. It was so macabre it could have been coming from an open, windswept grave on a black November night.

# 39

"O, let me not be mad, not mad, sweet heaven! Keep me in temper. I would not be mad."

William Shakespeare, *King Lear*

Cambridge Hill was a slob. Lived in his own shit. Disgusting. With his money he could have hired two-dozen domestics, but it looked like he only had someone come in occasionally. That occasion had not been recent.

The Body winced with distaste while maneuvering the piled and scabbed dishes in the kitchen, noted the overflowing ashtrays and scattered newspapers in the living room that was the size of a ballpark, swore at the stacks of unopened bills and invitations and junk mail piled all over the small eighteenth-century teakwood desk in what appeared to be Cam's ruined bedroom. Covers hung from the mattress to the floor. Discarded clothes were everywhere, covering every surface of furniture, dirty damp towels stood wadded and mountainous just outside the bathroom door.

Where would the script be? Under this stack of mail? No green cover in sight. Where—hell—where would he have put any extra copies?

He might have them in his office at the studio.

Getting in there would take so much effort. Might not be able to do it. Guarded too well, too much security.

Goddamn it, the script had to be here somewhere.

The Body toppled the stacks of mail. Envelopes fluttered to the floor and behind the desk. In the four drawers there was more mail, some of it opened, some not. Pencils, pens, paper clips, rubber bands, stamps.

No script.

The Body moved from the bedroom after peeking into the bathroom. The terrible mess in there made The Body's nose wrinkle. It smelled like mildew overlaid with men's cologne. Stunk worse than an old whorehouse. He must never wash his socks. There was a mountain of them all black, as tall as the damp towels. He probably bought new socks every week. Perhaps every couple of months he threw out the old stinking ones.

What a fucking pig.

It was in the library-study that the script was unearthed. This was no gentleman's library, no alphabetically arranged system of books in beautifully wrought wood shelves. Much handled and tattered paperbacks were squashed between hardbacks, magazines sprawled from shelf edges and over the floor, textbooks with broken spines were tilted precariously against vases full of dead flower arrangements and there were scripts literally everywhere. Stacked on the seats of chairs, spread three deep over a reading table in the center of the room, lying on the shelves, fallen open on top of magazines.

How did Cam ever find any damn thing in this chaos? He lived like a mad mystic. The Body imagined him going from one interest to another in the room, moving swiftly between an open encyclopedia to a magazine on a shelf to some scene in one of the myriad bent and littered scripts that sparkled with Post-it notes in three violently fluorescent colors.

*Pure and Uncut* had been bound in metallic green covers. The Body searched for twenty minutes amid the paper rubble before finding a copy beneath a weighty tome on criminal behavior.

Snatching it up, The Body grinned and thought if anyone were watching, he would think that grin malign. Got it. Got the plan and no one could take it away. No one would even know. Cam obviously hadn't looked at this particular copy of the script for ages. He had his own personal copies at the office, no doubt. This might have been an early working copy.

Now to get out of this place before Cam showed up. Get out where there was fresh air to clean away the stink of a life that obviously thrived in this massive disorder.

With the bound script, The Body finally possessed an outline of every step that needed taking to rob Karl of his precious life. No longer would The Body have to wait for the scene handed out daily. Now all the details for destruction were collected in one spot, in one metallic green folder. The Body could choose to skip scenes. Could choose to hurry Karl LaRosa to his demise, if that was called for.

The prospect was thrilling enough to make the exit from Cam's house as happy as a lighthearted dance through the air.

It was beautiful when a plan came together like a dream.

# 40

"A hallucination is a fact, not an error; what is erroneous is a judgment based upon it."

Bertrand Russell, *Logic and Knowledge*

Now tired and drained after the excitement of finding the script, The Body's mood spiraled into depression. While looking through the script in the nursery, bad memories crept into the forefront of the mind and demanded attention. The Body tried not to give in, but could think of nothing to replace or dispel the gloom. Gloom was not a state of mind, but a presence with shape and form. It seemed to come from the corners of the room, sliding from the shadows, insinuating itself through the very pores of the human body slumped in the chair at the child's desk.

Too hard to fight a phantom. Then let it come. Let the past swamp the present and take it away. When you couldn't fight, there was no alternative but to give in.

The Body glanced around the room from lowered lids, sneaking quick looks. Staring straight on might call attention to the self. Hallucinations always lay in wait, waking dreams that were more real than life. Most often they came when cocooned in the leather chair in the deprivation room, but sometimes the hallucinations pounced during normal time, time that The Body used to live life the way other people lived it.

From the wall at the head of the crib, the ghost of a child formed, rising from within the flat, white plaster. It was Michelle.

The Body whispered her name.

"Michelle. My belle."

The words from the old Beatles' song.

She floated from above the crib, settling down just on the floor in front of it. "This room is pretty," she said in her little girl's piping voice. "Can I stay here?"

She could not stay. If she stayed, at least for very long, The Body would die.

"You don't belong here. This isn't our old home. Go away, Michelle. Go away."

"But it's pretty here," she repeated. "I don't like it where I am. It's cold."

She was wet, her hair dark strings hanging about her face. She was bloated. She carried the sharp scent of chlorine and underneath that odor a sweetish, cloying smell of decay. She was dead. For many years she had been dead. Poor little sister.

Of course she was cold. Dead and alone, drowned on that sunny Hollywood day.

"I can't help you. Please go away."

Tears fell down The Body's face onto the open script. This is why there was no name. When alone and in the mind, the identity was The Body. Not twin or sibling, simply nameless. Just one aching shell of a body that had lost its soul the day Michelle died. Heartbreak all over again. It did not matter thirty-two years had passed. The pain was as great today as it was when it happened. A three-year-old never forgot, never let go. The wound remained raw and open, no way to heal.

"I'll just sit here," Michelle said, squatting and then sitting down on the floor. "I won't bother you." She rested her head on her little fists, staring at The Body.

On the day of her death thirty-two years ago, she had been arguing with her twin over possession of a big red plastic ball. She wanted to throw it in the pool. Both of them had been strongly admonished never to go near the pool without adult supervision. They did not know how to swim. They hardly ever had mommy or daddy around to teach them how. Mommy and daddy were movie stars. The parents were famous and busy, meaning the twins' care fell on the shoulders of live-in help. Nannies and housekeepers. No one wanted to play in the pool with the children, no one had time, "Too much to do, children, too much to do."

Time, it seemed, was too precious and too scarce for any of it to be shared with toddlers.

"I told you to put the ball back," The Body said now, weeping openly at the memory of that terrible day. "If you'd only let me have it."

"I just wanted to see it float in the pool," Michelle said. "Pretty ball. Pretty ball on top of the blue water."

She had the big ball in her chubby baby arms. She couldn't see where she was going or what was before her, how close she might be to the pool edge. Her twin came from the side and tugged to free the ball. "You can't go near the swimming pool. We'll get in trouble. Gimme it."

Michelle squealed and jerked away, refusing. She had always been the stubborn one. She stumbled, turned around trying to get her balance and still keep possession of the red ball. Her twin saw her falling. Reached out one hand to grab her, but it was too late. Her arms flew out to each side and the ball lifted into the air like a balloon.

Michelle hit the water first, falling backward, going under and sinking to the bottom. The ball bounced almost exactly on the spot where she hit. Her twin went to the pool's edge.

There was a screaming that went on and on. MOM . . . MOM . . . MOMMOMMOM!

Michelle was in the deep end, down under, her long hair swirling in the blue water like seaweed. She stared up through the water, eyes bulbous in shock, her mouth open in her own terrified scream. Her little arms made slow motion circles in the water as she kicked to reach the surface and air.

Her twin raised eyes to heaven, screaming, screaming, screaming for help.

Help came. But only after Michelle had swallowed water and lost air in her lungs. She bobbed face down in the still waters of the blue pool by the time anyone showed at its side. Not far away the big red ball rolled lazily over the wind-ruffled wavelets.

And still her twin screamed, unable to stop.

A gardener tried to revive her. Then the paramedics arrived and they tried, laboring in the heat, bent over her and sweating. Her twin stood by, going unnoticed, crying and whispering, "Save her, save her, save her." It was useless. Little Michelle was gone.

"Please go away," The Body cried. "Go away, go away, go away. I can't save you." It seemed no one could.

Michelle took pity after watching her twin cry and beg. She stood and floated toward the ceiling. She touched the top bar of the empty crib on her way. She moved toward the blank white wall, turned and waved, and disappeared through it into the beyond.

The Body had let the script fall to the floor. Had slipped from the chair to kneel and to keen in misery. Gloom had won. It had found its victim.

Michelle's twin called for help, screaming.

In the midst of the wail of despair, The Body shouted a name, cursing it.

Catherine shouldn't have killed the babies. Unlike the accident that took Michelle, the little twins in Catherine's body made no mistakes, presented no stubbornness that shoved them toward the brink of death. They were blameless. Murdered. For no reason. If Karl died because of those deaths so that Catherine would be convicted, then that is what it would take to clear the slate. She must pay for her terrible sin. It was not true the pregnancy was her concern only. It was not true that a fetus was a blob of cell structures and blood. Even in the first weeks a fetus already had a head, arms, legs, a body. A fetus was a human being dependent on its host for protection, for life.

How could she have had them aborted, those tiny twins? How could she have killed them in such a wanton, thoughtless way?

# 41

"Best friend, my well-spring in the wilderness!"
George Eliot, *The Spanish Gypsy*

Karl LaRosa was left alone for a week. He received no phone calls or notes from his tormentor, suffered no attempts on his life. There were no more bomb devices attached to the underside of the rental car.

It took that much time for The Body to search through the script and decide what scene to implement. During those days' filming on the set and location there was quite a hullabaloo about the missing actress, Marilyn Lori-Street. A police detective from missing persons was contacted by her friends. A few people from the film, including Cambridge Hill, were questioned about the last time she was seen. The detective seemed to be a tired, bored man going through the motions. He took a few notes, asked some desultory questions, and left.

Cam rewrote the scenes that included her, effectively writing her out of the movie by having Olivia's stalker character turn on her best friend and murder her. They used a stand-in actress wearing a wig. They never showed her face.

People on the film still discussed Marilyn and worried over her, but, as a topic of conversation, speculation on her whereabouts was beginning to lag. They were all too busy to give it the attention perhaps it deserved. Films couldn't just halt because one of the actors disappeared. It wasn't as if it hadn't happened before. The schedule went ahead at an inflexible pace.

After the week of planning, which gave Karl time enough to get back his Jaguar from the body shop, everything was set into motion again. After a lull in the eye of the hurricane the storm is greatest, The Body recalled. Karl might die from this attempt on his life. Once he was dead, the authorities would come looking for his killer.

And they would find Catherine Rivers. All the clues, for any halfway decent investigator, pointed to her involvement. She'd be arrested. She would pay for all her crimes. They might even suspect her of Marilyn's murder.

At this point in the script the fictional stalker had lost all patience. There was no longer any pretense that the man would find a way to love the rejected woman again. She meant to kill him, to even things.

Just as The Body meant to do.

If it didn't work, there were one or two more scenes upcoming that could be tried. Soon now, Karl LaRosa would be on the way to the cemetery. He might not know it, but he already had one foot in the grave and the other planted on flimsy ground.

Karl was thrilled to have his Jag back from the shop. It looked beautiful again. The detailed workmanship of the repair made the car look new once more. They had had to replace parts and repaint the car. The paint shone like liquid silver.

"Great work," Jimmy Watz said, sliding into the passenger seat. He had had a little time off and accompanied Karl to pick up the car. "These guys are worth the money."

"It's true, they are. I'm beginning to have some money problems lately, though, so this bill hurt more than it should have."

Jimmy listened while Karl explained the latest mishaps in his financial affairs.

"Okay," Jimmy said, "who do you know can use a computer and a modem like that? Got any old girlfriends who are techies?"

Karl shook his head. "That's what gets me. I mean, almost everyone I know owns a computer, but not many of us in the business spend our free time at home hacking around on them. I don't remember any woman I ever dated mentioning a real interest in computers or programming."

"Well, someone knows how to go about it, that's for sure. Isn't there anything you can do about it? Can't you turn your suspicions to someone?"

"I could if I could prove it. I don't know how to find that proof."

"You need some help, Karl. If someone can ruin your credit, get into the IRS database and show you owing back taxes, then you need some kind of electronic snooper who can follow the trail and find out who's doing it."

"Great. You know anyone like that?"

Karl drove them toward Malibu, handling the Jag casually, more at home behind the wheel than he had been in ages.

"Let me check around with some of my friends," Jimmy said. "I'll find you someone. This shit's got to stop."

"Ain't that the truth."

The conversation continued during the trip home and into Karl's house where he put some steaks under the oven's broiler and tore some lettuce in a big bowl for salad. Jimmy hung over the counter, drinking beer and just watching the meal preparations. He liked those times he and Karl batched it with no women around.

After dinner, with twilight settled all around the house, and the lights twinkling from beyond the repaired sliding glass doors to the patio area, Jimmy went to the refrigerator and found they were out of beer.

"I'll go to the store and get us one more six-pack. Hell, it's Saturday night Karl. I ought to be out laying some chick, the least I can do is hoist a few beers in consolation that I'm stuck with you tonight." He grinned and Karl laughed.

"Here." Karl threw Jimmy the keys to the Jag. "Take silver babe out there. Maybe one day when you're a big movie star you too can own a Jaguar."

Jimmy caught the keys and started for the garage. "If I do, it won't be an old one like yours, buddy boy. I'll have myself something just a little bit newer so the girls will go wild and all my nights will be jam-packed full with dates."

"That's a damn pitiful attitude to take toward women."

Jimmy gave him the finger and lumbered out the kitchen door.

Jimmy thought the brakes on the Jag were a little loose when he came to the first stop sign after leaving Karl's house. He shrugged, thinking Karl ought to get it back to the shop, see if they needed checking out. They'd had to change out all the tires so maybe the brakes were new and not set in yet. New brake pads sometimes made an awful racket until they were seated.

By the time Jimmy hit Highway One along the ocean, heading for the big all-night grocery about two miles distant, he had forgotten about the squeaky brakes. He thought he'd get two six-packs, not one, and some chips and dip. What the hell. Maybe they could turn on the tube and catch a ballgame.

He speeded up on the highway, feeling the breeze spinning through the windows. The crisp night air helped to sober him. He could smell the ocean, salty on his tongue and dry in his nostrils. He knew he was grinning like a monkey because the beer had made him feel good, feel easy for a change. He had been worried over Karl for too long. They both deserved one night of drinking and joking around and just relaxing.

He had the Jag up to eighty miles an hour before he noticed his speed and realized he was over the speed limit. Too much over. He put his foot on the brake pedal and eased it down, all the while checking his rearview to see if he could spot any patrol cars.

His foot went straight to the floorboard. The brake pedal seemed not even to be there.

A flash of panic lit a fire in Jimmy's brain. It was as if a white empty landscape opened up in his mind, swallowing all his faculties. No brakes? Did this mean . . . he had no way to stop?

He let up on the brake pedal and tried again. No dice. There were no brakes on the car. It was true. He had no brakes! He was going seventy-five miles an hour now with no way to stop.

He was coming up on a car traveling slower in his lane. He had to swerve over in the passing lane to keep from ramming it. The tires on the Jag sung along the blacktop with a whistling sound.

Jimmy had begun to sweat. The breeze coming in the windows did nothing to cool him down. He felt sick to his stomach and prayed the beer wouldn't back up on him.

No brakes. Brake line probably cut. Brake fluid leaked out.

No brakes, no way to stop.

He glanced down, wondering where the parking brake was

on the Jaguar. The moment his attention left the road, a car entered his lane from the right, cutting him off, expecting him to brake and fall back.

The Jag hit it with a bang, snapping Jimmy's head back. Then the Jaguar slid over into the center of the highway, and was slammed head-on by a late model GMC van.

Jimmy never knew what hit him.

He hadn't bothered to buckle his seat belt, not that it would have made a lot of difference.

On impact with the van, the upper half of his body went over the steering wheel and through the windshield. The Jag spun out again, hit the guardrail and flipped over and over through a drainage ditch. It took out four small cottonwood saplings, and, skidding on its roof for a hundred yards, plowed a foot-deep furrow through sand and gravel.

The wheels spun, the tires hissed as they rotated in air, and the engine sizzled. Jimmy Watz died from shock, head injuries, and a severed carotid artery, cut by the broken windshield, before he realized his legs were cut off from the crotch down.

# 42

"Life is a series of diminishments."
Coleman Dowell, *Mrs October Was Here*

Karl, frantic with worry, kept going to the front door to look down the street for Jimmy. Where could he have gone for the beer, Australia?

When the call came inquiring if he was the owner of a 1985 silver Jaguar, Karl choked. He could hardly answer the questions, his throat felt so tight. Jimmy Watz was dead. Accident on Ocean Highway. The Jag had been totaled. It had been in a collision and rolled several times. It looked like a gigantic sardine can with the label ripped off.

Karl told them who had been driving. He said yes, he would come identify the body.

Karl wanted to kill. He had no illusions this was a real accident. Jimmy had had a couple of beers, but he had not been drunk. He was a careful driver, a good driver. Once, as students in college together, he and Jimmy had taken a Christmas vacation trip across country. Jimmy was a helluva good driver. He'd saved their lives once on that trip when during a rainstorm a car lost control in front of them and spunout. Karl wasn't sure afterward if he could have been as sure and steady at the wheel under the circumstances. He'd been glad Jimmy had been driving the car.

No, the wreck was staged, that was a certainty. Karl didn't know what had happened, but it wasn't accidental, it was murder. It should have been him in the car, not Jimmy.

Now two people had died because of Karl. Two lives snuffed out.

On the way to the morgue in Jimmy's old 1968 fastback Mustang—driving too fast, feeling reckless with despair—Karl knew what he was going to do. As soon as it was morning, he was going to find the stalker. He wouldn't do another thing until he did that. He didn't care if his business went down the drain, if he went bankrupt, or if he ruined every relationship he had with women. He wasn't going to stop until he had Jimmy's killer. It ended here, now.

Cam, amazed by the scene Jackie Landry had just performed, called for a cut. He rarely complimented his actors because he had discovered praise tended to cause them to slack up. Cam might say, "That's a good take," but rarely did he feel moved to comment beyond that. This time he couldn't help himself. Jackie had been wonderful.

Cam called him over. It was the end of the day and the crew were wrapping up so they could go home.

Jackie looked like a dog about to get a slap on the behind from a rolled newspaper. Where was this guy's confidence? If he had balls, they must be tucked up high.

Robyn had been right; Jackie was meant for the part. He was putting out one hundred and ten percent. Olivia was having to really haul out the big guns to keep from being outshone by him. Ever since Robyn had had that talk with Jackie, the man made the celluloid sizzle.

"I just wanted to tell you how pleased I am with your work today." Cam watched him closely for his response.

Jackie grinned. If he had had a tail, he would have been

wagging it. Cam almost wanted to backhand him and tell him to act like a man, damnit. Show some spunk, for pete's sake.

"I've been trying to get into the character," Jackie said. "Maybe I finally got it."

"You know I don't usually tell actors how good they've done because it goes to their heads and they start fucking off. But I just wanted you to know that the scene you did today was excellent. It was top quality. It's going to look great in dailies."

"Thanks, Cam."

Cam watched him leave the stage set and thought maybe his shoulders were a little straighter, his head held a little higher. He couldn't figure the guy. He wasn't quite like any other actor Cam worked with. He wondered why he didn't know how good he was. It might be that he'd never had a chance to show what he could do before. His other pictures were box office worthy, but not blockbusters. Or maybe it was because his parents had been famous in the old days. Now that could sometimes pose a problem for young talent. How did you ever fill the old man's or old lady's shoes?

This film could move him right to the head of the class if he kept going. He'd get bigger salary offers than Stallone or Bruce Willis. He might grow into a star as lasting as Eastwood if he kept doing the kind of work he'd done today. He'd be better than his parents combined.

An assistant came up and said, "There's someone to see you in your office. Karl? LaRosa?"

Cam's mood shifted into shadow. "Okay, I'll see about it." What the hell was it now?

Thoughts of the head propped in the front seat of his Cadillac came unbidden to mind. Cam ran a hand over his face, washing it away. Karl couldn't know about that. No one knew about it. They'd be looking for Marilyn for a very long time yet.

The office door was open. Cam hustled to his desk and pulled out the chair there. He twisted around and faced Karl. "What's up? I got to get outta here in a minute, sorry, got some work to finish up."

"Cam, I want a copy of the script."

Cam's eyebrows rose in question then fell into a scowl. "Can't do it, bud. Under wraps."

"I'm not asking you, Cam. I'm telling you. I want a copy of the script. My best friend died last night in my car. The brake line had been cut. I'd just gotten it out of the shop, but they didn't do it. The police still think they might have made a mistake. They can't prove the line was cut or if it snapped in the wreck. They're telling me to file a claim against the shop; they can't bring charges unless there's a clear-cut piece of evidence. But I know it wasn't a mechanic's mistake. Someone was trying to kill me. Someone on your set did it."

"I'm sorry to hear about your friend, but I assure you . . ."

"No excuses, Cam. I don't get the script, I go straight back to the cops. I think they can get me a script, don't you?" Karl rose from his chair. "I probably wasted my time coming here. I should have told the cops what I know. How my life's been following your filming. I didn't want you to have trouble because I made a promise to someone. I know how much this project means to you and Robyn. I've kept it unofficial for her sake. I've tried to handle this on my own."

Cam leapt from his chair and circled the desk. He put a staying hand on Karl's shoulder. "Now wait a fucking minute. It's no problem getting you a script. Here, let me check . . ." He turned back and pulled out a key from his pocket. He unlocked a desk drawer and rummaged in it. Extracting a green metallic-colored binder, he grinned so wide his gums showed. "See, got one right here. You won't let it out, right? No one else reads it?"

"Give me a break," Karl said. He took the script, turned his back and left the office.

Cam noticed he was sweating. His armpits were wet and he smelled like a bricklayer. "Shit," he mumbled, watching Karl's back as it retreated across the soundstage. "What a fucker." What he thought privately was that it might be a good thing if whoever was up to tricks with the script actually succeeded. Karl looked like a hard-ass who needed a long walk off a short pier.

Karl sat on the sofa in his house skimming over the next scenes in the script of *Pure and Uncut.* The first he knew he was not alone was when a bullet came through the closed door of his bedroom, splintering the paneling. He flinched back and his gut tightened up. The script pages flapped shut in his lap.

Then there was a barrage of shots peppering the door and Karl was up in a flash, moving through the living room, leaping over furniture, heading for the hall and the study beyond. He heard wood and glass breaking behind him. The pops from the gun sounded muffled, as if someone were using a silencer. Karl's own gun was in the drawer of the bedside table in the room where the shots were coming from. He was unarmed. He must reach the phone, call for help.

He slammed the study door and locked it, then noticed what a flimsy push button indoor lock he had on the door. One kick could disable it.

No time to worry about what he couldn't change. He ran for the desk and grabbed the phone there. He was punching in 911 before he realized there was no dial tone. Oh Christ.

Gunshots came from outside the closed study door and the window behind Karl exploded. It sounded to his ears like a train had slammed through the wall. Glass fell all around him in a shivery transparent shower. Glass cut and slit his skin on his neck and arms. He dropped to the floor and crawled beneath the desk. He was breathing through his mouth, harsh rasping sounds of a man under siege. He'd never been more afraid in his life. For one instant he remembered watching on television the taking of the Davidian compound in Waco, Texas. The ATF in their bulletproof vests storming the building.

That's what he felt like now. Like David Koresh; outgunned, outmanned, doomed. Any second one of those many random shots might take him out.

There was a lull. Karl held his breath. Suddenly the shots came again, as if the person on the other side of the door had reloaded. The door must be riddled by now, holes all in it.

It finally dawned on Karl that whoever it was out there meant to terrorize rather than kill. If she wanted Karl dead, she could have simply opened the bedroom door, walked into the living room and shot him dead where he sat. He'd never known anyone was in the house. The damn alarm system had failed again.

The whole thing was mapped out in the plot of the script.

This didn't mean Karl was going to stand up and take a bullet. It just meant he understood something important about what was going on. While he puzzled over it, the gunfire stopped and this time didn't resume. After another five minutes of silence, Karl came out from beneath the desk and walked to the door. It was splintered and battered. One of the hinges had been blasted loose. Karl reached out for the doorknob, paused a second with his hand around it, then jerked it open. The door keeled to one side and he had to hold it up to keep it from snapping off the lower hinge.

Maybe now he'd be killed, though he thought not. He'd read this scene in the script just before shots erupted from his bedroom. The hero had not been shot in the script. He'd been forced to run, hide, and finally the shooter disappeared into thin air.

The hall beyond stood empty.

After searching the house, Karl knew the intruder was gone. Just like in the script.

Karl left the house through the kitchen exit to the garage. Started up the Mustang.

He was going to see Robyn. She had to help him.

She saw him coming from across the room. She was in Heaven, the top level of the Universe. A girl of Asian extraction sang slow, sad songs that had a hypnotic effect on the room. Embracing couples on the dance floor locked in swaying trances. Over at the end of the bar a man with a bad tic in his left eye kept sending signals Robyn's way. He was too paunchy for her. Naked he'd look like a slab of fatty beef.

She sipped at her third gin and tonic, ignoring the guy on the barstool and watching Karl make his way toward her. She knew he'd want to talk about Marilyn. How she'd warned him about the script and then came up missing. Robyn didn't know what to say about that. I'm sorry, she'd say, it's out of hand, she'd say, what can I do, what do you want me to do? Maybe she got scared, maybe she left town, who the hell knows where she went? Though it *was* passing strange that she would desert a film that could have made her into a box office name.

Karl looked the worse for wear. His tie was askew, his shirttail half pulled from the back of his trousers. He might be drunk. His eyes, underscored with puffy-looking bags, looked haunted. There was a day's growth of whiskers on his cheeks and his hair was mussed. Maybe he'd been mugged.

Robyn straightened, thrusting out her breasts, and happened to see the man at the bar give her a wolfish grin. She turned to the side in order to block him out.

Karl came right up to her and took her by the arm. "Come with me," he said, pulling her across the dance floor.

She held back and finally jerked her arm free. "Now wait a damn minute, what's this about?"

"We need to talk. Not here. Let's go."

"Karl, I don't have to do what you say anymore. Now let's go have a—"

"Come with me now." His voice rose enough that people around them looked over at her.

"Oh, all right. Let me get my purse." She found it lying on the bar and followed him down the stairs through the next level to the ground floor. Music pulsated at their backs. Robyn always wanted to wiggle her ass to the drum beats. She'd consumed just enough liquor to think how funny she'd look if she started doing that while walking and giggled to herself. Laughter sifted through the smoke and smiling faces greeted them as they moved toward the door. Mercy, how she loved this place. She'd live here if they rented out beds.

Outside the club they had to weave through a young crowd of gaudily clad night kids debating whether they wanted to stay to see the headliner or cruise some other place. A couple of the young Turks gave her a look that she appreciated. She smiled at them.

Karl had Robyn's hand, pulling her along behind him. She stifled the maternal urge that suggested she reach out and tuck in his shirt. He was no child. He wasn't even her husband anymore; what was wrong with her every time she got around him? He wanted to look like a slob, let him.

In the parking lot, Karl headed for a cherry red Mustang. What was he doing, having a flashback from the sixties?

When he reached the car, he turned around to face her. He took her arms just above the elbows and looked down into her eyes. "Jimmy's dead."

She knew she was slow on the uptake due to the alcohol, but no matter how she tried to roll those words around in her head she couldn't quite get them to come up lucky seven. Jimmy's dead, she thought, that's what he said. Jimmy is dead.

"Jimmy Watz?" She had known Jimmy almost as long as Karl. In fact the first time she ever met Karl, he was with Jimmy. They'd all been friends a long time.

"He took my Jag after I got it from the shop. He was going to get beer. The brake line was cut—I think it was cut. The police went over the car and say they can't be sure, but I say it was deliberately cut. Jimmy wrecked it on the freeway, the car rolled. Jimmy . . . he was . . . Jimmy was . . . Goddamnit, he was cut in two. They had to use the Jaws of Life to take out his legs."

Robyn felt the world drop out beneath her feet. Karl steadied her. She heard him say, "Whoa." She blinked a few times and understood then what Karl was telling her. Someone had rigged his Jag expecting him to drive it. But Jimmy drove it and Jimmy died. Jimmy was . . .

"Cut in two? Oh no. No."

"Robyn, you have to help me find out who did it. And there's something else . . ."

Robyn didn't think there could be anything else Karl could tell her that had the same importance as losing Jimmy. She and Jimmy kept in touch, even after the divorce. Jimmy knew how to love both of them without splitting his loyalties. He never said an unkind word about Karl when with her and she was confident he never uttered an unkind word about her when he was with Karl. Jimmy was her friend and she hurt all over right now. It felt like someone had just socked her in the chest.

"What else?" she asked, uninterested. All she wanted to do was go back into the Universe and get rotten, stinking drunk. She'd get flying-ace, falling-down drunk and go home to pass out so she wouldn't have to think another sensible thought for the next twenty four hours.

"Someone called me and said the body parts found all over Hollywood belonged to Marilyn."

Oh now, see, one unexpected body shot after another and the fighter goes down. Robyn dropped all the way this time. Her knees gave out and she collapsed. Karl eased her to the concrete parking lot until she was sitting, her legs folded beneath her. She hung her head crying silently.

"That's not in the script," she said. Hadn't everything followed the script? This didn't. The deaths of Marilyn and Jimmy had nothing do with the script.

"I know. I've read it."

"This wasn't supposed to happen."

"No. It wasn't."

She looked up at him where he squatted next to her. She noticed he held her hand and was patting it in an old-fashioned way, like a gentleman, like Errol Flynn in one of his Arthurian legend films.

"Someone cut Marilyn into pieces?" she asked. "And someone fixed the brakes on your car and killed Jimmy?"

"Yes, someone did. She killed Marilyn for telling me about the script. She killed Jimmy while trying to kill me. We have to stop her."

"Who?"

Karl leaned his forehead against the top of her head. He whispered, "I thought you could tell me."

# 43

"No more tears now; I will think upon revenge."
Mary Stuart, Queen of Scotland,
Attributed remark, 9 March 1566,
after the murder of her favorite, David Rizzio

It was almost noon with the sun like a gold globe hung as a centerpiece in the sky. Karl stood grieving at the graveside service for Jimmy Watz. Karl wore a dark suit and a snow-white shirt. A small white carnation perched on his lapel. He hardly heard the minister's words or noticed the other mourners. The sun was too bright, the pain too sharp, the loss too deep.

More than forty miles away, oblivious to death and burial, Olivia Nyad slowly removed her secretary's bra and cupped the woman's small pointed breasts in both hands.

"I'm glad you're not needed on the set today," Janice said, pushing back Olivia's hair.

"I'm glad too." Pat Connors nuzzled Olivia's spine just at the base where her hips began to swell. He then reclined easily on the bed, assessing the two women who would be his playthings for the day. Connors worked as a masseur for Hollywood stars. Olivia employed him periodically to come to her house. Sometimes, like today, he had a chance to do more than massage sore, tired muscles.

"You don't mind sharing?" Olivia asked Connors. She

moved from Janice's breasts to the erect nipples on Connors' chest. Her tongue flicked out again and again until she felt him shiver.

"Not a bit," he said. He pulled Olivia onto his chest. "Threesome's are a turn-on." He felt Janice slide a hand up the inside of one thigh. "Two birds in a hand, as they say."

Olivia gave her husky laugh. "First time I've ever been called a bird. A bitch, I understand. A bird, though . . . That's British, right?"

The trio spent the day sweating and rolling around on the bed. Fueled by any kind of drug they wanted to sample from Olivia's stash box, the three fell into a sexual frenzy. Positions were tried, sex toys were dragged out of the closet, and in another part of the house the telephone answering machine took a seemingly endless barrage of calls.

During a break when Olivia wandered to the kitchen for more champagne, the phone rang again. She swore and picked up the receiver. Interrupting her playtime was never a good idea. She barked, "Who the hell is this and what do you want?" into the phone.

Karl said, "Whatever you're doing, stop it. Meet me in Burbank in an hour."

She started to protest, but Karl overcame all her objections, as usual, and gave her the restaurant's address.

She hung up, mumbling to herself about how her chain was always yanked by Karl, the bastard. All he had to do was tell her to drop everything and come running and what did she do? She came running.

Her head swirling with crazy images, her thoughts zinging along a high wire with a feeling of accelerated speed, she stumbled toward the bedroom and her companions. "Okay, holiday's over. I have to make a run. Get dressed, get out, it was lovely. We'll do it again sometime."

Janice was used to Olivia's abrupt commands, but Connors, zoned out now on downers, said in slurred speech, "My bird's flying away. I want my bird."

Olivia threw his clothes across his naked, glistening body. "I said get out, honey. You want your bonus, you'll do what I say."

Janice kissed the back of Olivia's neck where she was bent over to start the water running in the shower. "See you later."

When Olivia exited from her bath, Connors was gone, the bed rumpled but empty. God, until now, the day had been a thrill ride. She hoped Karl wasn't on the rag.

Karl knew she was wired the minute she came through the door of the restaurant. She walked in a jittery stop-and-go fashion like some hophead kid hunting the next crack high. Her wide-eyed stare flicked here and there, searching him out. Once he was spotted, she fairly flew over. The perfumed breeze from her quick slide into the seat across from him wafted past his face.

He studied her dilated pupils. "What are you on, Olivia?"

She stretched her head back and flexed her shoulders. "Nothing much. Is that why you wanted me to meet you? To give me a lecture on the evils of drugs? If so, I have a bulletin for you. It's none of your business, Mr. LaRosa. In fact, your ass wouldn't be in such a tight pinch if you tried some yourself. A little recreation might get rid of that frown on your old Gloomy Gus face." She laughed, thinking herself right clever.

"This is important," he said, not wishing to be drawn into a debate. Olivia could be a hellcat if she felt the least bit threatened or put down. "I needed to talk to you sober."

"You think I'm not sober? Shit, Karl, since when did you get up on this high horse to see the rest of the world? I'm fine.

244

You wanna talk, talk. You don't wanna talk, I'm out the door. I left a splendid hard-on lying in my bed to come here today."

"Fine." He had never been fond of Olivia's vulgar manners. "Someone cut the brake line to my car, my Jaguar. I'd just gotten it out of the shop. My friend Jimmy Watz— remember Jimmy?"

She nodded.

"Jimmy drove my car to buy some beer three nights ago. He had a wreck going approximately seventy miles an hour. No brakes."

"Good grief." Olivia put a hand over her eyes and looked down at the table. When the waitress came for her order, Karl asked for hot tea.

"Olivia, you need to help me. I was supposed to be in the Jag. Because of me, Jimmy's dead. And he isn't the only one. Marilyn, the actress missing from the script you're shooting? The killer called me and said the dismembered parts found all over Hollywood belonged to Marilyn. I don't know if that's true because forensic homicide came up with zilch when they ran the fingerprints. And as far as I know they haven't found . . ."

"Her head," Olivia said.

"That's right."

"My god. You think someone on the set is the killer. I can see why you think that. It's the only thing that makes sense because most of what's happened to you has followed the script. Or is it you think it's me? You really called me down here because you wanted me to confess. Is that it, Karl?"

"If you did this, Olivia, it's time to confess, yes, it's high time."

Before he knew it was coming, her hand reached out and slapped him soundly across the cheek. He came up halfway out of the booth and felt like crawling over the table. He sat back down, breathing hard. His cheek burned like charcoal in a brazier. "I'm not taking any more bullshit, Olivia. What do you want from me? Isn't it enough two innocent people have died?"

She pushed from the seat and stood shakily. "That dog won't hunt," she said. She looked down at him and gave a grim smile. "You need someone to lay the blame on, look somewhere else. What about Robyn? She's the only one you ever fucking married. She always had the whole script. What about Catherine? Of the four of us—me, Marilyn, Robyn, and Cathy—she'd be my bet." She turned away and began to leave but turned and came close to him. She spoke in a low, steely voice. Her breath was sour from alcohol and whatever pills she had been taking all day. Just for a second or two, he was afraid of her.

"If you ever accuse me of murder again . . . if you ever accuse me of *anything* again, I'll never speak to you the rest of your lousy fucking life. I might have slept with you, I might have an old flame still burning for you, but I mean this. Don't do this to me again, Karl."

Karl watched her leave. He brought his hand up to his hot cheek. The waitress brought over the pot of tea and he poured himself a cup. They served good green China tea strong enough to open his nasal passages. He breathed in the bitter scent before sipping the tea. He felt too alone. Stranded without a friend in the world.

What was he to think about Olivia? He had ruled out Robyn. He had lived with the woman for several years. Would she kill him? She didn't even miss him from her life, why would she bother to hurt him?

Besides, unless she had taken a crash course in computer technology, she couldn't be the one snooping in his files, making changes that disrupted his whole life. She couldn't have disarmed his alarm system so many times, much less found and cut the brake lines on the jag. He knew her. Or he used to. She was about as mechanically talented as a crippled hedgehog.

No, Robyn had come to the point that she had everything she wanted out of life. The life she cultivated didn't include him. She had nothing to gain in hurting him. Nor would she have chanced Jimmy's death. She certainly didn't fake the shock she felt when told he'd died.

Maybe it wasn't Olivia either. It didn't seem to be Olivia. He knew she was a great actress, that at any time she might be acting, but the slap she had given him came out of deep hurt and heartfelt indignity. She couldn't have rehearsed that.

He had to admit though, he could hardly believe Cat might be the stalker either.

And if those women involved in the script didn't fit a stalker's profile, who did? What unknown enemy had he un-intentionally harmed so badly that his death was decreed?

He looked over the rim of his teacup and watched a family being seated not far from him. Mother, father, two children, a boy and a girl. The boy was blond and thin with wire-rimmed glasses which gave his eyes an owlish stare. The little girl was around three and she wore a party dress, all pink ruffles and bows. For the first time in a long while he envied the family life and wished he had made one for himself. Robyn hadn't been able to have children and she didn't want any anyway. Since his divorce, he had put away thoughts of a family. Could he settle down with Lisa, make children, grow old and gray and become a grandfather one day?

Well, he could, that's what Lisa wanted. He could if he could stay alive long enough.

After one more go-around with Catherine, he'd have to try to reorganize his thoughts. He might have to throw out all

earlier presumptions and start over again in another direction. Perhaps it wasn't a past lover at all, despite the mash
notes. The phone call he'd received still nagged at him. It
might have been a man. What if it was a man trying to set all
the evidence up to make it look like a woman was stalking
him?

Hell. A man!

Hadn't the voice on the phone been asexual, an indefin-
able gender with the voice tones low, but neither definitely
masculine nor feminine?

It could be anyone trying to kill him. Anyone at all.

The thought lodged in his brain and would not go away. It
was more frightening than the thought an old wounded lover
was out to ruin and kill him. If his stalker was a man, then
how could he ever determine the reason behind it? Nothing
so easy as a woman scorned to make the motives clear. But a
man? What had he ever done to deserve such an elaborate
plan? This seemed to be a mystery that was growing like a box
of poison mushrooms in a cellar; undercover, silent, and
deadly.

A headache bloomed just up from the back of his neck and
he rubbed his scalp there over the rounded ridge of bone. He
would see Catherine again and try to rule her out. One step at
a time, methodically, he would find out who had killed Jimmy
and Marilyn.

# 44

"She's gone. I am abused, and my relief
Must be to loathe her."

William Shakespeare, *Othello*

The Body woke in the closet. It was black as darkest night
though it must be early morning for the mind to feel so alert. A
breeze from the overhead fan stirred the air. Reaching out both
arms, The Body's fingers just brushed the walls on either side of
the mattress on the floor. It was understood that sleeping in a
small cramped space such as the closet in the child's room was
tantamount to returning to the womb. However, understanding
a psychological motivation did not always clear up the source of
the underlying need. The closet provided safety, enclosure, and
comfort, of course. A bed in an open room did not. Why the
small net of safety was so needful might have to do with seeing
Michelle's ghost (she never came to The Body in the closet) or
it might be that a return to *wombness* preserved the mind that
was attacked from all sides out in the wide, dangerous world.
There was nothing and no one in the closet to betray The Body.
There might be a stray single spider weaving a web in one of the
corners or around the base of the ceiling fan, but other than that
the closet belonged to one living being and no other.

It was time to sit up, crawl to the door, and greet the day.
There was nothing more refreshing than a full night's rest in

perfect surroundings to prepare a body for the ultimate scene.

On the chair sitting before the computer in the nursery the script lay open and face down. The Body took it up and flipped it over. Here was the climax. When acted on the silver screen, it would be a stunning piece of work. When carried out in reality, it would surpass the screen image by a hundredfold.

Karl LaRosa might have succumbed in any scene leading up to this one, yet he had survived. It was preordained that he survive until the end shot, the culmination scene, the denouement of the tale.

When the phone rang, The Body placed the open script on the white desk next to the computer and wandered into the kitchen where a wall phone hung next to a framed picture of a hummingbird frozen in flight over a bright red feeder.

"Hello?"

"Hi, glad I caught you at home."

It was Olivia. Bright as a cottontail bunny this morning, her voice sparkling with cheer.

"I just got up. What do you need?"

"You sound cranky."

"I'm not."

"Well, shake a leg. We have that scene today and I was wondering if you'd meet me early on the set so we could rehearse. I want to do it right."

"I guess I can go in early. When?"

"An hour? We'll have the place mostly to ourselves before catering gets there."

"Sure, okay."

The Body hung up carefully. Olivia, the hated one. Not as hated as Catherine, but no one was as hated as Catherine. Olivia was too damn pitiful to hate that much. She was talented, but ditzy and on top of that, a heavy drug user. Not that half the people in the movie didn't use drugs, but none with such uncaring abandon as Olivia. She had sometimes shown up for a shoot with her eyes so glassy Cam had to put off the filming until he had plied her with two pots of coffee and whatever drug might counteract the one she'd taken. If she was on tranks and lethargic, Cam got a few hits of speed for her. If she was high flying on cocaine or crank (or twice lately, when she admitted to having cooked just a little bit of smack, just a little tiny bit), he found something to bring her down. Not without cursing like a bandit whose treasure had been stolen. And stomping around and threatening to fire her off the film, but no one believed that, not even Olivia, who continued to abuse herself to the detriment of the project. Silly old bitch.

She had sounded too damn full of snap, crackle, pop for this early in the morning. Hell, dawn hadn't even broken and a pewter light heavy with falling dew still swirled over the lawns, flowerbeds, and white poplar trees in the neighborhood.

No time then to study the scene, to work out the plan for Karl LaRosa's swan song. It would have to be put off until tomorrow. One more day before the end could not matter one way or the other. That the final chapter was close gave The Body an electric feeling of power.

# 45

"Don't part with your illusions. When they are gone you may still exist, but you have ceased to live."
Mark Twain, *Pudd'nhead Wilson's New Calendar*

The babies would have given The Body a reason to live. The twins. The dead ones who would have lived in the nursery. That's what the new crib was for, the mobile, the colorful wallpaper. The Body believed Catherine loved him, loved him, loved him so much. He believed she would have his babies, she would marry him first, and have his babies.

But she left him and she killed the babies so that she could have an affair with another man. With Karl.

Oh, how The Body grieved. As much as for poor Michelle.

No one had ever loved The Body except for Michelle. Not mother or father. Not really. They were too busy with their professional lives to love their children.

Catherine had not loved him.

The twins would have. If she'd carried them to term and let him have them to raise. They would have loved him with such fierce loyalty that no one could have parted the three of them, ever.

As a child growing up, The Body had tried very hard to be like other children. But without Michelle, it was impossible.

It was as if half of him was missing. He was a shadow, superficial, not really all there.

He had a friend once. In junior high school. A boy named Davy Cotersill. He even told Davy about Michelle and how he missed her, how bereft he was yet. And Davy didn't make fun of him.

But then, after a few months of close friendship where he and Davy rode their bicycles everywhere together, and went to the same parties, and played tennis on their parents' tennis courts until after dinnertime, something began to happen. The Body noticed it first, but was unable to stop it from happening. He started first with the haircut. He went to the barbershop and had them cut his hair just like Davy's. Short on the sides, long on top. Then The Body found out where Davy's mother shopped for clothes and he had his own mother take him there and buy him a new wardrobe. He picked out the same style of jeans, the same shirts, belts, socks, and shoes. Finally, when Davy began to notice and look at him strangely, The Body had his father buy him a bicycle just like Davy's. Dark blue ten-speed Schwinn. When he took it over to show his friend, that's when Davy accused him of being some kind of clown.

"What's the matter with you?" Davy asked. "It's like you're sucking me in. It's like you're becoming me. What happened to your clothes, your hair, and now you got a bicycle like mine. Is this a joke or what? I don't like it if it's a joke. It feels funny looking at you now when you're starting to look like my twin or something."

The Body hung his head and scuffed his Reebok that was the same kind of Reebok that Davy wore. "I just like you, Davy."

"Well, it's okay to like me and it's flattering to be copied up to a point, but this is ridiculous! When school starts and you do this, other kids are gonna make fun of us. They'll think we're *dating* or something, for crying out loud."

"No, they won't, they won't even notice . . ."

"Yes, they will! They'll think we're fags. You're not a fag, are you? You don't want my body, do you?"

The Body felt the insult right down to his toes. He had never even entertained such nasty thoughts. Of course he didn't want to have sex with Davy. He just wanted . . . he wanted to be like him. He wanted to be like . . . someone.

They had had a big row and wound up swinging at one another. Davy's dad had to come outdoors and break them up. The Body went home with a bloody nose and never spoke to Davy again. He threw all his new clothes in the trash. He let his hair grow out long and scraggly.

He never tried to have a best friend again.

Because friends disappoint you. Sisters die on you. Lovers betray you.

Only his own children would have given him the kind of unconditional love he had always wished for. And Catherine never even asked him if he wanted those children. Before her pregnancy, if asked, he would have said a woman had the right to make that sort of decision on her own. But after it involved the loss of a set of twins he wanted in his own life—to save him from loneliness and despair—he realized he did not believe it was a woman's sole right to make the decision. The babies were half his! His sperm had created them. Their cells came from his cells, their genetic make-up came partially from him, and even the fact that Catherine had come up pregnant with twins had to do with him being a twin.

Once she had destroyed them, The Body could hardly go on. No use to reproach her. A modern woman. A career woman, like his mother. She wouldn't have listened to him. She probably didn't even know now how much pain she had given him.

Or how much she would have to pay for her sin against life.

If he knew of a way to murder her and never be suspected, he would have long ago done it.

The script was the only way he knew to bring harm to her. He had harbored his hate for all these years, through her dismissal of Karl, and her marriage and her new pregnancy, and the birth of her little girl, who he coveted. That hate had done something irrevocable to his soul, he knew that. It had warped him. It had left him half sane. He was functional in society, but not a part of it. He could never be right again because of her.

Finally, if he could finish up the shooting of the script and he could kill Karl so that Catherine was suspected, he might find a little peace. Or at least more than he'd ever enjoyed before. Michelle's ghost might not desert him, and his hunger for his lost children might not ever leave him, but at least Catherine would feel a little of what he had endured all these many lonely years.

The murders he had performed so far had left not a smudge of guilt on his conscience. He would feel nothing for Karl when he died, either. And nothing for what Catherine would be put through.

For The Body knew what to do once Catherine was out of the way.

He would take her little girl, steal away Barbara, and he would make her his own. If he could not have the babies who had been his flesh and blood, he would at least have a small child he could pretend was his own to share his life with and to be a father to. She was still young enough to learn to love him.

*Dear Karl,*

*I know you know why you were picked now. She'll be*

*blamed because it's her fault you're going to die.*

*Good-bye, Karl. It's been fun.*

*XXXX*

*OOOO*

Same cream-colored stationery, folded as usual in half. Karl read the note over again. It had been slipped between the windshield wiper and the glass on his new BMW parked in the lot next to his office.

Karl looked up at the roar of a car engine, fearing his death was coming in the form of a hit and run. He stood pinned between the BMW and the building, expecting to see a car racing toward him.

But no. The car he'd heard was on the nearby street and it was not turning into the lot. It sped away from the stoplight at the corner, leaving burned rubber and acrid smoke in its wake. Just some hotrod crazy kid.

Karl took a deep breath. How great it was to be alive—and he had to stay that way—on this balmy night.

He stared at the note again. Someone was going to be framed for his murder. That's what this was about all along. He'd been thrown off the trail with the love notes. Biggest mistake he'd ever made. One that was testament to his vanity. Who else, he had thought, would hurt me but a wronged woman? The stalker had depended on his vanity and ego to keep his identity safe. It had worked, hadn't it?

He had to tell this to the detective working on the case. Morales. The man who didn't believe Karl was in any real danger or that the department needed to expend a lot of time and effort running down the fingerprints they had lifted from his wrecked Jaguar.

Karl turned from the car and hurried back to the office to use the telephone. He was in such a hurry, he didn't bother to lock the door behind him although it was past office hours and all his employees were gone for the day. He had just gotten Detective Morales on his extension line when Karl heard the front door open, a few seconds of silence pass, and then the door closed.

"Hold on," he told Morales. Dropping the phone, he moved quickly around the desk and through his office door into the outer waiting room. His senses, tuned to any hint of a change in the routine, caused him to smell first the over-powering scent of gasoline, then he saw the smoke before the noticed the fire. He was faced in the waiting room with con-firmation of his fears. Flame rose in a line across the carpet from one end of the room to the other. The fire licked the walls and reached out for the upholstered chairs. His eyes widened in runaway fear. Something primitive and dark as a large worm turning over in his belly uncoiled so that his arms broke out in goosebumps and he felt paralyzed.

His heart kicked into an irregular rhythm. He gulped and smoke filled his mouth. The whole room was dimming and blackening with smoke. An oily, thick cloud of it streamed from the carpet and roiled in ugly, thickening corkscrews near the ceiling. He was forced back, the heat already intense, the flames licking and gliding like orange-red wraiths from floor to ceiling.

Turning, feeling himself drop into a dreamy state, every-thing set to slow-mo, he slammed the door to his office with a bang that sounded like thunder. The sound galvanized him. He grabbed the phone and yelled, "I'm in my office. It's on fire! The whole building's going to go up."

It was a moment before he realized his call had been put on hold. Muzak played over the receiver. He dropped the phone and panic overrode his thinking. Black smoke billowed from beneath the door. Soon the doorknob would melt and the door would turn into a wall of flame. He couldn't hear any sirens of fire trucks. Maybe no one yet knew the place was on fire.

What should he save? All his records were here. Had Lois backed them up on the computer and had she deposited the tape backups in the safety deposit box the way he had asked her?

Save nothing, get out, his mind screamed. Get out now!

Something that sounded like a small bomb blew up in the outer waiting room. The computer monitor. The whole place was going up.

Without further thought, he lifted the big desk chair onto his right shoulder and ran with it toward the window. He hurled it forward and brought both his arms up to protect his face from flying glass. The crash was drowned in the roar of the fire from the other room. The chair had gone through the glass and tumbled across the sidewalk to the gutter.

Karl looked back once before climbing over the jagged glass edge of the window frame. He saw fire had eaten through the door. Only then did he remember this scene from the script—all except the note left on his BMW. It was uncanny how the script showed the lead trapped in an office with the only way out a large window. He'd even used the office chair to break out. He'd had a feeling of deja vu from the moment he'd heard the outer door open. He should have been on alert, but how could he know when the stalker would try to implement the script scene? He might know what was coming, but never when.

As he stepped out into fresh air, his fear subsiding now that he was out of the fiery building, a blow fell on the back of his head. Karl slumped to the sidewalk, unconscious.

★ ★ ★ ★ ★

PERRY JOHNS: Detective Apollina, please. This is an emergency.

POLICE OPERATOR: Your name, sir?

PERRY JOHNS: Perry Johns.

POLICE OPERATOR: All right, hold a minute, while I see if the detective is in.

There's a suspicious crackling sound that draws PERRY's attention from the desk.

INTERIOR-FRONT WAITING ROOM: Front door snicking shut. Flame bursting from poured gasoline, leaping out of control, engulfing the exit.

CLOSE UP: PERRY standing in open door between waiting room and his office, shocked at the fire raging across the floor and moving up the walls.

INTERIOR-OFFICE: PERRY slams shut the door and rushes to grab up the phone.

PERRY JOHNS: Apollina! The waiting room's on fire. I can't get out the front of the building!

DETECTIVE APOLLINA: I'll alert the fire department. Do you have a window or a rear exit?

PERRY JOHNS: I've got a plate glass window. I'll have to break it out. I can't get from my office to the back door.

DETECTIVE APOLLINA: Someone will be right there. Get out now.

PERRY drops the phone, picks up the chair behind the desk and throws it through the wide window that faces the sidewalk. He crawls through, relieved to be away from the flames.

FADE OUT.


The Body raised the pipe again to strike a killing blow, but a car slammed its brakes on the street and pulled over awkwardly to the curb, the tires bumping up over the concrete lip. The grill halted no more than a foot from The Body. Time to go. No time to finish it.

He swiveled and ran away, throwing down the pipe as he ran. He turned down the next street at the corner, looking back over his shoulder to see the driver of the car wasn't following. A man had come from the vehicle and was squatting next to Karl.

The goddamn luck.

Karl did not come to until he had been moved away from the burning building so the firefighters could get their hoses across the sidewalk where he had been lying. He woke with a massive headache and his vision all out of whack. There were two Morales clones staring down into his face. So many teeth. So many eyes.

"You okay, buddy? There's an ambulance on the way."

Karl struggled to a sitting position. "I don't need an ambulance." He felt the back of his head where a goose egg knot had risen.

"You might have a concussion, need to get it checked out."

Karl remembered the note. *She would be blamed,* it had said. What if the bastard had left evidence somewhere near the building? The evidence could belong to Robyn or to anyone he'd ever dated. He couldn't let the fire inspector find it.

"Here. Help me up."

Morales took his arm and pulled him to his feet. Karl felt a little light-headed, but it passed. He stared at the building. Half of the roof was gutted. Smoke and an occasional cloud of sparks still streamed toward the night sky. The fire appeared to be put out, or almost. Firefighters still pumped in gallons of water.

Where would the stalker leave evidence? Near the front of the building where he'd entered, Karl assumed. He couldn't leave it inside in the fire, of course.

Morales was talking to a uniformed officer. Karl took his time walking slowly away from them, rubbing the back of his head, and toward the building. He passed over the thick snake-like water hoses and past two firefighters. They paid him no attention. Everyone was involved in doing their jobs. An investigator wouldn't arrive until later, maybe after the fire was completely out.

The front door was burned completely up. A gaping black hole spewed foul scorched odors of plastic wafting from within. Karl went closer, his eyes on the sidewalk. He saw light glinting off the pen. It was burnished stainless steel, a slim ballpoint, expensive. He leaned down and picked it up, stuck it in his shirt pocket. He looked for anything else out of the ordinary, but it was dark and he couldn't see a thing but puddles of sooty water speckled with flakes of burned material.

Karl wished he had the note, but it was gone. He had taken it with him inside when he first meant to call the detective. He could see it now in his mind's eye. He'd dropped it on the desk as he dialed.

Well, at least he had the pen.

Morales scared him by coming up from behind and placing a hand on his shoulder. "This is tough," he said. "Looks like a firebug. You smell anything in there when the fire started?"

"Yeah, gasoline."

"I want that list of women you were supposed to get together for me. I want it now."

Hell. How could he explain anything to Morales? It would sound insane. He nodded his head. "I'll get it for you."

Morales cocked his head and he gave Karl a curious stare. "You do want to find out who has been doing this, don't you? You could have been killed in there."

"Of course I want to know who it is. Why?"

"You just seem reluctant about the list. I've been after you to give it to me for three days."

"So you believe me now."

"Oh, you mean your friend's death in your Jaguar. Look, I'm not with the investigative team that checks out wrecks. I'm not the one who couldn't verify whether the brake line was cut or sheared during impact. I happen to be on your side, Mr. LaRosa, whether the wreck was accidental or not."

Karl nodded. He couldn't trust himself to speak in a civil manner with the detective. The whole police department had been completely ineffective in his opinion. They put him off. They didn't return his calls. They didn't follow up on his complaints. What was he supposed to do now, give thanks they finally believed he had a life-threatening situation on his hands?

"LaRosa?"

"Yeah." He had been drifting and he must have looked like a man in shock. His head felt as if a hammer was repeatedly pounding a nail into one spot at the back of his skull.

"You need to let the paramedics look you over."

"No. I'm fine."

He knew what he would do. He would find out who owned the stainless steel pen in his pocket. Then he'd have a direct line to the man who was so determined to kill him.

He ought to tell Morales. He ought to tell him about the phone call from the killer claiming to have committed the murder of Marilyn Lori-Street.

This wasn't just arson. Blood thrown in his office. Ransacking his house or wrecking his Jaguar.

People were dead.

"You don't look so good," Morales said, taking his arm.

Karl let himself be dragged over to the ambulance that had just arrived. Maybe they had some aspirin for the headache. Ibuprofen. Morphine! Any damn thing to stop the pounding.

"Is my BMW all right?" he asked Morales on the way to the open back of the ambulance.

"It's fine. The fire was controlled before it took out that wall."

"Sometimes I get lucky."

Morales looked at him and gave a toothy grin that brightened his dark Hispanic face. "I'd say you're one of the luckiest sons of bitches in town, LaRosa."

Karl couldn't dispute that.


"Look, I know it's late, but I've got to talk to you." Karl was on his cellular phone while driving the BMW toward North Hollywood.

"I was just going out," Cambridge Hill said.

"Don't. Don't go anywhere until I get there. Unless you want me to talk to the cops instead."

There was a groan. "Okay, shit, come on over then. Make it snappy."

The paramedics had given him three Tylenol tablets, but they weren't helping. Maybe he did have a concussion. Now his neck was so stiff he could hardly turn his head. When he did turn his head, his vision wavered. Hell. He was in no shape to argue with Cam. But he had no time to waste, either, headache or no headache.

Cam opened the door, took one look at Karl, and ushered him inside, clucking like a mother hen. "What the hell hap-

263

pened, man? You look like you've been run over by a tractor trailer."

"Close. My office was set on fire and I had to break out a window to escape. When I got outside, someone hit me over the back of the head with something. It felt like a sledge-hammer." He turned completely around to show Cam the swelling on his head.

"Jesus. That must hurt like a son of a bitch."

Karl faced him again. "I have the script now, but it's not enough, Cam. I knew the office fire was coming, but I didn't know when. I'm going to have to tell the police what I know."

Cam went up like a Roman candle. He seemed to grow five inches taller, he stuck out his chest, he paced like a wild man, running both hands through his hair. "Can't do that," he said. "Can't do that, uh uh, no way."

"Cam, listen. I read the fire scene in the script, but I had no idea it would happen tonight after everyone was gone. I made one dumb mistake. I had locked the office and was going to my car to drive home. I found a note on the wind-shield. I went back in to make a phone call and . . ."

"Someone poured gasoline in your office and set it off."

"Right. I'd forgotten to lock the door behind me. How many lives do you think I have left? And another thing," Karl said. "That actress you're missing? The guy who's after me killed her. It's because of me she's dead. We once had a fling, a short one, and she insisted I be told about the script. So this isn't just a case of harassment, Cam. You've got a murderer on the set. Are you going to let more people die for the sake of a movie?"

Cam was still pacing like mad. His hair rolled from the front into spikes toward the rear so that he looked like those oddball photographs of Einstein they put on T-shirts. He'd be comical looking if this was a comedy and not a situation where life hung in the balance.

"I know about Marilyn. I know about your friend, Jimmy. I know there's a fucking wacko on my set, they're all fucking wackos, you want my opinion." He gave a flourish of his hands. "Okay, okay, you get outta town." Cam had stopped and was pointing at Karl.

"What?"

"Just get outta town for a while, Karl. This will all blow over if you're not around, trust me on that. You bring in the cops and . . . and . . ."

"Maybe they'd stop this insanity," Karl supplied.

"No! They'd fuck up everything and you know it. I told you that already. I'd be under suspicion, my actors, my crew, everybody. You just leave town. You got a place to go? Listen, I have a cabin stuck way back in the fucking wilds, man, up in Montana. I go up there hunting elk and to get in a little skiing just to get away from this crazy goddamn place. I'll give you the keys, no one knows where it is, you'll be safe."

Karl began to shake his head.

"I'm telling you, Karl, this is what you've got to do. It's my life, this picture. You want to fuck me up, is that what you want? I promise, man, I promise you the minute I get the last shot in the can, you come back and we call in the cops. If they ask why didn't we tell them what we knew earlier, we plead ignorance. How they gonna prove otherwise? This is the only way it'll play. Okay? Let's do it my way. I'll take all responsibility for the decision."

"And if I don't?"

Cam gestured crazily in the air, turning half one way and then the other. He looked like a man about to blow a gasket. His color was high and he was breathing like a fire bellows. "I'm not going to beg you." His voice rose as he repeated it, stepping in close to Karl. "I am not going to fucking beg you. I'll tell you what I will do, though. You don't go off to Montana and let me do my film, you call in the cops now and screw this up, I'll make sure you really are ruined in this town. Now I don't like to threaten people, but you have to understand the wall I'm backed up to. You don't want to get me in that place, Karl. I get bad when I can't move around. So I'm telling you again, you take the keys to my cabin, you leave town, you stay out until I finish the film, and then I'll cooperate. It's up to you."

Karl knew what Cam could do to him. Despite the fact his business was going down the hole from the stalker fooling with his client base and his credit and his tax returns, it was nothing compared to what strings Cam could pull if he put his mind to it. Hollywood wasn't big enough for both of them if Cam went against him.

Karl walked away from Cam and the foyer in which they had been talking. He went into the living room and collapsed on one of the soft leather sofas. He ran a hand over his eyes. The headache was no better. He caught himself grinding down his teeth against the battering pain.

Cam followed and stood over him, a bear of a man, but he wasn't threatening Karl physically. He was, if anything, a dumbfounded bear, lost and crazy to know what cave to hide in.

Karl looked up at him. Saw his face, how seamed it was, how gray. "Okay, Cam. Get me the keys, draw me a map. I'll leave in the morning."

Cam reached out and clapped him hard on the back. It made Karl's brain rattle in his skull. The headache shifted right to the crown and sat there, thumping with his blood.

"Now you're talking," Cam said. He left the room and Karl heard him rummaging in another room. Going through drawers, it sounded like. Looking for keys.

"Montana," Karl said below his breath. "Hell." He leaned forward and put his head into his hands and closed his eyes. Maybe this was for the best. He could get some perspective. He could get out from under the pressure of being followed and nearly killed every few days. He hadn't realized how wearing the past weeks had been. The prospect of just running away, disappearing, was so appealing that it surprised him. He could easily go away at this point, leave town, and never come back.

Except he knew that was a lie. This was where his life was. Anywhere else he would be worthless. Only in Hollywood did he have a place he belonged. So he would come back.

"I found the keys," he heard Cam call from the other room. "We're in high cotton."

Karl drew the ballpoint pen from his shirt pocket. "Ever seen this before?"

"No, why?"

"Take a closer look. Maybe you'll recognize it."

Cam rolled the pen around between his fingers, scrutinizing it.

"Never saw it before. You gonna tell me why you're asking?"

Karl took it back and slipped it into his pocket. "No, it doesn't matter."

"You're leaving? Right away?" Cam handed him the keys to the cabin.

Karl came to his feet. "Yeah, right away."

# 46

"Perhaps the whole root of our trouble, the human trouble, is that we will sacrifice all the beauty of our lives, will imprison ourselves in totems, taboos, crosses, blood sacrifices, steeples, mosques, races, armies, flags, nations, in order to deny the fact of death, which is the only fact we have."

James Baldwin, "Letter from a Region in My Mind," *New Yorker* magazine

It was two days before The Body realized his prey was gone. The new BMW was missing from Karl's driveway. His new temporary office—in a building two streets away from the burned out shell of his old office—stayed closed. His house was empty.

Getting through the scenes on the set was torture. Concentration had flown the coop. Cam gave him hell, Robyn had a heart-to-heart talk with him—again. Olivia grew exasperated in their scenes together and once stalked off the set in a fury, screaming that she "hated working with goddamn pretty boys."

He would never forgive her for that.

His hands shook. He perspired and had to have his face mopped every ten minutes. He blew his lines. He missed his marks. His voice croaked and his movements were stiff. One day Cam threw half a tuna salad sandwich at him.

The Body tried to pry out of Robyn Karl's whereabouts. If anyone knew, wouldn't she? She was surprised he was missing. Her face crumpled like a crushed soda can when she learned he had not been seen in days. Hurt she hadn't been told he was leaving. Or worried something horrible had happened to him? She was no help.

The Body broke into Karl's new office and searched it. There was a new computer, but there weren't any clues in the files. He did find the employee records, all newly and neatly filled out, in a file cabinet. He had Karl's secretary's address and phone number.

On the night of the fourth day of Karl's disappearance, The Body called Lois.

"I need to get in touch with Karl LaRosa. Could you help me out?"

"I'm sorry, you need to call the office next week."

"I can't wait until next week. This is an emergency."

There was a pause. "Who is this and what is the nature of the emergency?"

The Body hung up. He should have known it wouldn't be that easy. Women were all bitches. You couldn't pry anything out of them with a crowbar big as a high-rise.

It was raining, nearly eight p.m. If he hurried over to her house he'd catch her still up. She would be coerced into giving up the information whether she wanted to or not.

He threw on a thin jacket to protect his shirt from the rain and ran to the car. She didn't live that far away.

She knew his face the moment she opened the door to him. Rain dripped from his fine blond hair into his eyes. He wiped it away and gave her a boyish grin. "Hi," he said, "nasty night, isn't it?"

"Uh . . . can I help you?"

"Could I come inside out of the rain? I have a message from Karl for you."

She unhooked the safety chain and allowed him entrance. She lived in a small, pastel-pink house set back from the street in a white gravel lawn. Her furnishings were modest, bargain basement stuff, but she wore a beautiful silk dressing gown, oriental, blue with red scaly dragons imprinted over the material.

He followed her to a tiny living area where an ivory nubby linen sofa faced a white, unused fireplace. She offered to get him a towel to dry himself off. He waited, standing on the pale blue and peach Indian throw rug.

He didn't know what he was going to do until she returned with the towel in her hand. He stepped forward as if to retrieve the towel, but instead caught her in an embrace, her arms pinned to her sides. She dropped the towel and gasped.

He looked down into her face. She was not a pretty woman. She was too thin, her chin too pointed, her nose and lips too tiny for her wide, flat face. But her eyes were exceptionally bright, black as a squirrel's, flaring with life. She said, "What are you doing?"

"Where's Karl? Tell me and I won't hurt you."

"Why would you want to hurt me?"

Now she was breathing hard, fear sliding into her eyes like a shaft of light breaking over a dark horizon.

He brought his arms quickly up and his hands circled her throat. He pressed both his thumbs into the cartilage of her windpipe, but not hard. "I don't want to hurt you," he said. "I want to know where Karl went. Tell me."

She tried to shake loose and he pressed his thumbs deeper. She tried to cough. His fingers tightened deeper into her flesh. Her hands were around his wrists, but he ignored them. She was not a big woman, not strong, not even as much of a challenge as Marilyn had been. With more pressure he could choke her. With a quick twist of her neck, he could break it.

"Okay, okay," she whispered. Her voice, cut off the way it was, sounded like a low, harsh wind blowing over a plateau.

Now her eyes watered. They glittered in the light from a lamp on the mantel over the dead fireplace.

He relaxed his hold on her larynx, but did not remove his hands. "Where?"

"He went to a cabin, Cambridge Hill's cabin."

"Where's that?"

"Somewhere in Montana."

"Where in Montana?" He was losing patience and his fingers tightened again.

"I don't know!"

He pressed so hard her eyes began to pop and she fought him, hammering at his upper arms with her fists. He relaxed his grip once more. She took in ragged breaths.

"Where in Montana? I won't ask again."

"Outside of Billings."

He grinned down at her. "You think I'm handsome?"

She blinked.

"Most women think I look like a young Robert Redford."

She tried to nod. She licked her lips.

"I could have played Louis in *Interview With a Vampire*. Don't you think so?" He bent down and nuzzled her ear. She arched her head away from him and he could feel her body trembling against his chest.

Just as he was pulling away from her neck where he had planted a kiss, he bore down with his thumbs hard and at the same time lifted her off her feet. She kicked and pummeled him. Her eyes were wild with fright, the wall eyes of a horse trapped in a burning stall. Her nails clawed his face and he just laughed.

Laughed and laughed.

Karl took along a laptop computer, his cellular phone, and the gun. He could still hardly believe he was packing a gun. He had bought it early in his troubled time with the stalker; he went into a gun shop and picked it out. He didn't like it at all, in fact treated it the way he might a poisonous snake he kept as a pet, handling it with great care. It made him feel safer, however, and that was the purpose of guns in the hands of law-abiding people.

He found books in Cam's little cabin, dog-eared paperback thrillers in a cardboard box set against the wall in the bedroom. There was no television or radio. There were no neighbors. Down the dirt and gravel road that led to the cabin tucked back into the woods was a small fishing pond and further on a rugged path led into forested hunting ground. The dirt road connected to a two-lane highway that wove into Billings, twenty-six miles distant.

Karl had stocked up on perishables, but overbought on canned goods. Cam's cupboards in the small open kitchen that joined the living area were full of every kind of canned food imaginable. He found tuna and salmon, beans, vegetables, yams, pickles, canned ham—enough to feed one person well into the millennium.

Karl had never taken a vacation. He hadn't left LA in years. His work was so demanding and he was so dedicated that he had forgotten the last time he took time off for himself. The cabin reminded him of the reasons he was a workaholic. It was *boring* to spend time doing nothing.

The first day there he missed being plugged in. The silence was pressing and made him slightly paranoid. Without the sounds of a city—the traffic roar, the ocean down at Malibu, the lights, the crowds—he found that his hearing overcompensated. He jumped at creaks in the wooden plank floor as he walked over it. He flinched when a breeze blew a fir limb against a window. He turned to find the source when the wind sung teakettle songs down the chimney.

Then there were wild animal sounds from the forest surrounding the cabin that he could not identify. Howls and cries, snorts and rumblings that put his nerves right along the razor's edge.

He thought he'd go crazy if he had to stay isolated too long. Cam had promised the script was almost finished. Five, six more scenes, he'd said, and we wrap.

It might take a week, two weeks. Longer than that and Karl thought he'd be climbing the log walls and scratching himself like a monkey. Reading the old paperbacks kept him entertained for a couple of days. He hadn't read a novel in . . . how long? Since college, he guessed. He had forgotten how many hours he could squander, lost in the pages of a novel.

Yet even reading began to lose its attraction after a while. It seemed to him Cam could have varied his reading habits a bit. Hell, where were the *Playboy* magazines and the copies of *Variety*? Even a *National Geographic* would have been appreciated.

It was cold during the nights at the cabin so that Karl had to build a fire in the fireplace for warmth and use two blankets on the bed. He chopped wood, amused at how bad he was at it, once nearly burying the ax in his own foot. He spent almost an hour imagining how he'd drive himself to a doctor from this ends-of-the-earth place if he really did manage to hurt himself.

He stacked the chopped wood neatly in cords on the front porch—panting, aching—and wondered why anyone romanticized the early years of the last century. It must have been a bitch to work this hard every single day.

He cooked, but nothing too complicated, swept the floors, washed his clothes in the tub and hung them from a clothesline he found in back of the house. He might have taken his laundry into Billings to be done for him, but too many Hollywood types took time off to visit in the town; someone would recognize him, word could get back where he was. He didn't want to have to answer questions or explain his presence here. All he wanted was to endure the hours until Cam called to let him know the film was completed.

Middle of the night, dreaming of swimming in the surf at Malibu with Marilyn. Every time he dove into the waves and came up, she waved at him from where she waded in the shallows. He was laughing, happy to know that her death was a lie. "Watch this," he yelled and dove again into a big white-crested breaker. When he came up, flinging his head to clear his hair from his eyes, he couldn't see Marilyn anywhere. He turned in a circle, treading water, but she was gone.

A hand wrapped around his ankle, jerking him into the deep. The water was green as new summer shoots of grass. Seaweed swirled before his eyes, tangled around his head. He tried to bend over to see if Marilyn had his foot and was playing a game. It was not Marilyn. It was a severed arm, latched onto his ankle, dragging him down . . .

He woke soaking with sweat, the covers heaped over his head. He threw back the blankets and that's when he heard someone at the door in the front of the cabin.

He wasn't ready for this. He hadn't expected it.

He fumbled for the nightstand, got the drawer open and his hand on the gun. It was a 9 mm Beretta, black, mean, and loaded with hollow-point cartridges. He flipped off the safety and pulled back the slide, chambering a round. The sound was like sheets of tin slapping against Karl's eardrums, loud and frightening.

Now he was sweating in earnest. It was dripping down his forehead and his neck. His palms were damp and he was afraid his finger would twitch on the Beretta's trigger, setting off an explosion.

There was no point in calling out and asking who was there. He knew who it was and why he was here. It didn't matter how the intruder had found out where Karl had gone. At this point all that mattered was living through the next half hour.

All vestiges of the dream world disappeared, wiped from consciousness. Karl's concentration narrowed. All his senses clicked into overdrive. His hearing was acute, his eyes saw everything—the gun in his hand, the sheen of sweat on his forearm, his bare feet moving over the polished wood floor, the doorway he approached, especially the doorway, a maw opening into pitch dark.

He could hear his footsteps crossing the floor, but overriding those secretive sounds was his heart, racketing fast as a jackhammer in his ears.

He put his back to the wall next to the door, the gun held before him and pointing to the ceiling. Suddenly he felt incredibly stupid. He felt like an actor playing a part. He had seen cops do this in a hundred movies and cop television shows. Back to the wall beside the door. Gun gripped with both hands, pointing to the ceiling.

God, if he could just get out of this cabin and to the rental car, he'd go to church, he'd take up religion, he'd get married, Jesus, and settle down and never lie with another woman but Lisa again.

Okay, he told himself. Do what the cops do. Play it

straight and maybe you'll live to see morning.

He took a deep breath, swung out into the opening and at the same instant reached through the dark for the wall plate and the switch there. He palmed it up. He expected light to fill his eyes, effectively blinding him for a moment. He even blinked in preparation. But darkness held. The electricity had been disconnected in some way. Hell, hell. Jesus, he thought, you're not listening. I thought we had a bargain. I wish you'd fucking listen when sinners beg for your help.

He had the gun pointed forward, swinging back and forth, hunting a target. His finger on the trigger tightened. It was too dark and there were too many shadows. He forced himself to wait. With the gun still and his breath held, he began to make out the dimensions of the room and the objects in it.

The room stood empty. The front door was closed.

Karl's heart stuttered in relief. And then his gaze was drawn back to the door. It eased open, in eerie slowness. A finger of moonlight crept along the floor like an animal sniffing out a lair.

Karl was in motion without thinking, crossing to the door, skirting the back of the sofa, passing the wing chair. His free hand clasped the doorknob and he jerked the door the rest of the way open.

There was no one there. He stared out into abysmal night. A wayward breeze rushed over him, chilling his bare sweaty chest. He shivered, lowering the gun slightly.

Perhaps he had not locked the door before retiring.

The small voice that was his instinct denied that explanation. He hadn't slept with his doors unlocked in years. He never failed to lock doors, most especially since his troubles had begun. Besides, the electricity was off. His enemy was here, he couldn't pretend otherwise, too dangerous to try fooling himself.

He stepped out onto the porch and when he did, the voice spoke. It was modulated and reasonable. It was male. It caused Karl to swivel toward it and pull the trigger without hesitation.

The resounding of the gunshot made his ears ring. He ducked back inside the semi-safety of the threshold. He might have just killed someone and the thought made his knees weak. He held onto the door facing to keep himself steady.

Just as he was about to step out again to find the dead or wounded body, the voice came again, closer.

"Because of you she killed my babies. They were *mine*."

The accusation was so fantastical, so nonsensical, that Karl lowered his head to think it over. Killed the babies? A man had babies and someone killed them? Because of *him?*

Had to wrap his mind around this because if he didn't he was lost in the whirlwind.

Then it came to him. It was like the sudden exposure of a cow's carcass in the middle of a ballroom of costumed people. The understanding swept over Karl with such ferocity that he opened his mouth and an utterance of disbelief passed over his lips.

"Catherine," he whispered.

"Catherine got an abortion after she left me. She left me for you. She killed our children for you. Did you think you could run far enough away to lose me? The ends of the earth aren't far enough."

Oh God, who had Cat been dating before him? Why couldn't he think? He knew about the abortion, he'd accused her of an immoral and selfish act in that regard. But he had not known the father. She wouldn't talk of it and he hadn't pressed her. He had convinced himself it was none of his business. That was her life before him. The pregnancy was her mistake and the abortion her decision. Millions of women aborted their pregnancies every year. Some used abortion as a weird form of birth control. Catherine had been pregnant with twins, but he'd had no business to be involved in that part of her life.

"Who are you?" he asked, now easing the door closed until there was but a crack six inches wide that he could hear through. He would not go out into the dark again and chance being the victim in this face-off. He was no cowboy, he wasn't even familiar with this goddamn gun. The Beretta scared the shit out of him. The first shot he had squeezed off had made his heart lurch. He was glad he hadn't killed the stranger on Cam's porch.

"Answer me," he repeated. "Who are you?"

"I'm The Body."

"The body?" Something in Karl's brain recoiled at the idea anyone would reply that way to a straightforward question of identity.

"The Body that floats on the water, dead. Dead. Dead. The Body that was rejected from the cunt's womb. I am the body of revenge for life ended cruelly."

"You're fucking crazy, man. I had nothing to do with Catherine's decision. You're in the wrong universe. Now leave me alone before one of us gets . . . hurt!"

The door slammed in Karl's face, causing his last word to come out a pained shout. His nose broke, crushing the cartilage to the side of his face, and immediately gushing blood. Lightning shot from the middle of his face into the center of his brain. He saw a sharp new sun, as if a floodlight had been turned on behind his eyes, and he couldn't see. He staggered back, bringing his hand up to his nose while at the same time his gun hand was pulling the trigger of the Beretta again and again and again. The shots were like cannons, booming and filling the room, reverberating off his head in successive violent waves. The gun barrel kept jerking up, to the side, down, and up again. He was crazy with fear and blindness and adrenaline.

He heard the man laughing and he swung to where he heard it and emptied the magazine until he was pulling a dead trigger, clicking it and clicking it like some mechanical toy gangster.

He backed up to the sofa. Blood covered his mouth so that when he breathed in a hot copper-tinged river filled his mouth and was spit out again.

Now there was a silence so loud, punctuated by his own gagging and spitting, that he twitched and turned this way and that, hoping for his vision to adjust.

The voice came from behind him. "It's her fault," the man said, and plunged something sharp, something wide, into Karl's flesh at the back of his waist. In that deadly moment, Karl twisted, throwing himself to the side and away, pulling his weight with one hand along the sofa back and the knife caught him in the muscle and fatty tissue, piercing all the way through to the front of him.

Now he jerked forward and the knife slid out, cutting deeper, and he was moving through the room to the bedroom, grabbing for the door, slamming it at his back and throwing his weight against it while he fumbled in the dark for the lock.

A thump hit the door, the body on the other side pushing as if the door had not yet been shut and now Karl had the lock in place.

Refill the magazine of the Beretta, that's what he had to do and fast, if he wanted to live. He ran into the end of the bed, bounced off, felt along it to the nightstand and reached into the open drawer. He had the cardboard casing off the cartridge box. He slumped onto the side of the bed, unmindful now of the blood flowing freely from his nose and the burning in his side. He worked out the magazine in the Beretta, grabbed a hollow-point from the cartridge box, dropped it. Fuck.

Now there were stealthy sounds coming from the locked door to the bedroom and the man on the other side was talking, but Karl wasn't listening. He heard a name, Michelle, and shut out the rest, picking up another hollow-point and managing to get it into the magazine, then another, and one more before he heard the door opening. Three. He had three chances to save himself.

He could see as well now as if the lights had been glowing overhead. He jammed the magazine into the bottom of the gun, turned, pointed, and pulled the trigger.

Once, twice, three times. The shots were right on, aimed perfectly, the gun held steady as the blasts ignited the room with sound, cordite smoke, and death.

The man was almost to the bed when it happened, almost upon Karl, his right hand raised, the knife descending. The hollow-point cartridges drove through gut and chest and knocked the man back, taking him onto his heels and off his feet and finally onto his back on the floor.

Karl rose from the bed, moaning as if he were the one shot, and went to his knees beside the prone body. He saw the hands were empty. The man had dropped the knife.

He was bleeding profusely, the front of his pullover darkening with blood. Karl knew him. It was Jackie Landry. The lead for Cam's movie. *The actor who was playing the part of the victim; he was playing Karl's role.*

280

Jackie turned his head to the side. Karl saw the glitter of his eyes and halted with his hand inches from the wounds. He didn't know what he was about to do, staunch the wounds? Change reality? Wave his hands over the body and heal it miraculously?

He drew back his hand and put it over the cut in his side and squeezed to hold it shut. This was for shit, this was fucking hell and for what? For insanity, he realized, it was a ballet from an asylum.

"I shouldn't be dying for her," the man said.

"She didn't do anything to you," Karl said. "I didn't do anything to you. This was no way to make things right."

The man turned back his head to stare at the ceiling.

Karl put aside the gun and this time he did reach over and place both his hands on the entrance wounds pumping blood from the dying actor.

In so many ways this was not following the script. He might have expected to die, for the villain died in the last reel, villains always died. Hollywood would have it no other way, but it should not have been at this man's hands, not here, not now, not without winning anything he had worked so diligently to win.

He focused on the ceiling and felt his heart bump his ribs and then clench, as if someone had reached inside and took it in a fist.

He called to her for help, pleading in prayerful silence that he not be left alone with this last scene. She came to him as he ended his plea, emerging as smoke from the rafters overhead, drifting down feathery soft and quiet, the way ghosts do. She rested on his torso, leaned over and stroked the tears from his cheeks with both her small hands.

"Come play with me," she said. "I've missed you so much."

He blinked away the tears and in his mind he answered. "I'm coming. I'm coming, Michelle. Help me now."

He strained forward and it surprised him that he came up from the floor so easily, wrapping his arms around his sister, and with her, drifting skyward and away.

# 47

"Every country gets the circus it deserves. Spain gets bullfights. Italy gets the Catholic Church. America gets Hollywood."

Erica Jong, *How To Save Your Own Life*

Karl stood with Lisa at the back of the theater. She was his bride and this was the first film they had seen together as a couple.

They had risen during the last scene and slipped to the back to stand with their arms around one another to watch the final moments of the premiere of *Pure and Uncut.*

It was difficult to watch the movie, but he did it for Robyn and for Catherine and for Olivia, and most of all, for Marilyn. She had been brilliant in it, even though her part had been cut short by her death. He thought she might have won an Oscar for Best Supporting.

It was most difficult of all to watch the screen when Jackie Landry was on. He was twenty feet tall and beautiful and brilliant. He was better than any actor Karl had seen in a drama in ten years. The audience knew, by the time the movie premiered, that Jackie was a murderer. Although Cam wanted to believe his film drew a packed crowd because it broke the mold and would usher in the new technology of movie-making, the truth was more sinister.

They had come to see the killer. The real killer. Jackie's insanity ensured that Cam's movie would break all box office records.

When the music swelled and the end credits rolled, the audience roared with thunderous applause. They began to noisily release themselves from the hydraulic platform seat belts and fill the aisles. Karl turned away and led Lisa out to the lobby. Though the wound in his side was completely healed, he still favored it, leaning a little, feeling the pucker of the stitched flesh.

Cam stood in the lobby with a woman who might have been picked up from a downtown bar. She wore a strapless, black, floor-length gown and too much make-up. It was obvious that Cam adored her.

Karl walked over with his hand extended. Cam took it, grinning to show the spaces between his big teeth. "I heard them," he said. "It's a fucking hit. Didn't I tell you?"

"It was great, Cam."

Cam turned to Lisa and took her hand. "I hear this is your wife."

Karl introduced her, smiling from ear to ear. She thought she might be pregnant and every time he looked at her he thought her radiant as a sunset.

"Karl's one lucky sumbitch," Cam said fondly.

The lobby filled and people crowded around Cam to congratulate him. Karl took the opportunity to take Lisa's hand. They slipped to the door that would lead them outside into the neon world that was the Hollywood night.

Once on the sidewalk, moving away from the waiting limousines and their drivers, Karl said, "I'm glad it all ended happily. It was a good movie, don't you think so?"

She squeezed his hand. "Yes," she said. "It was perfect."

Karl thought it not quite perfect, but he wouldn't argue. Had it been perfect, the script would not have possessed the seeds of destruction that had taken down so many innocent victims.

At least he had his life back and a future to look forward to.

And it would be, no matter how unpredictable and lacking in perfection, at least as normal from now on as he could make it.

"Promise me," he said, "that you'll never get a hankering to return to acting."

"I promise."

"Promise me you'll have at least one more baby for us."

"I can't promise that."

He laughed.

"Then promise me this."

"What?"

"That you'll always love me." He turned and took her into his arms.

"You know I will."

He thought that she would. Sometimes lives turned out just like fantasies after all, sappy and sentimental as the happy endings portrayed by Hollywood.

"I love this town," he said, kissing her once, and then walking at her side again. "God, don't you love this town?"